LIE NEXT TO ME

(A Millionaire's Love)

Sandi Lynn

Sandi Lynn

Lie Next To Me (A Millionaire's Love)

Copyright © 2014 Sandi Lynn

Cover Design by Cover It Designs

Photography by CJC Photography

Models: Nathan Tetreault & Alli Theresa

Editing by B.Z. Hercules

Dedication

This book is dedicated to my romance fans. Without each and every one of you, Lie Next To Me would not have been possible. I hope you enjoy reading Ian & Rory's journey as much as I did writing it!

Happy reading!

Love

He's not perfect. You aren't either, and the two of you will never be perfect. But if he can make you laugh at least once, causes you to think twice, and if he admits to being human and making mistakes, hold onto him and give him the most you can. He isn't going to quote poetry, he's not thinking about you every moment, but he will give you a part of him that he knows you could break. Don't hurt him, don't change him, and don't expect for more than he can give. Don't analyze. Smile when he makes you happy, yell when he makes you mad, and miss him when he's not there. Love hard when there is love to be had. Because perfect guys don't exist, but there's always one guy that is perfect for you.

Bob Marley

I fell in love with her courage, her sincerity, and her flaming self- respect. And it's these things I'd believe in, even if the whole world indulged in wild suspicions that she wasn't all she should be. I love her and it is the beginning of everything.

F. Scott Fitzgerald

Table of Contents

Chapter 1

The pain was unbearable, but I had to keep moving. I had to keep running because, if I didn't, he'd find me. I looked behind me as I ran through the streets; scared, alone, and in the dark as the mist of rain hit my face. There was no time to think and there was no time to stop. My shoes were soaked as they sloshed through the puddles of the dimly lit streets. As people passed by, they looked at me strangely. I kept my hand on my side as the throbbing pain continued deep inside me. I started to get dizzy, so I stopped in the alley and sat up against the brick wall. My breathing was shallow. I removed my hand from my side and held it up so the dim light could reflect on it. I gasped as the blood soaked my hand and dripped onto the cement. I started to shake, and I felt like I was going to lose consciousness, but I had to keep moving. As I stood up and leaned against the wall, I pressed my palm against my side and started moving out of the alley.

My mind kept flashing back to what had led me here in the first place. The fight, the rage, the look on his face that I'd never forget, and the knife plunging into my side. The sidewalk started to spin and the pain was getting worse. I didn't know where I was, and I didn't know where I was going until I bumped into a man, and he held onto me as I collapsed in his arms.

"Whoa, miss. Are you all right?"

I couldn't speak, and I started to fall to the ground. I felt him take my hand from my side as he picked me up, carried me a few feet, and slid me into the back seat of a vehicle.

"What the hell, Joshua?" I heard a low voice say.

"She's hurt and she needs medical attention. It looks like she's been stabbed."

"Call Dr. Graham, tell him what happened, and have him meet us at the house."

"Don't you think we should get her to the emergency room?"

"We can get back to the house quicker. Now let's go."

He wrapped his arms around me and pulled me down onto his lap. I felt the palm of his hand press against my wound as I flinched at the pain that shot through my body.

"Relax. We'll get you all fixed up," his low voice said. "Who did this to you?"

I tried to look up at him, but all I could see was darkness and shadows. My eyes slowly closed until I felt his strong hand grip my chin.

"Stay with me. Don't close your eyes. You need to stay alert."

"I—I can't," I whispered.

His grip on my chin tightened as he moved my head from side to side.

"You can and you will. It's not a request; it's a command. Do you understand me?"

Before I knew it, the vehicle had stopped and the door opened. After I was taken from the car, the man carried me inside and up the stairs.

"Lay her here, Ian, and let me do what I have to do," I heard another male voice say.

"Is she going to be all right?" the low voice asked.

"I'll do the best I can, but it looks like she's lost quite a bit of blood," he said as he cut my shirt up the side.

I tried to focus on what was happening, but I couldn't. Between the room spinning and the blurry faces, I just needed to close my eyes. I felt a prick on my skin and that was the last thing I remembered.

****

I slowly opened my eyes and took note of the oversized bed in which I was lying in. The sheets were soft and the pillows were fluffy. As I stared straight ahead, I noticed the beautiful green fabric that was draped amongst the four intricately carved cherry wood posts.

"You're awake," the low voice said as he walked through the door.

"Where am I?" I asked in a soft whisper.

He walked further into the room and sat down on the edge of the bed. "You're in my house."

"What happened to me?" I asked, since my mind was nothing but a ball of blur.

"Why don't you start by telling me your name?" he said as he sat on the edge of the bed and leaned over me.

I stared into his blue eyes as I answered him. "Rory. My name is Rory."

"Rory?" he asked with an odd look on his face.

"It's short for Aurora," I replied.

"It's nice to meet you, Rory. I'm Ian Braxton," he said as he got up from the bed and poured me a glass of water. "Here, take a sip."

I lifted my head as he held the glass up to my lips. The pain in my side was throbbing, reminding me of that horrific night.

"Good girl. Now, why don't you tell me who hurt you," he said.

I looked away because I wasn't about to tell him my troubles. He was a stranger, even though he did help me.

"How long have I been sleeping?" I asked.

"About two days. I'll ask you one last time. Who did this to you and why?"

"I don't know," I lied.

"You're lying," he said. "I don't like people who lie."

"And I don't like people who are nosy and think they can make everything their business."

He raised one eyebrow. "Hmm," he said as he stared at me. "Very well, Aurora. You'll tell me in due time," he said as he got up from the bed and walked over to the door. He put his hand on the handle and, before turning it, he turned around and looked at me. "I saved your life and now you owe me. That's how this works. I did something for you, and you'll do something for me."

He walked out of the room and shut the door behind him. I tried to sit up, but the pain was too intense. When I closed my eyes, all I could see was him, the look in his eye, and the pain of the knife that broke my flesh. I turned my head and looked out the large window. The French doors that led out to the balcony were beautiful. The only thing I could see from my lying position was the blue sky. I had no idea where I was other than the fact that the house was owned by a man named Ian Braxton. A sexy man. A man who stood about six feet tall with light brown hair and blue eyes that reminded me of the sky outside my window. The slight scruff that he sported on his face made him even sexier. His voice was one I'd never be able to get out of my head. Low, deep, authoritative, and permanently etched into my brain. The only voice I heard when I was scared, hurt, and alone. My eyes felt heavy and, just as I closed them, I heard the light squeak of the door opening. I opened my eyes and saw Ian standing over me.

"You need to take your antibiotics," he said.

"Antibiotics? For what?"

"So you don't get an infection from your stab wound. Do you remember what kind of knife it was?"

I closed my eyes, and instead of seeing darkness, I saw the stiletto blade he held in his hand after he stabbed me. My eyes flew open as a twinge of pain throbbed where my wound was.

"Are you all right, Aurora?"

"I'm fine," I said as I looked away.

"Is there something you want to tell me?"

"No. What would I possibly tell you?"

Ian sat down on the edge of the bed and stared at me. "You never told me your last name." He smiled as he held out his hand with the large red pill in it.

I lifted my hand and, when I went to take it from him, he closed his hand on mine. "You have no reason to be afraid of me, Aurora. I can keep you safe, but you need to trust me."

I nodded my head and he smiled softly as he opened his hand and I took the pill from it. He handed me a glass of water as I put the pill in my mouth and swallowed it.

"Sinclair. My last name is Sinclair," I said. "And my name is Rory. I hate Aurora, so please call me Rory."

The corners of his mouth slightly curved up when I said that. "You must be starving. I'll have my chef prepare something for you. What kinds of food do you like?"

"I'm not hungry," I said in a low tone as I looked out the window.

"It doesn't matter if you're hungry or not. You have to eat."

He was starting to piss me off, and I just wanted to be left alone. "Can you please just leave me alone?" I said with an irritation in my voice.

"Fine. I'll leave you alone, at least for now. But, make no mistake, Aurora, this is far from finished."

He got up from the bed and walked out the door. *What the hell was this guy's problem?* He seemed like some kind of control freak. He would be easy to resist if he wasn't so damn sexy. *Ugh…Rory, get the thought out of your head,* I said to myself. A guy like that would never be interested in someone like me. About an hour later, a man wearing a white shirt, black pants, and a chef's hat on his head brought me a tray with a bowl of soup and a plate of bread on it.

"For you, Miss Rory. I've prepared homemade chicken noodle soup and homemade bread for you. Everything you need is here on the tray," he said as he set it across my lap.

The aroma of chicken soup filled the air. "Thank you. It smells delicious."

"You're welcome. If there's anything else I can get you, please just push this button and it will ring down to the kitchen." He smiled.

"Thank you. What's your name?"

"My name is Charles, ma'am," he said as he walked out the door.

As the steam was rising up from the soup, I took my spoon and stirred it around the bowl. I despised chicken soup and for good reason. But, I was hungry, and because I didn't specify what I liked to eat, Charles probably figured that chicken soup was the safest bet. I brought the spoon up to my mouth and lightly blew on it to cool the soup off. It wasn't bad. I'm sure it was phenomenal, but since my hatred for chicken soup was so strong, I couldn't get past that it was just okay. Being in this place scared me. He scared me. He said I could trust him, but I didn't trust anyone.

Chapter 2

I desperately needed a shower. I looked across the room and at the closed door that was the bathroom. I carefully swung my legs to the side of the bed, and I slowly stepped one foot on the floor. I held my side where the wound was as I pushed myself up from the bed. I stood there for a moment and let the dizziness pass. As I slowly inched my way to the bathroom, I stopped in front of the full-length mirror that stood in the corner. My long brown hair was knotted and greasy-looking. My brown eyes were sunken in and it looked like I hadn't slept in days. My fair skin had a gray cast to it, and I just looked like total shit. I had no idea where the nightgown had come from that I was wearing, but it was pretty. A pretty satin and pink lace gown that stopped at my ankles was the only thing from keeping me looking like a homeless person. I silently laughed because I *was* a homeless person. Walking into the huge bathroom, that was bigger than the house I used to live in, I took down the straps of my gown and let it fall to the floor. I carefully removed the white bandage that covered the results of that horrible night. I felt sick to my stomach as I looked at the wound that would forever scar my right side. The dizziness started again, so I sat down on the toilet, waiting for it to pass. *Was I even going to be able to take a shower?* As I slowly removed myself from the toilet, I reached inside the shower, turned on the water, and stepped inside. I ran my hand along the beige marble walls as I looked through the triple glass doors that, if anyone walked in, they would be able to see me completely naked. In the corner were built-in shelves that held shower gels, shampoos, conditioners, razors, loofah sponges, and a sea salt body scrub. As I struggled to wash my hair, I heard a voice through the door.

"How on earth are you managing to take a shower? I know you can't wash your hair. I'm sure the pain is too much when you lift your arms."

He was right. The pain was too much when I tried to lift my arm. "I'm fine."

"No, you're not, and you shouldn't be in there alone. What if you fell or passed out or something?"

"I'm fine."

"Aurora, no, you're not! Now, I'm coming in to help you."

"Over my dead body, you are, Ian. Don't you dare open that door!" I yelled.

"Wrap one of the large towels around your body, then. At least let me shampoo your hair."

"Get one of your maids."

"They're gone for the night."

I took in a deep breath, and since I needed my hair washed, I was left with very little choice but to let him in and help me. I opened the shower door and stuck out my hand, grabbing the large towel from the rack. I wrapped it around my body, flinching in pain as the towel pressed against my wound.

"Okay, I'm covered. You can come in now."

He opened the door and looked at me as he started unbuttoning his shirt.

"What are you doing?"

"Taking off my shirt so it doesn't get wet."

As he unbuttoned the last button, he slid his shirt off his shoulders and set it on the counter. I stood there staring at him. Staring at the ripped, muscular man before me. His taut torso was perfection. Every ripped muscle was well characterized, as was the hint of his V-shape, which was slightly visible as his pants sat low on his hips. My eyes then diverted to his muscular arms, which were perfectly defined and strong. I remembered that much when he had carried me up the stairs that night.

"Do you like what you see?" He smiled.

I cleared my throat in embarrassment. "Yeah, sure. Now could you please help me?"

He walked over, opened the door, and asked me to hand him the shampoo from the shelf. As I handed it to him, he poured a small amount into his hand and began working it into my hair. I closed my eyes at the feel of his strong hands, massaging their way around my scalp. A tingling sensation started down below and my heart began pounding. Once he was finished shampooing my hair, he removed the showerhead from the wall and rinsed out the lather. I stood there, in a soaking wet towel, enjoying what this practical stranger was doing to me.

"Hand me the conditioner and I'll put some on your hair. After I rinse it out, you can wash your body. Unless you would like me to do that for you?"

"No, I can wash myself, thank you very much," I said as I handed him the conditioner.

After he rinsed my hair, he shut the shower door, and walked out of the bathroom, shutting the door behind him. I finished my shower and began to feel somewhat human again. I grabbed a dry towel, wrapped it around me, and opened the door. I was startled to see Ian sitting on the edge of the bed.

"Jesus, I thought you left."

"The name's Ian, sweetheart, not Jesus." He smiled. "I took the liberty of having some clothes and personal items delivered for you, since you have absolutely nothing. If you look in the drawer over there, you'll find some bras and underwear."

"How did you know what size I wore?"

"I looked at the bra you were wearing when I brought you here. By the way, I threw that one out. It was pretty nasty."

How dare him.

"I'll step out of the room while you change and then I'll help you brush your hair."

"Thank you, but I can brush my own hair," I said as I gave him a dirty look.

"Suit yourself and we'll see. You couldn't wash your hair, so what makes you think you can brush it?" He sighed.

He left the room and I opened the drawer that displayed five different beautiful bras, in different colors. A couple of them were plain, but the rest of them were made of lace and sparkles. Each bra had matching panties that came in twos. One a thong and the other bikini-style. I put on one of the lacy bras, and I walked over to the double doors and opened them, revealing a large walk-in closet with built-in shelves from floor to ceiling. I'd never seen anything like this in person; only in the movies. On the shelves were a few pairs of pants that were neatly folded and a few shirts that hung on the rack. I dug through until I found a pair of black leggings. I grabbed a long, pink shirt from the hanger and slipped that on first. Putting on my leggings was difficult, but I managed. Soon, there was a knock at the door and Ian peeked his head through.

"Decent?"

"Yes, and I thought you left."

"I wanted to stick around and watch you try to brush your hair. In the drawer of the vanity are the brushes and combs."

I walked over and sat down at the vanity, opened the drawer, and took out a large brush. I started with my ends first, so I didn't have to raise my arm any higher than necessary.

"For fuck sake, Rory, give me the damn brush," he said as he walked over and grabbed it out of my hand.

"Do you need to curse?"

"I apologize," he said as he gently brushed my long hair.

I stared out the window as each brush stroke relaxed me more and more. "How was your soup?" Ian asked.

"I despise chicken soup. But I will admit that Charles made it pretty good."

"Why do you despise chicken soup? Everybody loves chicken soup."

I was in such a daze from the way he was brushing my hair that I didn't even realize what I'd said.

"I used to love it at one time, when I was a little girl. But when it becomes the only food you are forced to eat every single day, you reach a point when you never want to eat chicken soup again."

The movement of the hairbrush stopped as he stared at me through the mirror of the vanity. I didn't realize it until I looked and saw his mesmerizing eyes staring back at me. "Why are you doing this?" I asked.

"Doing what?" he replied as he continued to brush my hair.

"Buying me clothes and helping me with my hair. Why?"

"You fell into my limo. What was I supposed to do? Kick you out and let you die?"

"You could have dropped me off at a hospital and left."

"Perhaps, but I felt you would be better off here, given your circumstances. It's not every day that a beautiful young woman falls into my limo with a stab wound. I was intrigued, and besides, you have no clothes; in fact, you have nothing."

I smiled softly as I looked at him. He called me "beautiful." No one had ever told me I was beautiful, except my mom.

"And there's her smile," Ian said.

He looked at his watch, set the brush down, took my hand, and helped me back to bed. "I have a date, and if I don't go and get ready, I'm going to be late. So if you'll excuse me, Rory, I'll see you tomorrow."

And just like that, he was gone. Ian Braxton had a date. *What would his date think about him harboring a wounded girl, helping her in the shower, and buying her sexy bras and thongs?* It didn't matter anyway; this was a world in which I didn't belong. As I lay down and turned my head towards the window, I closed my eyes and fell asleep to the sounds of the waves lapping against the shoreline.

When I awoke a couple of hours later, I couldn't seem to go back to sleep. I felt restless and like a caged animal, being cooped up in this room. When I looked at the clock, I noticed it was one a.m. I carefully got out of bed and opened the door as quietly as I could. I looked down the long hallway and to my right at the spiral staircase. I carefully pulled the door closed behind me, and I slowly walked down the stairs. I found my way to the back of the house and stepped outside the door wall. As I stood on the open patio, I breathed in the ocean air and light breeze that came my way. I sat down in the oversized lounge chair that faced the beach. As my mind began wondering if Ian was home, I heard laughter coming from inside the house. I slowly turned my head and caught a glimpse of Ian and his date heading up the stairs. I turned back and looked up at the stars that lit up the night sky. For the first time in my twenty-three years of life, I felt peace. I closed my eyes and thought about Ian walking up those stairs with that woman.

****

My eyes opened and I found myself covered with a blanket. I was still on the lounge chair. I slowly sat up as Ian came walking out onto the patio with a cup in his hand.

"I hope you drink coffee because I brought you some."

"Thank you," I said as I took the cup from him.

"Cream?" he asked as he held up the carton.

"Just a little." I smiled.

The morning air was just as breathtaking as the night air. I looked out at the calmness of the ocean as the sun was up, displaying its beauty in the clear blue sky. Ian took a seat in the lounge chair next to me as he sipped his coffee.

"When I came in last night and saw you sleeping here, you looked so peaceful, and I didn't want to disturb you. There's nothing like waking up with the warm morning air surrounding you."

"It's beautiful here." I smiled.

"How are you feeling, Aurora?"

I looked at him sternly because I'd asked him not to call me that. "My apologies. It's just Aurora is the name of a princess and, when you sleep, you look like Sleeping Beauty."

The pit of my stomach started to ache and my heart started to pick up its pace. *Why was he saying these things to me? Why does he keep saying I'm beautiful? I'm not. I'm nothing but an ordinary girl with a messed up life.*

"Thanks, but I'm far from it." I laughed softly.

Ian smiled and turned his head towards the ocean as I asked him a question that I wanted to know the answer to.

"How was your date last night?"

"It was fine. Why do you ask?"

"I'm just trying to make conversation, that's all."

"Why would you make my date the topic of conversation, Rory? Why not start the conversation by telling me who you are and where you're from and, most importantly, why were you hurt and who did it? Was it your boyfriend?"

I wouldn't look at him as I sipped my coffee and stared out into the depths of the ocean. "What makes you think I have a boyfriend?" I asked.

"Damn it, Rory. Why do you evade my questions?" he asked as he got up from his chair. He knelt down next to me and cupped my chin in his hand. "If you won't tell me, then I'll just find out for myself," he said as he got up and walked away.

The fact of the matter was that, growing up, I was never allowed to tell anybody anything. Everything about my life was a secret. As I was in deep thought, Ian yelled from the door.

"It's time for breakfast and you're joining us. So, come inside, now."

I turned and looked at him as he walked away. I got up from my chair and walked back inside the house. Mandy, one of the maids, showed me to the dining room where Ian and another woman sat. He stared at me as I entered the room and told me to have a seat.

"Rory, I would like you to meet Adalynn."

"Hi, Rory. It's nice to meet you." She smiled as she reached her hand across the table.

"Hi."

This wasn't the same woman I saw Ian with last night. Adalynn was beautiful. Her dark hair was long and her light blue eyes had a hint of gray in them, making them a stunning color. Her high cheekbones, almond-shaped eyes, and full lips gave her an exotic look. Mandy set down a bowl of fruit in front of me and poured some more coffee in my cup.

"I hope you like fruit. I wouldn't know, since you won't tell me a damn thing about you," Ian spoke.

"Leave the girl alone, Ian. She's been through hell and she doesn't need you to make her feel worse," Adalynn said as she winked at me.

"I do like fruit, Ian." I smiled.

"Well, there's a start. I finally know something she likes," he said with a cocky attitude.

I had had just about enough of his cockiness. I looked at him and tilted my head. "Why is it so important to you that you know about me? You're a millionaire. That much I've gathered just from being in this house and seeing the way you dress. I get the impression that you like to control things and people. You come off as arrogant and demeaning, and I'm not comfortable telling you about my lousy life and the shithole that I came from."

"Damn it!" he said as he slammed his fists on the table. "I saved your life!"

I threw my napkin on the table as I spoke sternly. "Maybe you shouldn't have."

I slowly got up from my seat and held my side as I walked outside and down to the beach. The sand felt like I'd always imagined it would. It was so soft and warm as I sat down and ran my hands through it. *Did I really mean what I said to Ian about he shouldn't have saved me?* I didn't know. Maybe I should've just told him so he'd leave me alone.

Chapter 3

Ian walked over to where I was sitting and sat down next to me. He brought his knees up to his chest and sighed. "You sure know how to make an exit."

"My name is Aurora Jean Sinclair. I'm twenty-three years old, and I come from a small town in Indiana. I want to thank you, Mr. Ian Braxton, for saving my life."

Ian looked over at me and smiled. "It's nice to meet you, Rory, and you're very welcome."

My hands were deep in the sand as I picked some up and held it in between my fingers. Ian stared at me for a moment before speaking.

"The way you're playing with that sand, I'd assume that you've never touched sand before."

"Only once."

He chuckled lightly. "Yeah, right."

I looked at him with all seriousness. "It's true. This is the first time that I've seen the ocean and the second time that I've felt the sand."

His eyes gazed into mine as he slowly shook his head. "You're dead serious," he whispered.

"All of this. The beautiful ocean air, the warm, soft sand, the peaceful sounds of the waves, you take for granted. To me, this is something I'll cherish forever because I thought I'd never be able to experience it."

I looked down for a moment as I could see the pity in his eyes. I didn't want pity. My life was what it was, but I refused to let it define me as a person. "That's only a small fraction of my life, Ian. I'm not sure you want to hear the rest."

He reached over and took a hold of my hand. I looked at him. "I've pressed my hand against your bloody wound. I've shampooed your hair in the shower. I brushed your hair for you. I've given you a safe place to stay. I don't think there's any harm in holding your hand." He smiled.

To be honest, I didn't want him holding my hand, because the feeling that overtook me when he touched me was overwhelming and frightening. I gave him a small smile and lightly squeezed his hand.

"What about your parents?" he asked hesitantly.

"I never knew my dad because I was conceived during a one-night stand. See, I was doomed from the start."

"Don't say that, Rory."

"My mom died when I was ten years old of pneumonia. We didn't have any money to pay the doctor, so she just didn't go and she died," I said as the tears swelled in my eyes. "My aunt took me and my brother in after the state took us away. She refused at first, but when she found out that she would get paid for taking care of us, she changed her mind. We lived in a two-bedroom house and my brother and I had to share a room. My aunt was a drug addict and she used the money the state sent her for drugs. The house was filthy and falling apart. I tried to clean it every week, but it didn't matter; she would just mess it up as fast as I cleaned it. She brought a different guy home every night. She'd have sex with them and they'd pay her either in cash or drugs. She didn't pay attention to us. She told my brother and I that we were only there for a place to stay and that she wasn't playing mommy, but we weren't allowed to tell anyone that. We weren't allowed to talk about our home life."

Ian squeezed my hand and looked down. "My God, Rory."

"We weren't allowed to have friends because they would see how we lived and my aunt couldn't risk it. I engrossed myself in my studies and tried to learn everything I could about the world, so one day, I could get out of that shithole."

"Who hurt you, Rory?" Ian asked.

I closed my eyes and freed my hand from his. "My brother, Stephen. You know what, I'm really tired, and I think I'm just going to go back to my room," I said as I got up and left Ian sitting in the sand as I walked back to the house.

I lay myself down on the bed as the tears fell down my face. Living that life was one thing, but having to tell someone was far worse. I was ashamed and embarrassed, but I survived and became strong because of it. I was finally out and there was no way I was going back, ever. I fell asleep for a while and, when I woke up, the beautiful morning was gone and the afternoon had brought in dark clouds and rain. I got up from the bed and stepped into the shower. I sat on my knees on the shower floor and brought my head down so I could wash my hair. Once I was finished, I got dressed and walked downstairs. As I made my way to the kitchen, Charles was in there cooking. I noticed a young man sitting at the table. I instantly had a flashback of that night.

"Good day, Miss Rory," Charles said as he stood over the stove, stirring something.

"Hello, Charles." I smiled.

"Rory, I'm Joshua." He smiled as he held out his hand.

I walked over to the table and shook his hand. "You're the one I ran into on the street."

"Yes, I am."

"Thank you for helping me," I said.

"No problem." He smiled. "I would've come up to see you, but I just got back from having a few days off."

"Miss Rory, please sit down and let me make you a sandwich," Charles said.

"Thank you, Charles, I'd like that. Do you know where Ian is?" I asked.

"I think he's in his study. Go through the living room and it's on your left," Joshua answered.

"Thanks, Joshua."

I walked out of the kitchen and found Ian's study. He was sitting behind a large cherry wood desk, typing on his computer. As I entered, he looked up at me.

"You're awake," he said as he looked back at his computer.

"My brother, Stephen, is a schizophrenic, and I brought him to L.A. to visit a doctor who was doing a trial study with an experimental drug."

His eyes looked away from his computer and straight at me. "Go on," he said.

"In order for him to be in the trial, he had to stop taking his meds one month prior to his appointment. We were in the motel room and I asked him if he could turn the TV on while I went and took a shower. He'd been irritable the whole way to L.A., and I knew it was only a matter of time before he snapped. I was just hoping that he'd been in the trial study before he did. Anyway, he told me that the voices in his head wouldn't let him turn the TV on. So I walked over and turned it on myself. He pushed me out of the way and turned it off. I told him to knock it off and to go lie down and get some rest. He started screaming at me and told me to stop telling him what to do. He said the voices were yelling at him to make me stop. I turned my back on him and, before I knew it, I felt the knife plunging into me."

I started to shake as I relived that night. Ian jumped up from his chair and grabbed me before I could fall. He wrapped his arms around me and held me as we slowly dropped to the ground.

"You're safe now," he said as he held my head against his chest. "He's never going to hurt you again."

As soon as I snapped back into reality, I lifted my head and looked at Ian. The only thing I could see were his perfectly shaped lips that I wanted to kiss. "I'm sorry," I said as I nervously got up off the floor and out of his arms.

"Don't be sorry, Rory. You have nothing to be sorry for."

I took in a deep breath. "Charles is making me a sandwich. I should go and see if it's ready."

Ian smiled. "Tell Charles to me make me one too, and I'll join you shortly."

I walked out of his study, embarrassed once again. As I walked into the kitchen, Charles had my sandwich made and sitting on the table. "Thank you, Charles. Ian asked if you'd make him one as well."

"You're welcome, Miss Rory." He smiled.

"Please, just call me Rory."

****

A few days had passed and every day I was feeling stronger. I spent most of my days sitting on the beach or by Ian's pool. Ian spent his days at the office, and I still didn't know what he did. He didn't offer any information and I didn't ask. When he'd come home, he'd shower, change his clothes, and go out on his nightly dates. More often than not, he'd bring the women back here, but they were always gone in the morning. The strange thing was the way he looked at me every time he left for the night. It was almost as if he was apologizing. Thoughts of him burned through me every second of every day.

As I was sitting by the pool, I heard Adalynn's voice coming from inside.

"There you are. I was looking for you."

"You were? Why?" I asked as I opened one eye and looked at her.

"Because I want to know if you're up to going out?"

"Going out? Where?"

"It's a surprise. Just tell me yes or no." She smiled.

To get out of this house sounded like a wonderful idea. But I was kind of scared at what Adelynn had planned, and I'd only met her that one time at breakfast. I agreed anyway because I was desperate to get away from here for a while, and I wanted a friend.

"Just let me run upstairs and change." I smiled.

As soon as I changed my clothes, I met Adalynn in the front, where her town car was waiting for us. "The first thing we're going to do is get our hair done. I thought we'd have girls' day out with some shopping and pampering."

"But I don't have any money," I said.

"Aw, sweetie, don't worry about that. Ian is paying for everything." She winked.

"Does he know about this?"

"No, not yet, anyway." She laughed.

I was really starting to like Adalynn. She was funny and she had an aura about her that gave off friendly vibes. "If he doesn't know, how's he going to pay?" I asked in confusion.

"Ian Braxton has accounts all over town. Don't worry, sweetie. He won't mind."

"How long have you and Ian been friends?"

Adalynn looked at me and smiled as she took a hold of my hand. "Ian and I have known each other since college. I'm sure he didn't tell you, but I'm his ex-wife."

My stomach dropped. "You and Ian were married?"

"For a short time. Only a couple of days."

"Why? I'm sorry, but I don't understand. Why wouldn't he introduce you to me as his ex?"

Adalynn laughed. "We don't talk about it. Ian and I have been good friends for years. Friends with benefits, if you want to know the truth, and one weekend we went to Vegas. We got really drunk and Ian said we should get married. I agreed, or should I say, the alcohol agreed, and we went to the chapel and got hitched. After we realized what we did, the next morning, we had it annulled the minute we got back. Neither one of us wanted marriage. It was just a random act, one drunken night."

"How many friends with benefits does Ian have?" I blurted out.

"Well, if you're asking if Ian and I are still doing it, the answer is no. We stopped all that a couple of years ago. I'm currently dating someone and we're very much in love." She smiled.

A sigh of relief washed over me when she said that. I didn't, in any way, feel threatened by her. I was just glad she wasn't sleeping with Ian. One less woman in this rich town to worry about. We pulled up to the salon and, once inside, we were immediately taken back to our stylists. Adalynn introduced me to her stylist, Renee. As I sat in the chair next to her, I heard a boisterous voice from behind.

"And you must be Rory!" he exclaimed as he clasped my shoulders with his hands. "I'm Benny and I'm going to be styling you today. Now, tell me what you're thinking."

"Nice to meet you, Benny. I just found out I was coming here, so I didn't have a chance to really think about what I want. What do you suggest?" I asked.

He ran his fingers through my long, brown hair, examining the ends. "Hmm...I'm thinking about two inches, long layers and caramel highlights. With your bone structure, it will look fabulous."

"That sounds perfect, Benny," Adalynn said.

"What do you think, sweetheart?" he asked.

"Sure. That sounds great." I smiled.

Two hours later and Benny was finished with my hair. He turned the chair around and I gasped when I saw myself in the mirror.

"Oh my God, Rory. You look fantastic," Adalynn said.

"Well?" Benny asked.

Tears began to form in my eyes as I stared at myself. "It's beautiful."

Benny helped me out of the chair and led me to another section of the salon. "Take a seat here, sweetheart, and Joey will be right with you."

I looked at Adalynn as she sat in the chair across from me. "What's going on?"

"You're getting your makeup done." She smiled.

Joey walked over and introduced himself. Adalynn said he was the best makeup artist in all of California. Once he was finished, I looked across at Adalynn, who had tears in her eyes. "You look gorgeous."

As I looked in the mirror, I stared at the girl staring back at me. I desperately wanted to cry happy tears and Joey knew it because he told me to look up at the ceiling so the tears wouldn't fall and I wouldn't ruin my makeup.

"You're gorgeous. You're a natural beauty and you don't need makeup, but with it, wow, all the men better watch out." Joey smiled.

"Thank you, Joey."

As Adalynn and I walked out of the salon, she put her arm around me. "You look simply stunning. You're a beautiful woman and don't ever let anyone tell you otherwise. Now, let's go buy you some clothes."

I was grateful to her for doing this for me. I felt like a charity case and I hated it. I'd always been a charity case. My aunt always led people to believe that no matter how hard she tried, she couldn't find a job. So, Stephen and I were always given hand-me-downs and people looked at us with pity.

Adalynn grabbed the clothes that I tried on in the dressing room and took them to the register.

"I don't know about this, Adalynn. It's really expensive."

"Listen to me, Rory. Ian is buying. He doesn't care. The man has more money than he knows what to do with."

"What exactly does he do?"

She looked at me with surprise. "He hasn't told you?"

I shook my head. "I don't know a thing about him. All I know is that he has money."

"Well, he certainly is rich." she smiled. "The thing about Ian is that he's a very private man. He likes to talk about business and not his personal life. We're close friends and there are still things I don't know about him."

"He likes women," I said as I looked down.

"Yes, Ian likes a lot of women."

"He brings a different one home almost every night," I said.

Adalynn looked at me and tilted her head. "You aren't falling for him, are you?"

"No, of course not. Even if I was, and that's a big if, a man like Ian Braxton would never be interested in me."

"Of course he would, Rory. You're a beautiful woman and you're kind. Yeah, maybe you're right. The women Ian seems to go for are total greedy bitches with sticks up their asses." She laughed.

I laughed with her as my side started to hurt. I placed my hand on it and sat down in one of the chairs.

"Are you okay?" she asked.

"I'm fine. I'm just a little sore."

Adalynn took my hand and helped me up from the chair. "Let's get you back to the house so you can rest."

As we walked through the door and into the house, Ian was coming out of his study. He stopped in the middle of the room and stared at me. He looked at me as if it was the first time that he'd ever seen me.

"What's wrong, Ian? Cat got your tongue?" Adalynn smiled.

Ian cleared this throat as he walked over to where I was standing. When he cocked his head, the corners of his mouth curved up slightly. "Rory, you look amazing." He brought his hand up to my hair and took a few strands between his fingers. "Your hair looks great. You had it cut and some highlights put in." He smiled.

"Yeah. It was Benny's idea."

"Ah, you saw Benny. He's the one who cuts my hair."

I looked over at Adalynn and she winked at me. "I need to go now. I have a hot date to get ready for," she said as she walked over and gave Ian a hug and kiss.

When Adalynn turned to me, I hugged her and thanked her for everything she did for me. She had done more for me in one day than anyone ever had in my life. I would always be grateful to her. For the first time in my life, I felt beautiful, and even a little bit sexy.

"Well, are you going to show me what I bought you?" Ian smiled as he pointed to the bags I was holding.

"Oh, sure. Let's take them to my room."

Ian took the bags from me and we walked up the stairs and into the bedroom. He sat down in the chair and crossed his legs while I showed him what he had bought, piece by piece. He sat there with a smoldering smirk on his face.

"What's that look for?" I smiled.

"Nothing. I'm just admiring the things you picked out. You look happy, Rory, and I can't help but feel that I had something to do with that."

I turned away from him as I hung the clothes in the closet. I didn't know what to say because the truth was that I was happy because of him. After hanging the last piece of clothing, I walked over to him and he stood up. I did something I never thought I would've done. I gave him a light kiss on his cheek.

"Thank you, Ian. Thank you for everything. You saved my life, and I do want you to know that I'm grateful for that."

He brought his hand to my face and gently stroked my cheek as his eyes stared into mine. "It was my pleasure saving you." He smiled. "Now, if you'll excuse me, I need to go finish up some work before heading out to dinner." He walked to the door, stopped, turned around, and looked at me. "You'll be joining me tonight at one of my favorite restaurants. Maybe you should change into one of your new outfits. We're leaving promptly at seven o'clock, so make sure you're ready," he said as he walked out of the room.

I stood there, trying to take in what he'd just said. He was taking me to dinner tonight. Not one of his other women, but me. A mixture of excitement and nervousness shot through my body at the thought of having dinner with him. It was just going to be the two of us. He was amazingly beautiful, but intimidating. His confidence was something I'd never seen in a person before. He walked with his head held high, as if he was the most important person in the world. Ian Braxton knew he was sexy, and he knew how to charm women. His charm was weakening me. I felt things that scared me. Things I'd never felt before.

Chapter 4

When we walked into Capo, we were promptly seated by a hostess named Bella, a tall, blonde-haired, blue eyed, lean and toned woman. She eyed me up and down as she handed us our menus. *How did I know her name?* Ian referred to her by it when he thanked her as she showed us to our table. I took my napkin and set it in my lap as I took notice of my surroundings. The restaurant wasn't overly large. It was just the perfect size for a quaint and quiet meal. The cherry wood floors, exposed rafters, and sconces that were mounted to the walls gave the dining room a warm feel. I picked up the menu from the table and opened it. I gasped when I saw the prices. Ian chuckled as he looked over his menu.

"Believe me, Rory, this is not expensive. Please order whatever you want."

I wasn't used to elegant food like this. I grew up on tuna fish, chicken soup, fish sticks, and macaroni and cheese. The waitress came over to take our drink order.

"What kind of alcohol do you like?" Ian asked me.

I blankly stared at him, as I had no clue. I didn't want to say gin and tonic because this restaurant was too fancy for that. I remembered what Carrie Bradshaw from Sex and The City always drank, and I ordered myself a cosmopolitan. Ian gave me a smile and winked.

"Bring a bottle of your finest cabernet and two glasses," Ian said.

The waitress smiled and walked away. "Do you know what you want?" he asked as he glanced over his menu.

"The chicken?"

"Are you asking me?" he asked.

"I'm sorry, Ian."

I apologized to him because I felt like an idiot. I knew nothing about fine cuisine. I couldn't even pronounce ninety percent of the menu.

"No need to apologize. The chicken here is excellent. In fact, I think that's what I'll order." He smiled.

As I picked up my cosmopolitan and brought the glass to my lips, I took a sip with the hopes that it would give me the courage to ask Ian what I've been dying to know. I took in a deep breath as I set the glass down.

"Is there something you want to ask me?"

"Actually, there is." I smiled. "What do you do for a living?" There, I finally asked him.

He stared at me as the waitress set down the bottle of cabernet and two wine glasses. Ian poured some in a glass, swirled it around, and then took a sip. He smiled as he looked at the waitress and told her it was perfect.

"I'm in real estate and development. I buy and develop property all over the world."

"So there's one thing I know about you." I smiled as I took another sip of my cosmopolitan.

"What else would you like to know?"

I wanted to bring up his brief marriage to Adalynn, but I wasn't sure if that was such a good idea. The waitress set our plates in front of us and I finished up the last of my cosmopolitan. If I was going to get through this dinner, I was going to need more alcohol.

"Would you like some wine?" Ian asked.

"Yes, actually, I would."

He poured some into the glass and handed it to me. Our fingers briefly touched and the sensation that jolted through my body startled me. I took a sip from my glass as I looked at Ian.

"This is really good."

He gave me a small smile and continued to eat his dinner. "I'm glad you like it."

"What about your family?" I finally got up the nerve to ask.

"What about them?" he replied.

I got the impression he didn't want to talk about his family, the way he answered me. I remembered what Adalynn said about him being a private person and not liking to talk about his personal life. I took another sip of wine. Okay, it was more than a sip and, before I knew it, the glass was empty. I could feel the alcohol working its way through my body.

"Tell me about your family."

"Why do you want know?" he asked.

"Why not? You demanded to know about my family life and I told you. So don't you think it's only fair that I know about your family?"

His eyes peered into mine as if he was contemplating what he was going to say. He cleared his throat before he began to speak. "Fair? There's nothing fair in life, Rory. You of all people should know that, with the kind of life you say you had."

Suddenly, his words hit me and I was confused. "What do you mean the kind of life I *say* I had?" I asked as I glared at him and grabbed the bottle of wine, pouring some into my glass. "Are you insinuating that I lied to you?"

"Not really. But your story is quite imaginative and a bit unbelievable."

I threw back the wine and set the glass on the table. My skin was on fire, not only by the amount of alcohol I drank, but because of Ian and his accusations. I was no longer afraid and I wouldn't let him intimidate me. I threw my napkin on the table as I got up from my seat.

"Thank you, Mr. Braxton, for enlightening me on what kind of person you really are. I will take my imagination and my stories and get the fuck out of your house and life," I said as I stormed through the restaurant. People were staring and I didn't care. I hoped they saw what an asshole Ian Braxton really was.

As I exited the restaurant, I didn't know which way to go, so I opted to go right. I took off my shoes and headed down the street. My head was spinning and my side was starting to throb. I began to pick up the pace so I could get as far away from Ian as possible.

"You better stop right now!" I heard a voice command.

I flipped him off as I continued my journey to God knows where. I started to slow down because the pain was becoming unbearable. Too much, too soon. I saw a bench on a cobblestone walk and I couldn't keep moving, so I sat down. Moments later, Ian sat down next to me.

"First of all, you will never embarrass me in public like that again. Do you understand me?"

Really? Is this guy serious? Who the fuck does he think he is talking to me like that?

I slowly turned my head so I was staring straight into his eyes – the eyes that made me weak every time he looked at me. Eyes that were serious, but with a little sadness behind them. Maybe it was more fear. I didn't know, but Ian Braxton showed his true colors at that table and I wasn't going to stand for it.

"No, I won't embarrass you ever again. So, don't worry, Mr. Braxton. Maybe the dozens of women you take out and bring home to fuck let you talk to them that way, but I'm not one of those women, nor will I ever be."

He turned his head and looked the other way. "Taking you to dinner was a mistake and I apologize. You're welcome to stay at my house, as a guest, for as long as you need to. I'm not that heartless to kick a woman out who has no place to go."

I started to stand up as a shooting pain knocked me back down on the bench. I held my side and took in a deep breath. Ian grabbed a hold of my arm.

"You've done too much. You're going to hurt yourself even more."

Ian pulled his phone from his pocket and told Joshua where we were. Moments later, the limo pulled up to the curb. I jerked my arm away from Ian.

"Don't touch me. I can manage myself."

"Wow, you're a completely different person once you get some alcohol in you," he said.

I slid into the limo and Ian shut the door. He walked around to the other side and climbed in next to me. I turned my head and looked at him.

"You're wrong. This is me, with and without alcohol. Perhaps I did lie to you about my past."

He didn't say a word the rest of the way home. I walked into the house and went straight upstairs to my room.

****

I sat on the edge of the beautifully marbled tub and ran the water for a bath. Sitting in the corner was a bottle of all-natural bubble bath in a lavender scent. I poured some under the running water, and the smell instantly started to calm me. I was furious at Ian for what he said and I felt betrayed. I stood up and stripped out of my clothes, looking into the mirror at my knife wound. I slowly stepped down into the gigantic bathtub and sank until I was immersed in bubbles. As I closed my eyes, images of Stephen invaded my mind. I'd taken care of him my whole life. I was startled by the sound of Ian clearing his throat. When my eyes flew open, I saw that Ian was standing next to the tub, looking down at me.

"What the fuck?!" I yelled as I covered my breasts with my arms. Not that he could see anything, anyway. I was still covered up to my neck in bubbles.

"Do you realize how many times you've dropped the F bomb this evening?" he smirked.

"Do you realize that I'm taking a bath and I'm naked? What the hell, Ian? Get out!" I exclaimed as I splashed water at him.

He took a few steps backwards to avoid getting wet, but it didn't matter; he got wet anyway.

"I just wanted to let you know that I brought up a laptop and set it on the desk in case you needed a computer."

"You couldn't just tell me that through the door?"

"I knocked and you didn't answer me. I wanted to make sure you were okay. I didn't want to be held responsible if something happened to you."

"I'm fine. Now leave," I said as I pointed my finger at the door.

As he turned around and walked to the door, I called his name.

"Ian."

He turned and looked at me.

"You're right. There's nothing fair in life. Life's nothing but a game of who will survive and who won't. I'm a pawn in a game of struggle and disappointments. A game that no matter how many times I go around and around, I'll never reach the end."

He didn't say a word. He just turned and walked out, shutting the door behind him.

Once I was finished with my bath, I climbed out and put on one of the satin nightgowns Ian had bought me. As I was brushing my hair, I saw the laptop through the mirror of the vanity. I took it from the desk and sat down on the bed. I pulled up local job listings and saw an ad for a coffeehouse that was hiring. They wanted experienced only. I had more than enough experience, considering I worked at a coffeehouse back in Indiana for four years. Needing paper and a pen, I got up and opened the drawer to the desk. I breathed a sigh of relief when I saw some sitting there. I didn't want to have to go downstairs and risk Ian asking what I was doing. I quickly wrote down the address of the coffeehouse and tucked it away in my new purse. As I climbed into bed, I reached over and turned off the light. My head was starting to throb and I needed to get some sleep.

"Stephen, is that you?"

"Help me, Rory. You promised you'd help me."

"Stephen, where are you? I can't find you. It's too dark."

"Rory. You promised me. You said you'd make me better and you lied. You lied, Rory," Stephen screamed as he stabbed me.

I screamed as loudly as I could and I heard Ian's voice in the distance. "Rory, wake up. You're having a nightmare," he said as he shook me.

My eyes flew open and I could barely breathe. I looked at Ian and then around the room, as I was curled up on the floor in the corner. My face was soaked with tears and my body was soaked in sweat. Ian was holding my arms and I was shaking. Suddenly, there was a woman standing in the doorway.

"Ian, are you coming back to bed, baby?" she whined.

I looked at her and then at him. I closed my eyes and slowly shook my head. "Go," I whispered.

"Get out of here. In fact, gather your stuff and leave," Ian said to the girl.

"But—"

"No. Don't say another word. Leave my house now!" he said.

The girl turned away in a huff and, in an instant, she was gone. Ian brought his hand to my face and wiped away the tears underneath my eyes.

"Are you okay?" he asked.

"It was just a nightmare. I'll be fine," I said as Ian helped me up.

"What was your nightmare about?" he asked as he followed me to the bed.

"It was nothing. Please, just leave me alone."

"Don't tell me it was nothing. You were screaming at someone to stop."

"It was only my imagination," I said harshly.

Ian stood up and shook his head. "You know what? I'm done being nice to you or even trying to be your friend," he said as he walked out and slammed the door shut.

I lay down and pulled the covers close to me as I grasped the edge and held on for dear life.

Chapter 5

The next morning, after I got dressed, I walked downstairs to the kitchen where Charles was making breakfast.

"Good morning, Rory. Would you like a fresh homemade blueberry muffin? They just came out of the oven thirty minutes ago. They're Mr. Braxton's favorite."

I don't know why he felt the need to tell me that. I didn't care what Ian's favorite muffins were. "I bet he makes you hand-pick the blueberries. It wouldn't surprise me."

"I heard that, Aurora," Ian said as he walked into the kitchen in his dark gray tailored suit.

God, he looked good. I rolled my eyes and took my blueberry muffin and coffee outside on the patio.

"Where are you going?" he asked.

"Out on the patio," I replied.

"Why can't you eat that here, at the dining table?"

"I like being outside, if that's okay with you."

"Suit yourself. I really don't care what you do."

I sighed and sat down in the lounge chair. As soon as I was finished, I walked upstairs, grabbed my purse and, as I was heading out the front door, Ian stopped me.

"Where are you going?"

"Just into town to walk around. Don't you have to go to your office or something?"

"How do you plan on getting to town?" he asked.

"I'm going to walk."

Ian chuckled as he shook his head. "Do you know how far that is on foot? I'm heading to the office now, so Joshua can drop you off wherever you need to go after he drops me at the office."

The last thing I wanted to do was sit in a car with him. I wanted to avoid him at all costs, especially after last night, but it was better than walking. At least, I thought it was.

"Fine," I said as I turned around and walked out the door.

We climbed into the limo and both sat in silence. "Joshua, you can drop off Miss Sinclair first."

"I thought you had to get to the office."

"I do, but it's no problem."

"Where would you like to be dropped off, Miss Sinclair?" Joshua asked.

"It's Rory, and here's fine," I said as he pulled up to the curb of an outdoor mall.

Joshua got out, walked around, and opened the door for me. As I was about to get out, Ian grabbed my hand.

"Here, you'll need this."

I opened my hand and looked at the wad of money he gave me. "I don't want your money, Ian," I said as I threw it down on the seat and got out of the limo.

I was still pissed at the fact that he doubted my past, but what really made me angry was how fast he went out last night and brought that whore to his bed. *Who the hell does that?* One minute, he's taking me to dinner and giving me a laptop, and the next he's fucking some girl in a room down the hall from me. The more I thought about it, the angrier I became. The least he could have done was have some common courtesy and respect. You would think that a well-bred man like that would have even an ounce of it.

I stepped inside the coffee house and looked around. It was crowded and all the tables were filled. The line of people was almost out the door. Behind the counter was a guy and a girl who looked like they were going absolutely crazy. The first customer in line was complaining that the latte she ordered wasn't made right. I walked up to the edge of the counter and stood there for a moment until the girl looked up.

"The line is back there?" she said.

"I know, but I'm just here to get a job application. I saw your ad online."

"Do you have any experience at all?" she asked.

"Yes. Back in Indiana, I worked at a coffee house for the last four years."

She stopped what she was doing and looked at me. "Okay, come behind the counter. This will be your interview because we need the help and you have the experience. I'm Jordyn and that guy standing at the register is Ollie. Hey, Ollie, say hi to—"

"Rory." I smiled.

"Say hi to Rory."

Ollie gave me a small smile and nodded his head. Jordyn told me that my job was to make the customers' drinks as fast as I could. About twenty minutes later, the crowd had cleared and everyone left happy. Jordyn turned and looked at me with a grin.

"You're hired. You're amazing! Isn't she amazing, Ollie? Tell her she's amazing."

"You're amazing and welcome to Java Hut." He smiled.

A feeling of excitement overtook me as I felt like this was the first step in starting my life over. "Thank you. I really appreciate it. You have no idea how bad I need this job."

"Well, judging by your clothes, I assume you like the finer things in life." Jordyn smiled.

"It's a long story."

"I'm going to run in the back and grab an application for you to fill out. You know, formalities and shit. So make yourself a coffee and go have a seat."

I smiled at her and made a caramel macchiato before taking a seat. Jordyn was a cute girl. I towered over her with my five-foot-seven-inch stature compared to her five-foot-two. Her blonde hair was cut into a cute bob style and she wore light makeup. She seemed to have a lot of energy and she acted really sweet. Ollie seemed a little more shy and reserved. He was cute with his longer black hair and bangs that swept to the side. As I sat at the table, Jordyn walked over and handed me the application.

"Here, just fill out the required information. Can you start tomorrow?"

"Yes. Tomorrow will be great," I replied.

"The position is part-time for now, but I might need you for extra hours."

"That's fine. I want to work as much as I can." I smiled.

"You, my friend, are awesome. It's so hard finding anybody who wants to work these days."

I looked over the application and when it came to me putting down my address, I realized I didn't know it. *Shit.* I had to think of something quick. I left it blank and finished the rest of the application. I got up from the table and walked over to where Jordyn and Ollie were standing.

"I just moved here a couple of weeks ago and I'm staying with a friend and I don't know the house address."

"Oh, no problem. You can get it when you go home and then fill it in tomorrow when you start." She smiled.

"Thanks, Jordyn. I'll see you tomorrow morning," I said as I walked out the door.

Now what? I walked around the corner and did a little window shopping, and when I was finished, I sat down on a small wooden bench. I had no clue how I was getting back to Ian's house. I had no phone and no money, so I couldn't even take the bus if I wanted to. I sat there for about an hour, trying to formulate a plan, when suddenly, a black limo pulled up to the curb and the window started to roll down.

"I'm guessing you need a ride home." Ian smiled.

"What are you doing here, Ian?"

"I'm not stupid, Rory. I knew you had no way of getting home, so I had Joshua keep tabs on you. Now get in."

I rolled my eyes as I got up from the bench and climbed into the back of the limo. Ian looked at me and smirked.

"Did you have a nice day?"

"I had a great day, thank you. I thought you told me last night that you were done being nice to me," I said as I cocked my head.

"I certainly couldn't leave you stranded in a strange place. I'm not that mean."

Ian Braxton confused me. On one hand, he was a complete asshole, but on the other, he had a sweet side – a side that I wished he would show more often.

"Aren't you going to ask me how my day was?" he asked.

"How was your day, Ian?" I sighed.

"Fantastic. My day was fantastic, Aurora."

"Rory." I sighed.

"Let me tell you why my day was fantastic. I just closed a multi-million dollar deal that had been in negotiations for over a year and, to celebrate, I'm taking you to dinner."

"Remember what happened the last time you took me to dinner? You said it was a mistake and I ended up walking out."

"I do remember, since it was only last night, and I know that tonight will be different, right?"

The truth was that I was starving, and I hadn't had anything to eat all day except a blueberry muffin and coffee.

"Dinner sounds nice and there's actually another reason to celebrate." I smiled.

Ian tilted his head and gave a small smile. "Another reason? Are you going to tell me?"

"Yes, I am. At dinner."

He arched his eyebrow as he looked at me. He was so sexy and I hated myself for thinking it. We pulled up to the front of the restaurant and Joshua opened the door for me. As I stepped out, Ian held out his arm. I looked over at him and saw that he had a cocky grin on his face. I hooked my arm around his and we walked inside. The restaurant was very casual, almost like a family dining place. It was sure a big difference from the restaurant he took me to last night. As we were seated in the booth, I looked at him and twisted my face.

"What's that look for? I don't mind it. I think you're adorable when you do that. But, why are you looking at me that way?"

"I was just wondering why this restaurant. It seems very beneath you to dine in a restaurant like this."

Ian chuckled. "Well, it's not my first choice of a restaurant, but I thought you'd be more comfortable here since it's more—"

"More what, Ian?" I sternly asked.

"More your type of restaurant," he said as he waved his hand in the air. I knew he did not just say that. Yep, he said it, and I could feel my skin starting to burn with anger. I took in a deep breath and remained calm. I was hungry and I wasn't going to let his arrogant ass ruin my dinner.

"That's so sweet of you, Ian." I smiled as I tilted my head. "You are so thoughtful to go slumming to make me comfortable."

"Now, Aurora. That's not what I meant. You took that remark the wrong way."

"Did I, Ian? Then maybe you should explain to me what you meant."

The waitress walked over and asked us if we were ready to order. Ian looked at her and asked her nicely to give us a few moments to look over the menu. Ian opened his menu and, while he glanced at it, he tried to explain his words.

"All I meant was that last night's restaurant was fine dining at its best. This place is more, very casual dining, I guess you could say."

"You mean 'lower class' because that's what I am."

Ian looked up at me from his menu and stared into my eyes. I stared back. He was searching for something inside me. But he wouldn't find anything. It was nothing but a dark, cold, lonely place.

"I never said that, Rory. Don't put words in my mouth."

The waitress came and took our order. God, I was starving.

"I have something for you," Ian said as he reached into his suit pocket.

He held a cell phone in his hand and he extended it across the table towards me. I looked at it and then at him. I was shocked that he would give me a phone.

"What's this for?" I asked.

"For you. You can't be walking around without a phone. What if I needed to get in touch with you or you needed help? My number to the house, office, and my cell phone are already programmed in, and so is Adalynn's if you need to speak to her."

"Thank you, Ian, but I can't accept it. You've done enough already."

"Nonsense. You need a phone, Rory. Just take it and don't mention it again."

"I'll pay you back when I get my first check."

Ian took a sip of his water and, as he set the glass down, he looked at me strangely. "What do you mean when you get your first check?"

"That's the news I wanted to tell you! I got a job today. I'm working at Java Hut, and I start tomorrow morning!" I smiled.

Ian looked down. "I see. Why did you feel the need to go and get a job? I don't think you're fully healed yet."

"I'm fine, and I'm in less pain every day. In fact, I'm going to start running again. I got the job because I need to start over. I need to get my life back on track, and I need to find my brother. In order to do that, I need money."

Ian looked at me and paused before speaking. "You sure have a lot of needs." He smiled.

I couldn't help but smile when he said that because the smile on his face was something that captured me every time.

"You mentioned that you run."

"I used to run every day until—" I stopped as I looked down at my food.

"It's okay, Rory. You just took a little break. You'll be running again soon. Maybe we can go running together," he said.

"You run?"

"Yes. I run along the beach every morning."

"I've never seen you run."

"That's because I'm up and out at the crack of dawn. You're still sleeping." He smiled.

"I'd like that," I said.

The way Ian looked at me after I said that was different. I saw something in his eyes that I'd never seen before: a glimmer of light.

Chapter 6

We headed back to the house and Ian said he had some work to do, so he walked straight into his study and shut the door. I went upstairs to change into more comfortable clothing and then went and sat in the lounge chair on the patio and stared out into the night. Listening to the waves lap against the shore was peaceful. I began to think about Stephen. My mind wandered back to when Stephen and I were living in that house. As I was slowly closing my eyes and starting to drift off, I was startled by Ian's loud voice behind me.

"Why didn't you tell me that your brother is your twin?"

"Jesus, Ian, you scared the shit out of me. What the hell does it matter and how did you find out?"

"It doesn't matter how I found out. What matters is that you aren't being honest with me and I want to know what else you're hiding."

A rage began to brew up inside me as I contemplated whether or not to go off on him. I opted for going off on him. I shot up from the chair and stared directly into his eyes as I pushed my finger into his chest.

"I've been honest with you about everything. I'm sorry I didn't tell you Stephen is my twin brother and it wasn't something I was trying to hide. Do you know how embarrassing it was even to tell you that it was *my* brother who attacked me and that he's schizophrenic? You already think I'm trash as it is," I yelled, and turned and walked away.

As soon as I stepped through the door and into the kitchen, Ian grabbed me and pushed me up against the wall, holding my arms above my head. "Don't turn your back on me, Rory. I'm sorry. I don't think you're trash. I think you're broken and I can fix you," he whispered in my ear.

His hot breath traveled down my neck and my body went into a near convulsion. I wanted him, but I knew if anything were to happen, it would destroy me. I would become too emotionally attached and when he got tired of me and moved on, I wouldn't recover. He brought his face to mine as he stared into my eyes.

"I'm not broken. I'm shattered. I'm a million tiny pieces that would take longer than forever to piece back together. So please, do me the favor and don't even try," I whispered.

His grip on my arms lightened as he let go and took a step back, giving me one last look before he turned around and walked away. I stood and placed my hand on my neck where his hot breath had touched me. I took in a deep breath and walked upstairs. Tomorrow was the day I start my life over, alone.

****

"Rory, I need you. I need your help. I'm sorry I hurt you. You know it wasn't my fault. You promised you'd always take care of me. You said that no matter what happened to us, you'd always be there."

"Stephen, where are you? I can't see you. I'm trying to find you."

"Rory, I don't believe you. You lied to me, Rory! YOU LIED TO ME!"

"I'm sorry!" I screamed as I felt hands gripping my arms.

"Rory, wake up."

I could hear Ian's voice in the distance as I was running through the woods. He was telling me to wake up, but I couldn't. I ran, calling Stephen's name and looking every which way for him.

"Damn it, Rory! Wake up!" Ian yelled.

My eyes flew open. I was out of breath. My heart was racing and the only thing I could do was throw my arms around Ian's neck and beg him to hold me. I broke down and sobbed as I buried my face into his neck. I wrapped my legs around his waist as he held me tight.

"Shh, it was only a dream. Calm down. No one is going to hurt you anymore," he whispered as he kissed the side of my head. "Come on; let's get you back in bed," he said as he lifted me up and carried me.

As soon as he laid me down, he sat on the edge of the bed and began pushing the strands of my hair behind my ear. "You have nothing to fear."

"I need to find him, Ian. He's crying out for help. I can feel it. He's in trouble."

As he gave me a warming look, he ran the back of his hand along my cheek. "We'll talk about this in the morning. Get some sleep," he said as he got up from the bed.

When he started to walk away, I reached out and grabbed his hand. I didn't want to be alone. I wanted him to stay with me and comfort me. As much as I hated to admit it, I needed him at that moment.

"Please stay with me tonight."

Ian turned around and looked at me. I could see the hurt in his eyes as he spoke, "I'm sorry, Rory, but I can't." He walked out of the room, leaving me there, scared, lonely, and starving for comfort. I began to get the impression that I wasn't the only one who was shattered.

The next morning, I got out of bed, showered, and headed downstairs. As I walked into the kitchen, Ian was just walking through the door. He had just come back from a run. He was dripping in sweat and he looked even sexier. I quickly diverted my eyes to the coffee pot because I couldn't face him after last night. I was hurt and confused by his actions. One minute, he was all over me and the next, he was pulling away.

"Good morning. How did you sleep?" he asked as he wiped his face with a towel.

"Not good," I replied as I poured some coffee into my cup.

"How are you getting to work?"

"I'm going to call a cab."

"A cab costs money. Something you don't have any of. Joshua will drive you in or you can take one of the cars if you know how to drive."

"You have cars?"

"Yeah, I have three of them. Actually, Joshua will drive you in and I'll drive myself to work."

I gave him a small smile as I took a sip of my coffee and waited for Joshua to show up.

"I need to go and shower. Good luck today," he said as he turned and walked away.

Something was off with Ian Braxton that morning. He was moody. I'd already picked up on that, but there was more going on with him than he was letting on.

Joshua walked into the kitchen and smiled. "Are you ready to go?"

"Yeah. Just let me grab my purse."

As I sat in the back of the limo, I pulled out my phone and pulled up Adalynn's name. I sent her a text message, telling her about my new job. A few moments later, she replied.

"That's great news, Rory. To celebrate, I'm taking you to dinner. Text me with the time you get off and I'll pick you up."

"Thank you. But that's not necessary, Adalynn."

"Nonsense. I'll be there and you better be hungry."

"Fine. But next time, I'm paying."

"Deal."

I asked Joshua to drop me off around the corner because I didn't want to risk Ollie and Jordyn seeing me step out of the limo. They would begin to ask questions and I wasn't ready to answer them. I walked through the door of Java Hut and saw Jordyn standing behind the counter with a big grin on her face.

"Welcome, Rory! You have no idea how excited I am that you're part of the Java Hut team!"

"Thanks. I'm happy to be here." I smiled.

Jordyn showed me around the coffeehouse and showed me how to work the register. It was pretty much the same cash register I used back in Indiana, so it only took a few minutes to learn.

"Where's Ollie?" I asked.

"He's still at home sleeping. He doesn't come in for another couple of hours."

"The two of you live together?"

"Yeah, we've been dating on and off for about four years." She smiled. "Oh, by the way, do you have your address?"

"Oh, yeah," I said as I grabbed my purse from under the counter and took out the small piece of paper.

Jordyn looked at it and then at me. She looked back down at the address and then at me again. "This is where you live?"

"Yes. Why?"

She started to speak, but couldn't. It was funny watching her try to spit out the words. "This is Ian Braxton's address. You're staying with him?"

Fuck. How the hell does she know that's his address? I looked down as I nodded my head. "Yes, I'm staying with Ian. How do you know his address?"

"I'm a journalism student at UCLA and I did an interview with him about three months ago for the university magazine.

His office was under construction, so we did the interview at his house. Are you dating him?"

Great. I hadn't even been there twenty minutes and the questions about my life were already starting. "No, Ian and I are not dating. We're just friends and he was kind enough to let me stay with him because I didn't have anywhere else to go."

"He's a very intimidating man. Have you met his father yet?"

"No," I said.

Jordyn laughed. "That man is piece of work, let me tell you. While I was interviewing Ian, his father came over and rudely interrupted our meeting. He told me that I was insignificant and to step outside while he had a conversation with his son. I'd never met anyone so rude in my life."

"Ian's never talked about his family," I said.

"How long have you been staying with him?" Jordyn asked.

I knew if I answered, more questions would be asked, and I didn't want to get into it with a girl I'd only known a day. In fact, I didn't want to get into it with anyone.

"Only a couple of weeks. I'm just a guest and I barely see him."

A rush of people walked through the door, and that distracted Jordyn from asking me any further questions. Ollie came in as scheduled and the three of us got along well. I could easily see myself becoming friends with them. My shift had ended and I said goodbye to Jordyn and Ollie. Before I walked out the door, Jordyn handed me my schedule and, surprisingly, I had tomorrow off. I gave a wave goodbye and walked out of Java

Hut. I saw Adalynn's car parked at the curb and I climbed in with a smile on my face.

"I take it you had a great first day of work," she said.

"It was good. It felt good to work again." I smiled.

"Well, I hope you're hungry, and I hope you like Mexican, because I've been craving it all day."

"Mexican sounds good." I smiled.

****

As Adalynn and I were sipping margaritas and eating chips and salsa, I decided to ask her about Ian's father. It really bothered me what Jordyn had said about him and I wanted to know if it was true.

"Tell me about Ian's father," I said.

Adalynn looked at me strangely and as if I had just touched on a taboo subject. "Why do you want to know about Richard?"

"My friend, Jordyn, from Java Hut did an interview with Ian about three months ago and she said that she met his father and he was the rudest person she'd ever met. I guess I was just curious, since Ian hasn't mentioned him. I didn't know if they were close or not."

Adalynn picked up her glass and looked at me. "Ian and his father are very close. Richard can be mean and crude. He has very little respect, if any at all, for women. I think that's where Ian gets his attitude from. Ian's mother passed away when he was eight years old and left Richard to raise their only child. After she died, Richard never remarried. He just bounced from woman to woman. From what I hear, he has women all around the world that drop everything when he comes to town."

"Wow. He sounds like a real gem," I said. "I guess that explains why Ian is always with different women," I said as I looked down.

Adalynn put her hand on mine. "Rory, I get the feeling that you're falling for Ian and it's not a good idea. I don't want to see you get hurt. He's a charmer and he'll make you fall hard and fast. But, in the end, he'll break you."

A small smile escaped my lips as I removed my hand from hers and took a sip of my margarita as I lied to my friend. "Don't worry, I'm not falling for him. He can't break me anymore than I already am. No one can."

Adalynn told me that she had just started her own magazine company called *Prim* and she was hoping, as she put it, to kick *Vogue*'s ass out of the water. Her goal was for *Prim* to become one of the most respectable and high-powered magazine companies around. She told me that Ian had helped her get it off the ground and that he was a major contributor. I admired Adalynn a lot.

"Oops, look at the time. I better get you home."

I pulled my phone from my purse, and I noticed I had 35 missed calls and 45 text messages; all from Ian. I looked at Adalynn as I showed her my phone. Her eyes widened as she looked at me.

"Well, I'm going to say that Ian was trying to get a hold of you."

As soon as I went to call him, my phone died. Adalynn drove me back to Ian's house and as soon as we walked through the door, Ian came storming through the living room.

"Where the fuck have you been?! And why the fuck didn't you answer your phone?" he screamed.

"Calm down, Ian. She was with me. I picked her up from work and we went to dinner."

"Don't tell me to calm down, Adalynn."

"Leave her alone. We had a good night and you're not going to ruin it. Now, I have to go. I'll call you tomorrow, sweetie." She smiled as she hugged me.

As soon as the door shut, Ian's glare burned through me. "Do you know how many times I tried to call you, not to mention all the text messages I sent you?"

"Yeah, I do. I saw it when I pulled out my phone from my purse."

"Then why the fuck couldn't you answer?!" he screamed as he stepped closer to me.

"I didn't hear it ring."

"You didn't hear it ring? Do you even have the ringer volume turned up?" he continued to yell.

He was frightening me and it threw me back to a night when I was a child. I started to shake as I ran up the stairs and into my room, heading straight for the corner where Ian had found me the past few nights. I sat with my back against the wall and curled myself into a ball. I closed my eyes tightly and buried my head, trying to escape the memories of that night. I heard the door handle turn and my heart started beating faster than it already was. I cried as I whispered over and over, "Please don't hurt me. Please don't hurt me."

I felt a soft touch on my hands. "Oh my God, Rory. I would never hurt you. I'm so sorry," he said as he wrapped his arms around me and held me. "I was just so worried about you and when you didn't answer your phone, I immediately thought you were in danger and I couldn't find you. I felt helpless."

"He wouldn't stop screaming. 'Who do you think you are, spying on us? I think I need to teach you a lesson little girl,' and he grabbed me by my hair. My aunt came in the room and told him to leave me alone and not to waste his time on a piece of shit like me."

"Jesus Christ," he said as his grip tightened around me.

I finally started to calm down. As much as Ian had scared me moments before, he was now comforting me. His voice and touch were both warm and apologetic. I broke our embrace and wiped my eyes. Ian took my face in his hands.

"I'm sorry. I didn't mean to scare you. Please don't ever fear me. I will never hurt you."

I stared into his eyes as he desperately apologized to me. "I'm sorry," he whispered as he brought his lips to mine and kissed me softly.

His hand wrapped around the nape of my neck as his kiss grew more intense. A low growl came from the back of his throat as I parted my lips and he slipped his tongue inside. I reciprocated and he went crazy, like an untamed beast. He halted and looked at me, breathless from our kiss.

"I want you so bad, Rory. I want to fuck you. I want to taste your sweetness and I want to bury myself deep inside you."

He had me at the first "I want." I had never wanted anything or anyone more badly in my life than I wanted Ian Braxton inside me. I knew it would change me and I didn't know if I was ready for it. I sat there, breathless and aching, as I smiled at him.

"You sure have a lot of wants."

Ian chuckled and put his forehead on mine. "Do you want me, Rory? Do you want me to fuck you? I need an answer," he said.

"Yes. I want you."

"You want me to what, Rory?"

He was putting me on the spot because I never had said that to anybody and I was feeling embarrassed. But, I managed to spit out the words if it would get him to touch me again.

"I want you to fuck me, Ian."

He took in a sharp breath and closed his eyes while he held the back of my head. "Not tonight. I need to make sure you're strong and fully healed. I can't risk hurting you, because when I fuck you, sweetheart, I'm going to take you on a ride you'll never forget and do things to you that you've never experienced before."

Did I just hear him correctly? Did he just say "not tonight"? I didn't have the strength to argue. He was playing me and I wasn't going to stand for it. Ian Braxton had taken me to another world, even if just for a few moments. He made me get lost in him, in his scent, and his charm. I was tired of being the weak person, succumbing to what people wanted and what they needed. I was no longer going to be a victim of my life.

I pushed him away while I stared into his eyes. "You're right, Ian. Not tonight."

Chapter 7

I set my alarm for five thirty a.m. Today was the day I was starting my daily run. I went into the bathroom and splashed some cold water on my face as I examined my swollen eyes from last night. I changed into some yoga pants, threw on a t-shirt, and went downstairs. Charles was in the kitchen, preparing breakfast. It smelled like blueberry muffins again.

"Good morning, Charles." I smiled as I opened the fridge and grabbed a bottle of water.

"Good morning, Rory. Blueberry muffins will be coming out of the oven soon. Would you like one?"

"No, thank you. I'm heading out for a run. Have you by any chance seen Ian yet this morning?"

"He's out for a run himself." Charles smiled.

Damn it. I thought I could be up and out before he was. "Thanks, Charles. By the way, please don't mention that you saw me this morning."

"I won't, Miss Rory. Have a nice run."

"Oh, and one more question. Which way does he usually go when he runs?"

"If you're trying to avoid him, I'd go left." He winked.

A smile fell across my face as I opened the door and turned left. I took it easy at first. Since it was my first time attempting any sort of exercise after the incident, I didn't want to push myself, so I started to jog slowly. The sun was just starting to rise as I jogged along the shoreline. I took in deep breaths of fresh ocean air as a slight wind swept across my face. This was perfect. I was relaxed and, for the first time in so long, I felt peace. I picked up the pace, just a little, as I was doing okay. Today was the day; my day of renewed strength and a new life. The first thing I needed to do was move out of Ian's house. As much as I had wanted him last night, I knew that it would've been a mistake. A man like Ian Braxton and a woman like me would never work. We were on opposite sides of the spectrum. We were from different worlds and nothing would ever change that. I needed to get back to the motel that Stephen and I had stayed at. I had left something behind and I had a feeling it would still be there. I ran about three miles before the cramping in my side started. I stopped and faced the ocean as I grabbed my side and bent over, trying to ease the pain.

"You overdid it," Ian's voice said.

I stood up straight and put my hands on my hips. "Nah, I'm good. Three miles isn't bad for a stab victim."

"Three miles is too much for the first time. I would've gone with you had I known what time you were going."

I stood still, staring out into the depths of the ocean. I didn't want to turn around because I couldn't face him after last night. I could still feel his moist lips on mine, and I wanted more. Before I knew it, I felt his hands clasp my shoulders from behind.

"Are you ready to head back?" he spoke softly.

The flip in my belly, causing the familiar ache down below, was back. His simple touch was enough to excite me. I needed to stay strong. Today was the day; my day to never let anyone control me again.

"I'm ready," I said as I walked away without even so much as a glance at him.

"Are you mad at me or something?" he asked as he caught up with me.

"No. Why would you ask that?"

"I'm not stupid, Rory. I can tell something is wrong with you. You won't even look at me."

I stopped dead in my tracks and turned to him. "There, I'm looking at you. See? Nothing's wrong."

"Don't be bitchy. I don't like bitchy women."

"Really? I'll have to remember to be extra bitchy then."

"What the hell is the matter with you?" Ian said as he grabbed my arm and pulled me back. "Why the attitude? Is it because I wouldn't fuck you last night? Is that what this whole bitchy attitude is about? I told you that I won't risk hurting you and I thought you would appreciate that."

Strong. Stay strong. "I do appreciate it, Ian. I'm sorry." I smiled softly.

He tilted his head as he brought his hand up to my face. He took his finger and softly traced the outline of my lips. "I don't regret kissing you last night and I won't regret kissing you now," he said as he brushed his lips on mine. His kiss was soft and light. He looked at me and smiled. "I think Charles made some blueberry muffins. Let's go have one."

As soon as we got back to the house and walked through the patio doors, Ian stopped, looking at a man sitting down at the table.

"Dad, I didn't know you were back from your trip."

"Hello, son," he said as he glared at me.

"Rory, this is my father, Richard. Dad, this is Rory Sinclair."

"Nice to meet you." I smiled as I held out my hand.

Richard just looked at me with cold hard eyes as he dismissed the fact that I had my hand out to greet him.

"Okay then," I said as I put my hand down and walked over to pour a cup of coffee.

"Tomorrow night is the annual company gala. Have you decided who you're bringing as your date?"

My stomach instantly felt sick when I heard Richard ask that. "No, Dad. I haven't decided yet."

"I think you need to bring that hot blonde. You know; the one with the huge tits? She's good arm candy for you, son, and there's going to be a lot of press there, so if you haven't already, give her a call and ask her."

Ian looked away from his father and over at me. I wanted to run out of there so badly, but I didn't want to make it obvious that this conversation was hurting me.

"So, Rory. What kind of name is that?" Richard asked.

"Dad! That's enough," Ian snapped.

"It's okay, Ian," I said. I walked over to the table and sat down across from Richard. "It's a nickname. My real name is Aurora."

"Well, that's not any better," he chuckled.

Wow, Jordyn was right. This man was a complete asshole.

"Ian, I need to speak with you. Let's go into the study."

Ian looked over at me, but didn't say a word. He walked out of the kitchen and followed his father to his study. After a few moments, I quietly made my way to the study and listened outside the door at their conversation.

"Who the fuck is that girl and why is she here?" Richard snapped.

"That girl is my houseguest because she was badly injured and she needed medical attention."

"Is she better now?"

"She's better."

"Then get rid of her. You don't need some lowlife hanging around your house and your money. And you better not even think about bringing that girl tomorrow night."

"I'm not bringing her, so don't worry," Ian said.

My heart broke at that moment. Not because Ian wouldn't ask me to go with him to the gala, but because he didn't defend me. I needed to get out of here and away from Ian as quickly as possible. I ran up the stairs to my room and took a quick shower. When I was finished, I sent a text message to Adalynn, asking her if there was any possible way she could drive me to the motel. I didn't have any money for a cab and there was no way

I was asking Joshua. She sent me a text message back, saying that she'd be here within the hour. I quickly got dressed and then headed downstairs.

Ian was walking up the stairs as I was walking down. "Hey. You look great." He smiled.

"Did your father leave?" I asked.

"Yeah, he just left."

I pushed Ian out of the way as I continued down the stairs. "Rory, I'm sorry for the things he said to you. He can be an ass sometimes."

"He's more than an ass and don't apologize for him. I'm used to it, anyway."

"Rory, wait," he said.

I walked out the front door and sat on a bench that was near a pond in the front of the house. A few moments later, Ian came outside, carrying his briefcase. He walked over to where I was sitting and stood over me.

"I'm leaving for the office now. Maybe tonight, we can have dinner here. I'll have Charles cook us something nice."

"That sounds nice, but I think maybe the hot blonde with the huge tits would enjoy it more. You're calling her anyway; ask her over for dinner and then you can take her upstairs and fuck her. Oh, wait, that would be tomorrow night after the gala. I believe you don't fuck the same girl two nights in a row."

"Rory," he said as he slowly shook his head.

"Don't you have an office you need to get to?"

He turned away and climbed into the back of the limo that was waiting for him in the driveway.

****

"Seriously, Rory, this neighborhood is not one I like to travel to," Adalynn said nervously.

"I know. But it's all I could afford."

Adalynn pulled into a parking space at the motel and leaned over the steering wheel, looking out the window. "Do we have to get out?"

"Yes, Adalynn, we need to get out. I have to talk to the clerk in the office. I will warn you, it smells pretty bad in there."

"Gee, thanks for the warning. I never would've guessed." She smirked.

We walked into the motel office and it reeked of cigars. The man sitting behind the counter was overly large and bald and he had a limp when he walked.

"What can I do for you beautiful ladies?" He grinned.

I explained to him that I had left something in the room that my brother and I had stayed in a couple of weeks ago. He glared at me as he bit down on his cigar.

"Sorry, no can do, pretty girl. If you want to get back into that room, you'll have to pay for it."

"Are you kidding me? I only need to retrieve something that I left behind. I won't be more than five minutes."

"You're talking two weeks ago, pretty girl. Those rooms have been cleaned and cleaned again. If you would've left something behind, we would've found it."

I sighed and put my elbows on the counter. "Listen, you mother—"

"We'll pay for the room. How much?" Adalynn interrupted.

"Adalynn, no. He's ripping us off."

"Now *you're* a smart cookie," the man said as he winked at Adalynn. "It's fifty bucks for the night."

I shot him a look, as I knew he was overcharging us. "I only paid forty dollars. You raised your price within the last two weeks?"

"Inflation, sugar. Gotta keep up with that damn inflation." He smiled. "Now which room was it?"

"Room 205," I said.

The man stared at me when I gave him the room number. "That's the room that had blood all over the floor. It stained my carpet."

"I'm sorry. I cut my foot and I had to go to the hospital."

"That boy that was with you. He up and left without checking out and he left the blood all over the place. I'm sorry, but if you want back into the room, I have to charge you extra for the mess you left."

I started to speak and Adalynn interrupted me. "Here's two hundred dollars. Give us the fucking keys so my friend can get what she left and we can get out of this shithole."

"Like I said, smart cookie." He smiled as he handed us the key to the room.

Adalynn and I went to Room 205. She inserted the key and opened the door. "Jesus, Rory. How the fuck could you stay here?"

"I didn't have a choice. It was all I could afford," I said as I walked over to the bed. I pulled it away from the wall and stuck my hand behind the headboard. I felt around until my hand touched the tape that I had put there when Stephen and I had first arrived. I ripped off the tape and pulled out an envelope filled with cash. I looked at Adalynn and smiled.

"I can't believe that's still here," she said with wide eyes.

"Do you think in a place like this they actually pull out the bed and clean behind it?"

"Good point." She laughed.

"I taped it here when Stephen was in the bathroom. I didn't want him to know that I had it because he would've stole it. I didn't have time to grab it after he stabbed me."

Adalynn looked at me with sympathetic eyes. "I'm so sorry you had to go through that. Didn't you have a suitcase or anything?"

"Yeah, but I'm sure Stephen took that when he left. I have to find him, Adalynn. He's dangerous and he needs help," I said as I looked down at the bloodstained carpet.

"Ian can help you find him. He has resources and connections."

"I don't want Ian's help, ever. He's helped me enough, and it's time to move on," I said as I opened the door and walked outside.

We gave the key back to the overly large man and got out of there as fast as we could. I reached into the envelope and pulled out some money.

"Here, I want to pay you back for the motel," I said.

"Rory, no. You're going to need all of that money for whatever it is you're planning. Just forget about it and do what you have to do."

I sighed because I knew if I argued with her, she'd end up winning anyway. So I thanked her and changed the subject.

"I met Ian's father this morning."

"Oh, he's back from his trip? How'd it go?"

"He was repulsed by me and my name and, the sad part was, Ian didn't even defend me."

"Ian can be an ass and, as for Richard, pay him no attention. The man has issues and wouldn't know a proper woman if one stepped on his face. Now, where do you want me to drop you off? Something tells me that you don't want to go back to Ian's house."

"Can you just drop me off at Java Hut?"

Adalynn pulled up to the curb and before I got out of the car, she grabbed my hand. "I'm having a birthday party Saturday night and I want you to come. It'll be your first Malibu party."

"Thanks for the invite, Adalynn, but I wouldn't fit in."

"You will fit in, Rory. I want to celebrate my birthday with my new friend. Please come."

There was a hint of desperation in her voice when she asked me. She had done so much for me and it wouldn't be right if I turned her down. "Of course I'll come. I wouldn't miss your birthday." I smiled.

"Great! You can come with Ian, or if you'd prefer not to, I'll text you my address."

"Text me your address and thank you again for taking me to retrieve this," I said as I held up the envelope.

"You're welcome. I'll see you Saturday."

I shut the door and Adalynn drove away. I walked into Java Hut and asked Ollie for a chai tea latte.

"Hey, Grayson, this is Rory. Rory, this is Grayson. Today's his first day back from vacation."

"Hi, Grayson." I smiled as I held out my hand.

"It's nice to meet you, Rory. I look forward to working with you."

Ollie handed me my tea and I went and sat down at the table. Jordyn came out from the back room and as soon as she saw me, she sat down across from me.

"What are you doing here on your day off?"

"I was out and about and needed some chai." I smiled as I held up my cup. "Do you have a newspaper or something? I want to look for an apartment."

"I have my iPad. You can use that," she said as she got up from her chair.

She set her iPad down in front of me and pulled up the listings of apartments for rent in the area. I looked at the prices and shook my head. "I can't afford any of these apartments."

"I may have something for you," Jordyn said. "Let me call my dad."

She stepped away from the table as I sat there and contemplated on what to do. There was no way I could continue to live here. A few moments later, Jordyn sat back down and smiled.

"I may have just the place you're looking for. It's not much and it needs to be cleaned up, but I think you could do wonders with it and it's super cheap."

"Seriously?" I asked excitedly.

"Follow me," she said as she led me out the door and over to the next building. On the side of the building were a set of black, wrought-iron stairs that led to a door up above. The store below was a bakery and you could smell their bread from the street. Jordyn inserted the key into the lock and opened the door. She flipped the light switch as we walked inside.

"It's not much, but I think with some help, you can make this place a nice home."

"Jordyn, I don't understand," I said as I looked around.

"My dad owns this building and Java Hut. He didn't want the hassle of renting this place out, so he never did anything with it. I explained to him your situation and he said you're more than welcome to fix the place up and he'll only charge you $100 a month, water included. So, all you'll have to pay is gas and lights and, in this little place, that won't be much."

I didn't know what to say. I was stunned at the generosity of Jordyn and her father. I looked around. To the left side was the small kitchen area with a stove, sink, refrigerator, and a small counter top. A few feet down was a closed door, which I had guessed to be the bathroom. I opened the door and just about died when I saw the filthiness of it.

"Okay, so that needs some cleaning up," Jordyn said as she pinched her nose closed.

The bathroom had a toilet, sink, and a bathtub. No more than one person could be in there at one time. I walked over to a large window and pushed back the curtains. The sunlight that filtered in was amazing. It really brightened the whole place up.

"I'll take it." I smiled.

"Great. I'll let my dad know, and Ollie and I will help you fix it up! I love to decorate." She smiled as she hooked her arm around me.

I smiled back at my new friend, but worry started to consume my mind about Ian's reaction when I tell him I'd be leaving. I couldn't stop thinking about last night and what he said to me. He wanted me and, when he touched me, I wanted him too. But if I let him have his way with me, I would be the one who would be destroyed, not him.

"Earth to Rory," Jordyn said as she waved her hand in front of my face. "Where were you?" She laughed.

"Sorry. I was just picturing this place all done."

"I'll bring some cleaning supplies with me tomorrow and, after our shift, we can come up here and start cleaning. I'll get Ollie and a couple of his friends to help."

"Thank you, Jordyn. I'm so grateful for your help."

"That's what friends and co-workers are for." She smiled.

Chapter 8

"How was your day?" I heard Ian ask as I stood on the shoreline and let the water soak my feet.

"It was fine. How was your day?"

He walked over and stood next to me. I looked down and saw that he didn't have on any socks or shoes. In fact, he was dressed in khaki shorts and a cotton shirt. I looked him up and down.

"Is there something wrong with me?" he asked.

"No. I'm just not used to seeing you dressed so casually."

Ian laughed as he pushed my hair behind my ear. "What did you do today?"

His fingers brushed against my ear, which resulted in shivers riveting throughout my body. I was going to have to tell him sooner or later about what I did and what I was doing.

"I went back to the motel Stephen and I were at so I could retrieve something I left behind."

Ian cocked his head and glared at me. "How did you get there and what did you leave behind?"

"Adalynn was kind enough to take me, and I left an envelope of money taped to the back of the headboard."

"And it was still there?" he asked, in shock.

"Yeah. Like I told Adalynn, do you really think places like that pull out the bed to clean?"

"Well, I don't know which motel you were at, so I really couldn't answer that."

"Let's just say it's like Motel Hell and Adalynn was repulsed." I smiled softly.

"That was smart to hide your money. Why didn't you mention it sooner? I would've taken you to get it."

"I was too busy trying to heal, I guess."

"I'm truly sorry for my father and the things he said. I think maybe the three of us should have dinner together so he can get to know you better."

"He doesn't need to get to know me, Ian. You stood there and didn't say a word to him. You let him treat me like a piece of shit, so you're just as bad as he is. But like I said earlier, I'm used to it and didn't expect anything else."

"Rory, please."

"No! There's no 'please.' What's done is done. The sad thing is I thought we were friends," I said as I started to walk away.

"We are friends," he said as he lightly grabbed my arm and stopped me.

I turned around and looked at him. "Really? Because the last time I checked, friends stick up for each other. And by the way, I'm moving out," I said as I turned and walked away.

"What do you mean you're moving out? Where the hell are you moving to?" he yelled.

I ignored him as I walked to the house and up to my room. It wasn't too long before he came storming into the bedroom. "Where are you moving to?" he demanded.

"I'm moving to an apartment by Java Hut."

"You can't afford any apartments over in that area," he yelled.

He was angry that I was leaving and I couldn't understand why. *Was he lonely? Or did he like having someone here he could control?* "Calm down, Ian. I won't tell you anything unless you calm down."

He stared at me for a moment and then ran his hands through his hair. He walked over to the bed and sat down. He buried his face in his hands and, for a moment, my heart started to ache. I walked over, sat down next to him, and put my hand on his leg.

"It's a small apartment upstairs from a bakery next to Java Hut. Jordyn, the girl that hired me, her father owns it and is letting me stay there for $100 a month. I just need to clean it up a bit."

Ian sighed and looked at me. "Okay. When are you leaving?" he asked.

"I don't know yet. I guess whenever I can get the place cleaned up. Is that okay?"

He brought his hand to my face and ran the back of it across my cheek. "You are more than welcome to stay here for as long as you want," he said.

I closed my eyes at his touch as I took his hand and pressed it firmly against my lips. "Thank you. Thank you for everything."

"You're welcome," he whispered. "Say you'll have dinner with me. I'll grill us some steaks and we can open a bottle of wine, sit on the patio, and have a nice dinner."

"You can cook?" I smiled.

"Yes. Can you?"

"Yeah. I can cook."

"Good. Then you can help me." He smiled as he got up from the bed and held out his hand. "Let's go kick Charles out of the kitchen."

I put my hand in his and we walked down to the kitchen. "I'm giving you the rest of the night off, Charles. Rory and I will be cooking dinner."

"Are you sure, sir?" Charles asked in amazement.

"Yes, I'm sure. Enjoy your night."

Ian walked over to the refrigerator and pulled out a couple of steaks. I followed behind him and took out everything I needed to make a salad. I washed the lettuce while Ian started the grill. He went downstairs and came back up with a bottle of cabernet.

"See this bottle here?"

"Yes." I smiled.

"This is a vintage cabernet that I had flown in from France. So, I really hope you like it because it was very expensive."

"And if I don't like it?"

"Well, just humor me and pretend you do." He winked.

I couldn't help but laugh softly as I cut up the tomatoes. It was amazing to me how sweet Ian was being especially after I told him I was moving out. It also made me wonder how many women he did this with. As I was in thought, I felt a sharp pain in my finger.

"SHIT!" I yelled as I held my finger.

Ian came running inside. "What happened? Are you all right?"

"I just cut my finger. I'm okay."

"You don't look okay. Let me see," he said as he took my hand. "Rory, in order for me to look at it, you need to let go."

I was scared. I didn't want to let go. "Ian, seriously, it's no big deal."

"You're scared; I can tell. It'll be okay. Just let me see if you need stitches. Please, Rory."

His pleading eyes forced me to let go and show him my finger. He looked at it and smiled. "I think you're going to survive, since it's barely bleeding."

He walked over to the drawer and pulled out a Band-Aid. As he removed it from the wrapper, he asked me to hold up my finger. I did. He softly kissed it and put the Band-Aid securely around it.

"There, all better."

"I'm sorry. I overreacted," I said as I looked down.

"You didn't overreact and it's understandable with what you've been through," he said as he pressed his lips against my forehead. "I have to go check on the steaks. Do you need me to finish the salad?"

"No, I can finish it."

Ian smiled and walked outside. He smiled a lot tonight, and he was making me fall deeper for him. I finished the salad and set it outside on the table. I cut up a fresh loaf of bread that Charles had made earlier in the morning, boiled some redskin potatoes, seasoned them, and set them on the table while Ian set down the plates and silverware. He brought the bottle of wine outside and poured some into my glass. He handed it to me as I sat down.

"Now remember, pretend." He winked.

I took a sip and smiled. "It's perfect."

"No pretending?" he asked as he held up his glass.

"No pretending. I truly like it." I smiled as I brought my glass to his.

The steak that Ian grilled was prepared to perfection. I cut into it and took a bite. He stared at me as I chewed. "Is something wrong?" I asked.

"I've sort of gotten used to having a house guest. It's going to be weird around here when you move out."

I looked at him and pursed my lips together, smiling softly as I replied. "You have house guests almost every night, Ian. You won't miss me."

"Those women aren't guests, and I will miss you, Rory. Whether you want to believe it or not, I will miss having you around here."

"Your dad will be happy when I'm gone."

"Fuck him," he snapped.

I could feel an argument coming on and I wasn't going to let that happen. I wasn't about to ruin our perfect dinner.

"Adalynn invited me to her birthday party Saturday." I smiled.

"Ah, yes. That's this Saturday. I was going to ask you if you wanted to go with me."

"Why didn't you tell me that she's your ex-wife?" I blurted out.

He set down his fork, wiped his mouth with his napkin, and stared at me. He picked up his glass and slowly brought it to his lips, staring at me the whole time he drank his wine.

"She told you about that, eh?"

"Yes. And I couldn't help but wonder why you didn't tell me when you introduced her to me."

Ian sighed as he took a bite of his steak. "It was a mistake and it only lasted two days. We were drunk out of our minds. I seriously don't remember anything about that night. People make mistakes. We did and we took care of it. Adalynn has been a long-time friend and that's it. I don't see her as anything but that. I never have and I never will. Trust me when I say that marriage will never be in the cards for me."

"Never?" I asked.

"Never!"

"Why not?"

"Marriage is overrated. Who wants to be tied down like that for the rest of your life?"

Now I was starting to get some insight on his feelings and, so far, I didn't like what I was hearing. "Can I ask you something?" I asked.

"Sure, go ahead."

"How many actual girlfriends have you had? Not ones that you just bang and kick out. I mean, a real girlfriend who you take to dinner, movies, dancing."

Ian chuckled. "None."

I gasped as I looked at him and he smiled in amusement. "Seriously, Ian."

"Seriously, Rory. I don't do that kind of stuff. I'm not interested in any of that crap. Women, to me, are good for one thing and that's to fuck. The flowers, romance, expensive gifts; it'll just wear you out and drag you down. It'll lead you down a road that eventually splits and then you're forced with the decision of which way to go."

I was taken aback by his words and I didn't know what to say. I was nothing but stunned and disgusted by what this hot and sexy man sitting across from me had just said. He had no respect for women whatsoever and he had just showed me his true colors.

"Do the women you frequently bed know this?"

"Of course they do, and I like how you're so polite about the way you refer to them." He smiled.

"I'm willing to bet your father is the same way," I said as I sipped my wine.

"Yes, he is the same way. He's been that way since my mother—"

Ian stopped what he was going to say and threw back the remaining wine that was left in his glass.

"Your mother what?" I asked. "Died?"

His eyes shot up at me and, as he stared into my soul, he calmly said, "Since she left us."

I had to stop and think for a minute because I distinctly remembered Adalynn telling me that Ian's mother had died. He got up from the table and grabbed my plate.

"Stay here and I'll bring out dessert."

I reached for the bottle of wine and poured some in my glass. Just when I would start to let my guard down and feel somewhat normal, Ian always managed to fuck things up and instantly my guard would go back up. I guess it was better that I found out now what kind of man he really was. He came back with two blueberry muffins on a plate. I looked at him and he smiled at me. I don't think he thought he said anything wrong. I believed that he was okay with his disrespect of women. I felt sick to my stomach.

"Is something wrong?" he asked as he sat down.

"Adalynn told me your mother died and you're telling me she left? Which is it, Ian?"

He leaned back in chair. His defenses were up, I could tell by the way he looked at me.

"Why were you discussing my family with Adalynn?"

"Because you refuse to talk about anything with me. The only thing she said was that she passed away when you were a child."

"I don't know you, Aurora, so why would I want to tell you about my family and my past?"

Calm. Stay calm. Breathe. "For someone who doesn't know me, you sure are hell bent on fucking me."

Ian laughed and nodded his head. "Yes. Yes, I am, because I do believe you are deliciously fuckable."

Okay, that was it. That was the last straw with this so-called man. I got up from my seat, walked over, and wrapped my arms around his neck as I leaned into him and began dragging my tongue lightly across his smooth skin. His scent was driving me crazy. A clean, fresh scent with a touch of musk.

"God, Rory, what are you doing?" he moaned.

"Your scent drives me insane and I can't help myself," I whispered as I continued to explore his neck and run my hands down the front of his shirt.

He grabbed ahold of my arms and pulled me onto his lap. He smiled as he kissed my lips. His erection was underneath me, grinding against my ass as I sat firmly on his lap. His hand found the edge of my shirt and it traveled up until he cupped my breast. Our kiss was passionate and I didn't want it to stop. He had me in a trance, but I couldn't lose sight of what I was doing.

"Rory, you have me so hard. I'm almost positive this is the hardest I've ever been," he whispered. "I need to feel your pussy. I want to feel how wet you are."

He moved his hand slowly from my breast to the front of my pants. His hand began its journey down south and, as he reached the lace of my panties, I grabbed his hand and broke our kiss.

"This is where I stop you, because I'm not a woman who's only good for a fuck. I'm more than that and I'm not one of your cheap whores who gives in to your every demand. I won't be used, and this is one vagina you'll never have!" I yelled as I got up and began to walk away. But I wasn't finished. I stopped, turned, and looked at him one last time. "For the record, I hate blueberry muffins," I said as I ran into the house and up to my room.

I went into the bathroom and locked the door. As I started the bath water, I poured some bubbles under the stream of water. I was shaking. I needed to calm down, but I couldn't. My heart was racing as I undressed and stepped into the bathtub. The water was warm and the scent of jasmine and lavender filled the air. Tears quickly filled my eyes and then fell down my face. I was startled by a light knock on the door. I didn't respond when Ian called my name. There was a moment of silence and then he started talking.

"My mother left me and my father when I was eight years old. She left me, her only child, for a man who lived in New York. I'll never forget that day. It was a Friday, and she kept me home from school. She said we were going to have a fun day together and it was just going to be her and me."

I stepped out of the bathtub and wrapped the towel around me. I walked over to the door and gently placed my hand on it as I sank to the floor and listened to Ian's story.

"She took me to the carnival that I'd been asking to go to and she went on every ride with me, even though she hated them. We went to the park, had lunch, and then we went for ice cream. She took a lot of pictures that day and, when I asked her why she was taking so many, she wiped a tear from her eye and said because it was such a special day with just the two of us that she always wanted to remember it. When we got home, she had her suitcase sitting in the foyer. I asked her if she was going on a trip. She knelt down in front of me and hugged me tight. She told me that she was going on a trip and, when the time was right, she'd come back to get me and I could go with her. But, she never came back. I waited for years for my mother to walk back through the door and she never did. Maybe even at thirty-three years old, I'm still waiting."

My heart broke listening to him. I could hear the sadness and anguish in his voice. *How could a mother just leave her child like that?* As much as I hated him at the moment, he needed me, and I wanted to hold him. I wanted to comfort him like he did me. I got up from the floor and opened the door. I looked around the room and he was gone. I quickly got dressed and walked downstairs, looking throughout the house for him. He wasn't anywhere to be found. I stepped outside on the patio and looked towards the beach, thinking maybe he'd be there, by the water. He wasn't. I went back upstairs, grabbed my phone, and sat on the edge of the bed.

"Ian, where are you?"

I waited ten minutes and he didn't respond. So I sent him another text message.

"Please, Ian, come back so we can talk. I'm sorry."

I climbed into bed and held my phone to my chest. I waited for a response that never came, and Ian didn't come home.

Chapter 9

My eyes flew open and I was drenched in sweat from the nightmare again. The sun was just starting to rise and little specks of light began to filter through the window. I picked up my phone, which sat on the pillow next to me, and looked at it with the hopes that there was a message from Ian. There wasn't. After I climbed out of bed, I opened the door and walked down the hall to Ian's bedroom. My heart was racing with nervousness, as I didn't know what I'd find on the other side of the door. I put my hand on the knob and turned it; carefully and slowly, I opened the door. The room was dark with dark gray walls and carpet. In the middle, sat an overly large bed with a black comforter draped across it. I walked further into the room and took a closer look at the bed. Attached to the headboard were chains with wrist cuffs attached to them. I ran my hand across the black comforter and down to where the ankle cuffs were attached to the end of the bed. *What the fuck?* My eyes diverted over to the wall, where a black wrought-iron shelf hung with several hooks. Sitting on those hooks were blindfolds, whips, paddles, and handcuffs. Half-burnt candles sat upon the two nightstands. I walked over and opened one of the drawers, only to find matches, several bottles of lubricant, and a variety of vibrators. I opened the next drawer and it was filled with different types of condoms. This room was probably his sex room. I was repulsed by it, but turned on at the same time. I quickly left the room and walked downstairs to the kitchen, where Charles was making a pot of coffee.

"Good morning, Miss Rory. How was your evening and dinner with Ian?"

"Just lovely," I said with a fake smile. "Have you seen Ian this morning?"

"No, I haven't. He's usually up and running by now. Maybe he slept in today."

"Yeah, maybe," I said as I poured a cup of coffee.

"Will you be eating breakfast, Miss Rory?"

"No, Charles, not today, and please just call me Rory."

I took my coffee and went upstairs to find Ian's bedroom. I looked at the closed door, which was straight ahead from the stairs. The room next to mine. I walked over to it and with the same carefulness. I slowly opened it, peeking my head inside to see if Ian was sleeping. The king-sized bed was fully made and it didn't look like it had been slept in. His bedroom was enormous and the wall where his bed sat was nothing but windows from floor to ceiling. The view of the ocean was the most beautiful view I'd ever seen. His room was made up of neutrals, a mixture of pale gray walls with white molding and darker gray accents. I looked at the time on his clock and realized that I needed to get ready for work. As I walked back to my bedroom, I sent Adalynn a text message.

"Good morning. Ian isn't over there by any chance, is he?"

"No, why do you ask?"

"We sort of got into an argument last night and he left and, from what I can tell, he never came home."

"Listen to you. You two sound like an old married couple. Don't worry; Ian will turn up when he wants to."

"Thanks, Adalynn."

I couldn't think about Ian anymore. I needed to focus on moving out of here and finding my brother. I got dressed and took a cab to work. Jordyn had surprised me by telling me that two of her male friends who owed her a big favor were painting my apartment.

"There's a cute little secondhand furniture store down the street if you want to go look after we get off work," Jordyn said.

"That sounds great." I smiled.

"I have something for you," Jordynn said as she pulled something from under the counter. "Here, last month was my birthday and I got a new one. This one is only a year old and I want you to have it because I'm thinking you don't own a laptop."

I couldn't believe Jordyn was giving me a laptop. "Jordyn, no. I can't accept this."

"Yes, you can, Rory. Just take it. It's been sitting in my closet for the last month."

"At least let me give you some money for it."

"Don't be silly. Consider it a housewarming gift." She smiled.

I hugged her and we went on with our workday. I kept checking my phone with the hopes that Ian would message me. He didn't. So, I decided that I would send him one more text message.

"Ian, you haven't responded to my last two texts. Please let me know you're okay."

My shift ended and still no word from Ian. I sighed as I grabbed my purse, and Jordyn and I walked down to the secondhand furniture store. The good thing about shopping in Malibu at a secondhand store is the stuff is practically new. Since the space was small, I had to be creative. I found a beautiful cream-colored leather sofa sleeper, a matching end table, and a small, round coffee table. I didn't need a dining table since it was just going to be me. I asked the sales girl if she could hold my furniture until I found a way to get it to my apartment. Jordyn said that a couple of her friends had trucks and they'd help out. I hated to impose on people, but I really had no other choice. I owed Jordyn big time. I called a cab and went back to Ian's.

When I walked through the door, there was a woman standing in the foyer. She was blonde and, when she turned around, I saw that her tits were huge. Damn it. I forgot about the gala. Her dress was unflattering, as it made her look fat. She smiled and introduced herself as Nikki.

"You must be Ian's house guest?" she said as she snapped her gum.

"Yes, I'm Rory. Is Ian upstairs?" I asked as I pointed.

Just as she was about to answer, Ian came down the steps. He stopped and looked at me.

"Did you get my messages?" I asked.

"Yeah, I did. Now, if you'll excuse me, Nikki and I have a gala to attend."

He put his hand on the small of her back and led her to the door. As he walked out, he turned his head one last time and looked at me. It wasn't his apologetic look this time. It was a big fat "fuck you" look. He shut the door and I stood there in tears. I had to get out tonight. I couldn't live here anymore. I ran up the stairs as my heart beat rapidly. I grabbed a duffel bag that was sitting on the shelf in the closet and started stuffing some clothes in it. As I packed some things from the bathroom, I called a cab. I took a blanket that was sitting on the chair in the corner and shoved it in my bag. As I held it in my hand, I stood and looked around the room that had been a source of comfort to me over the past couple of weeks. A tear streamed down my cheek as the honking of the cab horn came from the driveway.

****

I inserted the key into the lock and opened the door to my new apartment. I flipped on the light switch and admired my half newly painted walls. I set my bag down and looked around at the empty space that was mine. The paint and supplies were in the corner of the room, so I decided to finish painting since I had nothing else to do. When I brought the can of paint over to the counter, my phone beeped. I pulled it from my pocket and noticed a text message from Adalynn.

"What's going on between you and Ian? I asked him why he didn't bring you to the gala instead of that blonde bimbo and he yelled at me and told me to mind my own business. Did something happen?"

I really didn't know what to say to her, so I opted for the easy way out.

"It's a long story. I'll explain it to you over coffee."

Sandi Lynn

"Okay, but you're still coming to my party on Saturday, right?"

"I wouldn't miss it for the world."

I pulled out the rest of the paint supplies and finished painting my walls. I took a step back and looked around the room as I yawned in exhaustion. I looked at the time on my phone; it was already one a.m. Ian had to be home by now and I bet he'd brought that girl home with him. I washed up in the kitchen sink, spread the blanket on the carpet, and curled up into a ball and fell asleep.

The chiming sound of my alarm jolted me out of a sound sleep at five thirty a.m. It was the time I had it set daily so I could get up and go running. I picked up my phone to check my messages and nothing. *Did he even realize I'd left?* I bet he didn't because he was probably too busy getting off in that room with the blonde. The thought burned through me like a gasoline fire. I shook it off and dug through my bag for my yoga pants and a t-shirt. I quickly changed, put on my running shoes, and went for a run. The morning air was brisk as I ran down the street, over two blocks, and down to small beach where an exercise class had just started. My ponytail swung from side to side as I jogged across the beach, trying to forget about Ian. He occupied every bit of space in my head. As much as I needed to forget about him, I couldn't. I wanted to forget about him because a man like him spelled trouble and heartache. He'd already broken my heart and we were nothing but friends, or at least we used to be. I jogged back to the apartment because I had to start work in an hour.

The day passed quickly and I really enjoyed working with Jordyn and Ollie. The two of them were so cute together. You could tell that he was totally in love with her. That was

100

something I'd wished for my whole life; to be loved. Jordyn grabbed my hand and took me outside Java Hut.

"Come on. I want to show you something." She smiled as she led me upstairs to my apartment.

As soon as she opened the door, I heard "surprise!" I took a step back and covered my mouth with my hands in excitement as I looked around my fully furnished apartment. Jordyn hooked her arm around me.

"I had the guys pick up your furniture today while we were working. SURPRISE!"

I was overcome with emotions because I didn't know what to say. Everyone was being so generous and helpful. "Thank you. I don't know what to say."

"You've already said it." Ollie smiled.

After everyone left, I ran my hand along my new couch, smiled, and sat down. I stared across the room, taking in that this place was mine, all mine. I was getting kind of hungry and I needed some things for the apartment, so I put on my shoes and went to the local Target to stock up. I was browsing in the clothing department when I came across a beautiful black lace dress that would be perfect for Adalynn's birthday party. I looked at the price tag and smiled when I saw that it was well within my price range. It might not have come from Nordstrom, Saks, or any other high-end store, but it was pretty, and I loved it. After I arrived home and my arms felt like jelly from carrying all those bags, I preheated the oven for the frozen pizza I'd bought. Once I put everything away, and when my pizza was done cooking, I took it from the oven and sat down on the couch with my laptop. I did something I had no business doing; I googled Ian Braxton. The fact was that I missed him. *Why? Why did I miss someone who only thinks women are good for one thing and one thing only?* Before stupid words came out of his mouth, he was kind and caring. Every time I thought of him, all I saw was his smile. The headline that grabbed my attention was: '*Who will tame Malibu's most eligible playboy?*' It was right above the picture of Ian and a woman on each arm. The picture was dated a month ago. *Could someone like Ian even be tamed?* I picked up my phone and almost sent him a text message, but I didn't. I brought up his name and stared at the flashing cursor that was waiting for me to type something out. After I closed out of it, I set my phone down, unfolded the couch, put the new sheets down, and crawled under the blankets as I cried myself to sleep.

"Rory, I'm in trouble," I heard Stephen's whisper over and over again.

"I'm looking for you, Stephen, but I can't find you. You need to follow my voice."

"You promised me that you'd take care of me, Rory. You promised."

"You hurt me, Stephen. You hurt me really bad."

"You lied to me, Rory. You lied!"

Stephen's scream jolted me awake. My skin was drenched in sweat and my face was soaked with tears. It took me a minute to realize that I wasn't in bed and that I was crouched in the corner of my new apartment. I was shaking, like I did with every nightmare. The only difference with this nightmare was that Ian wasn't here to hold me and calm me down.

Chapter 10

A few days had passed and then it was the night of Adalynn's birthday party. We had been texting back and forth over the past couple of days. She asked me if I needed anything and when I told her that I was doing fine, she didn't believe me and came over with a bunch of kitchen items, extra sheets, towels, and washcloths. We had lunch and not one word was mentioned about Ian. She had told me that her birthday was a no-gift birthday party and I'd better not buy her anything. I didn't listen because everybody deserved a little something on their birthday, so I bought her a silver bracelet. Nothing expensive. Just a little thank you. I really thought that Ian would have either called or sent me a text message asking if I needed a ride to the party, but he didn't. I still hadn't heard a word from him since that night he spoke about his mother. Thinking about seeing him tonight made me nervous, but I had a plan. My plan was to not look at him, talk to him, or even be in the same room as he was. It wouldn't be difficult because I was sure he was bringing one of his hookers to keep him company.

I stood in front of my bathroom mirror and put on my makeup. I played with my hair and tried different styles before I decided just to curl it. After curling the last strand of hair, I ran my fingers through the loose curls and sprayed them with hairspray. I slipped on my black lace dress with the three-quarter-length sleeves and sweetheart neckline. It was the type of dress that hugged my body and showed off my hourglass shape. I felt sexy and confident as I looked in the mirror. As the cab pulled up to the curb, I put on my black heels, grabbed my purse, and took in a deep breath as I shut the door.

When the cab pulled up the long, winding driveway of Adalynn's house, nervousness settled in. The valet opened the door and helped me out of the cab. There was a couple who pulled up behind me, so I let them walk ahead and I pretended just to blend in with them. The oversized doors were opened by a really hot guy wearing a black tuxedo. He was older, but extremely handsome, and definitely someone you could sit and stare at all night. He looked at me and smiled as I walked through the door.

"You must be Rory," he said as he lightly kissed my hand.

"Yes, I am." I smiled.

"It's nice to finally meet you, Rory. I'm Daniel, Adalynn's boyfriend."

I wasn't surprised. As beautiful as Adalynn was, I knew her partner would be equally as gorgeous.

"It's nice to meet you, Daniel." I smiled.

"There you are! And, oh my God, look at you. You look amazing," Adalynn said as she flitted across the room and hugged me.

"Happy Birthday," I said as I handed her the small gift bag.

"Now what did I tell you?" she pouted.

"It's nothing big. Just a token of my appreciation for everything you've done for me."

"Aw, you're just too sweet. Come in and have a drink. There are some people I'd like you to meet."

She led me to the living room, which was filled with men in suits and women dripping in diamonds. I felt so out of place. I scanned the room to see if Ian was there, but I didn't see him. There was no way he wouldn't come to Adalynn's birthday party. After leading me through the living room and introducing me to some of her friends, Adalynn and I walked out onto the patio and I stopped dead in my tracks as I looked a few feet in front of me. Ian was staring at me. There was no expression on his face at all. Just a blank stare and dead eyes. My stomach began doing flips and I wanted nothing more than to run away. I grabbed a glass of champagne off the tray as the waiter walked by and started to sip it as I turned away. I couldn't even bring myself to give him a small smile or wave. I was angry at him for ignoring me the way he did and it stung to look at him.

After meeting more of Adalynn's friends, I walked to the corner of the property, where it was quiet. I felt so out of place with all these rich people, even though some of the ones I met were nice. I walked over to a beautifully lit gazebo that sat in the middle of a large flower garden. I could hear the soft music that was playing throughout the entire property. I sat down on the bench and took off my shoes. My feet were already killing me in those heels. As I admired the flowers that surrounded me, the mixture of colors and the beauty of them made me feel both happy and sad.

"You look beautiful," a familiar voice spoke softly from behind.

My heart started racing and my belly did flips. I closed my eyes for a moment before I turned around and looked at the sexy man standing in my presence.

"Thank you, Ian."

"Do you mind if I sit down?"

"No. Have a seat."

This was awkward and uncomfortable. Why would he talk to me now? He had his opportunity and I didn't know if I had it in me to struggle to be nice to him.

"I like your hair curly like that. It's very pretty."

"Thanks." I smiled as I looked down.

"How are you, Rory?"

Stay calm. Don't give him attitude. Breathe. Be nice. "I'm fine, Ian. How are you?"

I really wanted to ask him why the fuck he cared how I was now and not a week ago when he chose to ignore me and my text messages.

"I'm okay. How's your new place working out?"

"It's great," I lied as I looked at him.

"Are you still having the nightmares?"

"Yeah, every night."

He folded his hands while he looked straight ahead. "I think you need to talk to someone about what happened to you. I know someone who may be able to help you. She's a good friend of mine."

I bet she is. "Thanks. But I don't think so. I couldn't afford it anyway."

"You wouldn't have to worry about that," he sighed as he rested his elbows on his thighs and cupped his face in his hands. "I'm sorry, Rory. I'm sorry for ignoring you."

Suddenly, my heart started to slow down and beat at its normal pace. It took a lot for him to come over to me and apologize. I put my hand on his and he turned his head and looked at me.

"I'm sorry too."

"Unchained Melody" by The Righteous Brothers began playing. "Would you care to dance?" he asked with a slight smile.

"I would, but I don't know how," I replied as I looked down.

"Then I'll teach you."

Ian took my hand and helped me up. He wrapped his arm around my waist and pulled me close. He then wrapped his hand around mine as we swayed back and forth.

"Just follow my lead." He smiled.

I was nervous as all hell. I'd never danced with anyone before. I started to ache down below for him. His strong hand wrapped around mine, and when our bare flesh touched, it sent shivers throughout my entire body. I slowly closed my eyes and concentrated on not stepping on his feet.

"For someone who doesn't know how to dance, you're doing very well."

"Thanks. I'm trying really hard not to step on your feet."

"Ah, well, I wouldn't mind if you did."

I looked up at him and smiled. The song had ended and so did our dance. He let go of me and my hand and I walked down the steps of the gazebo and stood in front of all the big and beautiful flowers. I ran my finger along the petals of hydrangeas and then bent down to smell them.

"I take it you love flowers," Ian said.

"I do. They represent life and growth. As long as you give them tender loving care and everything they need, they'll thrive. Like people do in life. Even if the flower starts to wilt, it can so easily be brought back to life."

"I never looked at flowers that way," he said. Ian put his hand on the small of my back as he stood next to me and looked at the array of flowers.

He put his hands in his pocket, turned around, and started to walk away. When he was a few feet away, he stopped in the middle of the grass and stood there. "I miss you, Rory," he said as continued to walk away. His words stabbed through me much like the knife had.

I blurted out, "Tomorrow morning, six a.m., I'm going running if you would like to join me."

He stopped again and stood there. "We'll see."

And just like that, he left. I walked back up to the house and, when I stepped inside, I saw Ian kiss Adalynn on the cheek and walk out the front door.

"Why did Ian leave?" I asked.

"He got a call and said there was something he had to do," she replied as she shrugged her shoulders.

I stayed long enough to sing "Happy Birthday" and have a piece of cake. It was getting late and I wanted to get home, so I called a cab, said my goodbyes, and left.

As my alarm went off, I rolled over, fumbled to find my phone, and turned it off. I noticed I had a text message from Jordyn.

"I had to switch your day off from Tuesday to Monday because one of the girls quit last night. I hope you don't mind. Enjoy the next two days."

I smiled as I got out of bed, went into the bathroom, and stared at the bags under my eyes from another nightmare and sleepless night. Maybe I should take Ian up on his offer to see a therapist. I changed into my running clothes, threw my hair up in a ponytail, and looked at the clock. It was six a.m. I guessed Ian wasn't coming or he would've been here by now. I should've known better than to get my hopes up where he was concerned. I sighed with disappointment and opened the door. I gasped when I saw Ian sitting down on the steps.

"It's about time," he said with his back turned.

"It's six o'clock right on the dot and why are you sitting on the steps? You could've knocked," I said as I walked down and stood in front of him.

He got up from the step and stared at me. He took his thumb and lightly swiped it under my eye. "Another nightmare last night?" he asked.

I nodded my head as I stared into his eyes. "Come on; let's get going. You lead," he said.

I ran my usual course. The only difference today was I had a hot and sexy millionaire by my side. "I was thinking that maybe you could give me the phone number of that therapist you know."

Ian smiled as he looked over at me. "Of course. I'll give you Dr. Neil's number when we get back to your place."

"Thank you."

"How are you feeling?" he asked as we continued jogging.

"I'm feeling good. I barely feel any pain anymore."

"Good. I still want you checked out. I called Dr. Graham and he said he'll be at the hospital all day and just to stop by."

"That's not necessary, Ian. I'm fine."

"Well, you may think you're fine, but you could have some internal damage. Let's have Dr. Graham check you out to make sure you're okay and then we'll never discuss it again."

I laughed lightly because of Ian's authoritative tone. "Yes, sir!" I said with a deep voice.

"Are you making fun of me?" He smiled as he glanced at me.

"No. I would never make fun of Ian Braxton." I winked.

He ran into me and almost knocked me over.

"Really, Ian?"

"Really, Rory." He smiled.

I bumped my body against his and laughed as he almost took a tumble. He looked at me and shook his head, then stopped. I stopped with him, as we were both out of breath. "You almost knocked me over," he said breathlessly as he pointed his finger at me.

"So. You almost knocked *me* over." I smiled.

"I'm starving. Let's go get some breakfast," he said as he tapped me on the nose.

"Okay. Where do you want to go?"

"I know this great café that's not too far from your apartment."

"Would it be okay if we walked?" I asked. "I'm kind of tired."

"Are you feeling okay? Do you hurt?"

"I'm fine, Ian. Just a little tired, that's all."

I looped my arm around his and he looked at me for a moment and then smiled. We walked to the café and sat down at a table outside. I ordered a bagel sandwich and Ian ordered eggs and a blueberry muffin. I silently laughed because of his love for blueberry muffins.

"Did you really mean what you said last week?" he asked.

"I said a lot of things. Which are you referring to?"

"About hating blueberry muffins. Do you really hate blueberry muffins, Rory?"

His look was so serious. I think if I would've told him that I didn't like them, he'd cry. I sat there and stared at him while I bit down on my bottom lip.

"Well?" he asked as he cocked his head.

"No. I don't *hate* blueberry muffins, but I prefer the chocolate chip ones."

The corners of his mouth curved up slightly as he took a bite of his muffin. "I'm confident that I can get you to change your mind about them."

"You can try." I smiled.

We finished up our breakfast, Ian paid the bill, and we walked back to my apartment. As we walked up the steps, Ian placed his hand lightly on my back. The touch of his fingertips through my shirt sent a tingling sensation throughout my body. I inserted the key in the lock and opened the door. I stepped inside and invited Ian in.

"Well, here it is. My apartment. I know it's smaller than your bathroom, but it's mine."

"It's—it's nice."

"I honestly didn't expect you to like it because it's not fancy and big like you're used to."

"Seriously, Rory. It's nice. Except, where's the bedroom?"

Of course that was the first thing he'd ask, because I was sure sex was the only thing the man thought about.

"There is no bedroom."

Ian looked at me strangely and walked around the apartment. "Do you sleep on the couch?"

"It's a sofa bed. I pull it out every night and put it back every morning."

"Oh. I see."

"I know it's hard for you to believe that people live like this, Ian, but not everyone is rich and can live the luxurious life you do."

"I assure you, Rory, my life is far from luxurious."

I saw a flicker of pain in his eyes when he said that. "I want to talk about that night and what you told me about your mother."

"Ah, I was wondering when you were going to bring that up," he said as he put his hands in his pockets. "There's nothing to discuss and I just want you to know that I've never told anyone that before. Not even Adalynn. As far as she's concerned, she thinks my mother is dead. Which, to be honest, she is; at least to me."

The sadness and loneliness in his voice bothered me. I walked over to where he was standing, looped my arm around his, and laid my head on his shoulder.

"I'm sorry she left you like that."

"Me too. Maybe I'd be a different person if she'd stayed," he said as his lips softly kissed my head.

I reached my hand up and gently stroked his face. His eyes studied me for a moment before he leaned closer to me and his lips caressed mine. He moved his hand from his pocket and up to the side of my face. He held it gently while he teased my lips with his. He pulled away and looked at me as if he was asking my permission to keep going.

"We need to talk," he whispered as he gently nipped my bottom lip.

I didn't want to talk. I wanted him. I wanted to feel him inside me. I hadn't felt this way before and I never wanted anyone so bad in my life. These feelings and aches were new to me and I wanted them satisfied, even if it was just for one night.

"I don't want to talk," I whispered back as I licked his lip.

A low growl came from the back of his throat as he picked me up and took me over to the couch, sitting me on his lap so I could feel the bulge that was pulsating in his pants.

"Did you mean what you said?" he asked as I tilted my head to the side and his tongue explored my neck.

"I said a lot of things."

"The one about me never having your pussy?"

His hand traveled up my shirt as his fingers pulled down my bra cup and took my hardened nipple between his fingers, tugging and pulling. "Christ," he moaned. "Answer my question, Rory."

Fuck. Fuck. Fuck. I grabbed his hand and stopped him. "I want you, but I'm scared."

"Why are you scared?"

"I've only had sex twice in my life and it was not good."

Ian looked at me sympathetically and wrapped his arms around me. "You don't need to feel scared and I can promise you it'll be the best experience of your life. I'll make you feel so good, you'll never want me to stop."

His words hit me like a ton of bricks and reality set in. If I had sex with him, I wouldn't want him to stop. But he would have to, because I wouldn't be the only woman he was fucking.

Instantly, I felt sick and I pulled away from him. "You said we needed to talk. So talk."

"I want you, Rory. I want you in a way that's different from the other women."

The only thing that was going through my mind was that room and all the things that sat inside it. I was so scared that he was going to tell me he wanted me to be his sex slave because that was one thing I wouldn't do. Not for him or anyone.

"When I fuck you, I don't want there to be anything between my cock and your pussy. I want to feel you and be inside you naturally; skin to skin, flesh to flesh."

I slowly shook my head because I didn't get what he was trying to say. "I'm sorry, Ian, I don't understand."

He smiled softly as he pressed his lips against my forehead. "I don't want to wear a condom. I'm asking you if you would be willing to get on some type of birth control so I wouldn't have to wear one."

"You've been with too many women, Ian."

"I know. I'm clean. I'll have Dr. Graham show you the reports. I'm going to be totally honest with you, Rory, and I hope to God you believe me. I've never not used a condom with anyone, ever."

"Yeah, right, Ian."

He took my face in his hands and stared into my eyes. "I swear to you."

"Why me, then? Out of all the hundreds of women you've had sex with over the years, why me?"

"I don't know," he said as he scooted me off his lap and got up from the couch. "The only thing I know is I want to have sex with you and I don't want to wear a fucking condom. I want you to get on birth control so I don't have to worry about you getting pregnant."

"I have a question for you," I said.

"Go ahead."

"If I get on birth control and have sex with you, would there be more to us than just sex?"

I already knew the answer to that, but I wanted to hear him say it.

"I've already told you that I don't do 'us,'" he said as he walked over and sat back down on the couch. "I can give you great sex and I can help you out, but that's as far as I'll go. I'm sorry, Rory."

"Thank you for being honest with me. Let me think about it."

"Okay, just don't take too long. I'm a very impatient man. I want you, and when I want something, there's no waiting." He smiled as he ran the back of his hand across my cheek. "Now go grab some clothes and I'll take you back to my house so we can shower before we go and see Dr. Graham."

Chapter 11

"It looks like your knife wound healed up nicely and there's no internal damage," Dr. Graham said as he patted my hand. "You're a lucky girl. You could've been killed."

"She's lucky we found her." Ian smiled.

Ian helped me off the table and he thanked Dr. Graham for seeing us. As we were leaving, Ian's phone rang. He pulled it from his pocket and told me to keep walking and he'd catch up with me. I reached the front doors and saw his limo pull up to the curb. Joshua got out and opened the door for me. I climbed in and looked back to see if Ian was coming. Suddenly, the other door opened and Ian slid in next to me.

"Everything okay?" I asked.

He grabbed my hand and interlaced his fingers in mine. "Yeah, everything's fine. It was just a business call." He leaned over and softly licked my lips before the strength of his mouth fully enveloped mine and we were locked into a passionate kiss. He pushed me back until I was lying on the down on the seat and he was on top of me. He undid the button on his pants and then took my hand, bringing it down the front of his pants. He was rock hard. I clasped my hand around his dick as he made that sexy growl noise. He broke our kiss and stared at me.

"I want to finger fuck you and I want to feel you come."

The ache I'd been feeling down below every time I saw him needed to be satisfied, and I was so turned on, how could I say no? I nodded my head as he smiled at me. His fingers tugged at my pants as he moved them down my hips. I lifted up my ass to help him out. Once he was satisfied that my pants were down enough, he took his down so I would have better access to his throbbing cock. My hand started moving up and down his shaft slowly as he threw his head back and moaned.

"Christ, Rory," he said as he leaned down and brushed his lips against mine.

His hand made its way between my thighs and slowly up to my wet spot. Just the slight touch of his fingers there made me want to come instantly.

"You're so wet. God, I love that you're so wet," he whispered as I tilted my head and his mouth explored my neck.

His fingers deftly circled around my clit, making it almost unbearable to control myself. I began to moan, which excited Ian even more. He pushed my legs further apart as he inserted his finger. "Oh my God, Rory, you're so tight. You're so beautifully tight."

I was gone. He took my body to another dimension. He moved his finger in and out of me while circling my clit with his thumb. I arched my back as he plunged another finger inside me, stretching me, pleasuring me, and bringing me to the brink of an amazing orgasm. I tilted my head back as far as it would go as my hand moved up and down his hard cock and my thumb circled his tip.

"Come for me, Rory. I want you to say my name when you do."

"Ian," I screamed as his finger hit the spot. My body shook like never before and I tightened myself around his finger.

Sandi Lynn

"That's it, baby. I can feel it. I can feel your come all over me," he said breathlessly as he removed my hand from his cock, took it in his, and jacked himself off while he continued to finger-fuck me until he came all over my shirt. He collapsed on top of me as we tried to catch our breath.

"You better make your decision quick, because after that, I need to be inside you and I won't fuck you with a condom on," he whispered in my ear.

He sat up, took my hand, and helped me up. He opened the console and took out some tissues. He looked at my shirt and started to wipe his come from it.

"Sorry," he said with a smirk.

"It's okay. I can wash it."

I reached down, grabbed my pants, and pulled them up. After Ian cleaned himself up, he pulled up his pants and then wrapped his arms around me, pulling me into him.

"I hope you enjoyed how I made you feel."

Was he kidding? Couldn't he tell how much I enjoyed it? "Of course, Ian. It was amazing."

I desperately wanted to ask him about the room. But I was afraid that he'd be mad if he knew I saw it.

"That was just the appetizer. You'll get the full course as soon as you give me your decision and then your appetite will be fully satisfied."

I smiled as I pressed my lips against his shirt because I knew he was right.

****

Joshua pulled up to my apartment and Ian followed me inside. "Take off your shirt and give it to me so I can have Mandy wash it."

"It's okay, Ian. I can wash it."

"Rory." He smiled as he ran his finger down my jawline. "It's not a request; it's a command. Now do it."

He had a way of hypnotizing me with the tone of his voice and his mere touch. I pulled my shirt over my head and stood there while his eyes stared at my breasts. He brought his hands up and cupped my bra while he took in a sharp breath.

"You're so beautiful, Rory, and I can't wait to have you, savor you, and save you from your insecurities and fears."

"I don't need saving, Ian."

"Yes, Rory, you do." He smiled as he kissed my forehead and took my shirt from my hands. "I'll get this back to you. I have to go." And just like that, he was gone.

I sighed as I pulled another shirt from the drawer and put it on. I walked over to the stove and put on some water for tea. The feeling of Ian's touch was still all over my body. I needed to talk to Adalynn, so I called her and asked her if she had time to stop by.

"I don't know what to say, Rory. Ian is Ian and he'll never change," she said as she took a drink from her glass.

"You mean he'll hurt me."

"Not intentionally, but yes, he will hurt you. I've seen the devastation he's left behind when it comes to women. I've seen the tears, the heartache, and the pathetic begging. I don't want you to have to be subjected to that."

"What about you?" I asked as I sipped my wine.

"I knew how he was, and I was okay with that because I didn't want Ian for anything more than great sex. We stopped having sex and became even better friends. Just be careful. If you want to get on birth control so Ian doesn't have to wear a condom, then make sure you're fucking him for the right reasons and prepare yourself for a bumpy ride. I'll be honest with you; I'm not surprised. I've seen the way he looks at you and it's different from anything I'd ever seen from him."

I smiled softly as I poured some more wine in both our glasses. "I need to ask you about the room in Ian's house."

Adalynn looked at me with a smug grin. "Did he show you that room?"

"No, and he's never told me about it either. I happened to open the wrong door one day."

"He usually keeps that room locked. It's odd that is was open. So, what do you want to know about it?"

"Have you and Ian been in there?"

Adalynn let out a light laugh. "Of course; that's the only place Ian brings women, unless he's out of town or something. Did the room freak you out a bit?"

"Yeah, actually it did."

"Don't worry. It's all harmless fun and amazing sex. Ian likes to be in control and he likes to be kinky. It's nothing to be scared of and if you don't want anything to do with that room, just tell him. Are you okay, Rory?"

"Yeah, I'm okay. I just have a lot on my mind."

She reached over and hugged me. "Listen, I have to get going. Daniel and I have a hot date filled with bubble baths, chocolate, and lots of mind-blowing sex!"

"Have fun." I smiled as I walked her to the door.

"Trust me, darling, I will." She winked. "Call me if you need me. My advice to you is, fuck Ian, if only for the reason that you'll always wonder what it's like if you don't, but don't get emotionally involved."

"Thanks, Adalynn," I said as I shut the door.

I took a hot shower, changed into my nightshirt, and climbed into bed. I lay there, thinking about Ian and what happened between us today. I reached for my phone and sent him a text message.

"Goodnight, Ian."

A few moments later, he replied.

"Goodnight, Rory. I hope you sleep well."

A smile fell upon my face when I read his message. It was too late. I was already emotionally involved. I closed my eyes with a smile on my face and fell asleep.

"Stephen, what did you do?"

"I'm sorry, Rory, I didn't mean to. It wasn't my fault, Rory."

"Oh my God, Stephen!"

"You have to help me, Rory. You have to protect me."

I woke up in a sweat, shaking and remembering every vivid detail of that night. I couldn't breathe as I sobbed into my hands. I needed Ian, and I needed to be held by his strong arms. I stayed in the corner and reached for my phone, which was on the floor in front of me. With shaking hands, I hit Ian's number. It rang and rang until he finally picked up.

"Rory, what's wrong? Are you okay?"

"No," I managed to cry out. "I—I—"

"I'm on my way over. Stay put and don't move. Do you understand me?"

He hung up before I could answer. I crawled across the floor to the door and unlocked it. I quickly made it back to the corner and brought my knees up to my chest. I had buried that nightmare years ago and suddenly, it was back. I heard the door handle turn and Ian ran into the apartment and straight to the corner. He got down on the floor and wrapped his arms around me, hugging me and holding me tight.

"It's okay. No one is going to hurt you. You're okay," he whispered.

I couldn't say a word. I just cried into his chest. He picked me up and carried me to the bed. As he laid me down, he climbed in next to me. He sat up and I rested my head on his lap.

"I'm calling Dr. Neil tomorrow and you're going to see her," he said as he stroked my hair. That was last thing I heard.

****

My eyes flew open at the sound of the opening door.

"Good morning," Ian said as he walked over with a brown bag and two cups of coffee.

"Morning," I replied as I got up and walked to the bathroom.

After I finished peeing and splashing my face with cold water, I walked back into the living room and Ian had the couch put back together. He gave me a small smile and held out his hand as I walked towards him.

"I brought us some coffee."

"Thank you, Ian," I said as I took the cup from him. "What's in the bag?"

"Let's see, shall we?" He smirked.

He reached inside the bag and pulled out a large muffin. "A chocolate chip muffin for you and a blueberry one for me."

"Thank you. I'm sorry about last night. I didn't mean for you to come all the way over here. I never should've called you," I spoke as I looked down.

"Rory, don't apologize. You were scared, and I hate that you're alone in this tiny place. Something was different with you last night. Was it the same nightmare you've been having? Because you were completely out of it."

I couldn't tell him about this nightmare. The one I buried deep inside my head so many years ago so I wouldn't go crazy. "Yeah, it just lasted a little longer than usual."

"I called Amanda and she agreed to see you this morning."

"Who?" I asked.

"Dr. Neil. Dr. Amanda Neil. You need to talk to someone. These nightmares can't continue."

Ian's phone rang and he pulled it from his pocket and held up his finger, asking me hold on. He looked at me with a strange look like something had just happened. Then Ian said something to whomever it was on the other end that was odd.

"Let me talk to her first. Keep an eye on him and I'll get back to you in a few minutes."

He hung up and continued to stare at me. His eyes displayed an empathetic look as he spoke.

"Rory, I found your brother."

"What?" I said as I shook my head in disbelief.

"He was living in a homeless shelter. I had my men take him to the hospital. He needs help, Rory."

My mind was racing and I started to pace back and forth. "Is he hurt?"

"No. Physically, he's fine," he said as he wrapped his arms around me and held me. "Get dressed so we can go."

I lifted my head and kissed his lips. "Thank you," I whispered.

Ian closed his eyes and took in a sharp breath. I went into the bathroom and changed out of my nightshirt and into some clothes, threw my hair up, and put on some light makeup. We walked out the door and headed to the hospital. Once we arrived, I explained who I was, and Ian and I were shown to the room where Stephen was being kept. As I walked through the door, he turned his head and looked at me. A small smile fell upon his face as he whispered my name. I gulped as I stared at him, lying there, strapped to the bed. My brother, my twin brother, was a mess, not only physically, but emotionally. He hadn't shaven since the last time I had seen him and he looked dirty. Tears filled my eyes as I walked over to his bedside and put my arms around him.

"Stephen, thank God you're okay."

"Where've you been, Rory?" he whispered. "Why did you leave me?"

The tears that filled my eyes fell down my face as I held his hand. "You hurt me, Stephen. I had to go."

Just as I said that, Ian walked up behind me and clasped my shoulders.

"I didn't mean to hurt you, Rory. Just like I didn't mean to hurt Mom."

I froze as I felt Ian's grip on me tighten. "I know you didn't, Stephen. You're sick and you need help. I'm going to get you the help you need."

"Rory, tell them to let me go," he pleaded.

The tears were now pools of water as I leaned in closer to him and whispered, "You're going to be okay. The doctors are going to help you."

A man in a white coat walked into the room and introduced himself as Dr. Michaels. He was a psychiatrist and he came in to talk to me about Stephen.

"You must be Stephen's sister, Aurora?" he said as he held out his hand.

"Yes, I'm Rory, and this is Ian Braxton."

We shook hands and Dr. Michaels went over his assessment of Stephen with me. I already knew what he was going to say and I was scared.

"When Stephen was brought in, we had to sedate him. He was violent, disoriented, and screaming your name. We found a medical emergency card on him and spoke to your aunt in Indiana. She filled me in on his history. Has he ever hurt you?"

I closed my eyes and Ian spoke for me. "He stabbed her a few weeks ago. That's how they became separated."

"Your aunt said that she didn't know you were leaving. She woke up one day and the two of you were gone," Dr. Michaels spoke.

"It wasn't her business. I was the one who'd been taking care of him my entire life. I brought him to L.A. for a trial on a new drug for schizophrenic patients. He'd been off his current meds for a while and he snapped."

"I see," he said as he wrote it down in Stephen's chart. "Stephen needs round the clock medical care and he needs to be in a place where he's monitored at all times and won't be a danger to himself or anyone else. I believe your brother's condition is worsening or we're dealing with more than schizophrenia. I'm suggesting Hudson Rock Psychiatric Hospital. It's about an hour from here and it's one of the best in the country. He'll be tested, start new medication and therapy."

"How much will this cost?" I asked

"You don't need to worry about that, Rory. I'm taking care of it," Ian spoke.

"I'll go get the paperwork for you to sign. I'll be right back," Dr. Michaels said.

He walked out of the room and I turned and looked at Stephen. My heart broke for my brother like it had every day since I could remember.

"They're going to lock me up, aren't they? I won't ever see you again."

I undid the straps that were holding him down. "Rory, what the hell are you doing?" Ian snapped.

I laid my head on his chest and Stephen brought his arms around me. Ian stood close. "You're going to a wonderful place where you'll be taken care of. You'll meet new people and you'll get the help you need. I'll come visit you all the time. I promise. I won't let you down. Do you understand, Stephen?"

"I'm sorry I hurt you, Rory. I went looking for you, but I couldn't find you. I wanted to tell you that I was sorry."

"I know you're sorry, Stephen."

"I'm tired, Rory. I want to go to sleep. Will you sing to me?"

I started to sing the song that always calmed him down and helped him sleep, "Over the Rainbow."

"We'll go to that land someday, won't we, Rory?"

"Yes, Stephen, one day," I whispered and I continued to sing.

Ian took a hold of me and sat me up. "He's asleep, Rory. Let's step out for a moment."

He handed me a tissue, took my hand, and led me out into the hall. We walked around until he found an empty room. He led me inside, shut the door, and then wrapped his arms around me as tightly as he could. He buried his face into my neck and whispered, "I'm so sorry that you have to go through this. But, I don't want you to worry. I'm taking care of this for you. Stephen will be well taken care of and you can visit him every chance you get."

"I can't have you pay for it, Ian. You don't even know him. You barely know me."

He broke our embrace and stared at me. "You're my friend, and I help my friends. I'm helping you and Stephen and there will be no more discussion about it. Do you understand me, Rory?"

I rolled my eyes at him because once again, he was using that commanding tone. "Yes, I understand."

"Don't roll your eyes at me. As cute as it makes you look, I can't stand that." He smiled.

I sighed and told him we better head back to the room. Stephen was still asleep when we walked in. Dr. Michaels came in behind us and went over the paperwork with me. He said that he was going to keep Stephen here overnight and that he'd be transferred to Hudson Rock tomorrow morning.

"You may come here tomorrow morning and ride with him to Hudson Rock so you can say goodbye and see for yourself that he'll be well taken care of."

"We'll be taking him in my limo so Rory can spend some time with him," Ian said.

I took the pen from the doctor and signed the papers to commit my twin brother to a psychiatric hospital and cried while doing it.

"I know this is hard, but it's the best thing for him," Dr. Michaels said as he put his hand on my shoulder and then left the room. I looked over at Stephen as he opened his eyes.

"Don't cry, Rory. It'll be okay. You can't take care of me anymore and I know that now."

"I'm sorry, Stephen. I have to go now, but I'll see you in the morning," I said as I kissed his head.

"Bye, Rory."

I ran out of the room as fast as I could and down the hallway until I found the exit. I ran down the sidewalk. I wouldn't stop running. I couldn't stop running. Ian caught up with me and grabbed me. He held me so tight that I couldn't move.

"Stop, Rory! You need to stop, right now!" he whispered in my ear.

We were near a park and people were watching.

"People are staring. Now, I'm going to let go of you and I'm going to take your hand, and we're going to go sit under that tree over there. Okay?"

I nodded my head, and Ian did exactly what he said he would. He took my hand and led me to the big oak tree. As we sat down underneath it, Ian looked at me and smiled. "Have you calmed down?"

I nodded and laid my head on his shoulder.

"Talk to me, Rory. Tell me what's going on in that pretty little head of yours."

"I let my mom and my brother down."

"How did you let them down? None of this is your fault. I heard Stephen say that he didn't mean to hurt you or your mom. What did he do?"

I took in a sharp breath. The air around us was getting cool. "One night, I was on the couch watching TV and my mom was in the kitchen with Stephen. All of a sudden, I heard her scream and a crash on the floor. I jumped up from the couch and Stephen was standing over her, holding a bloody knife. He had stabbed her in the leg. The way he looked at her was so blank, like he wasn't even there. She started to back away from him, and I could see the fear in her eyes. I told her that I was calling 911 and she screamed at me not to. She told me to take the knife from him. I remember standing there, shaking uncontrollably. I took tiny steps towards him as I asked him to drop the knife. I'll never forget the look in his eyes when he turned his head and looked at me. He dropped the knife and curled up in a ball on the floor next to my mom. She said that if we told anyone what Stephen had done, they'd take him away from us and she couldn't let that happen. So, she took him to the doctor to have him evaluated and told them about his hallucinations and conversations with himself and they diagnosed him with schizophrenia."

"Christ, Rory," Ian said as he laid me down so I was on my back and my head was in his lap.

I looked up at him as he stared down at me and gently wiped the tears from my eyes with his thumb. "I have no words. I think that once we get Stephen situated and you know he's going to be okay, you can start to heal physically and emotionally. What about your aunt? Does she know any of this?"

My eyes left his as I looked down and started picking at the blades of grass. "Yes. She came over right after it happened and helped my mom take care of the wound. It was only a few months later that she passed away from pneumonia. My aunt didn't want anything to do with us. She said that Stephen was evil and needed to be locked away. Personally, I think she was afraid of him."

"That's understandable, considering what he did to your mom," Ian said as he played with the strands of my hair.

"The night my mom died, she called for me to come in her room. When I went in there, she told me to sit down next to her on the bed. She reached up and put her hand on the side of my face.

"'My beautiful Aurora. I need you to promise me something. I need you to promise that you'll always take care of Stephen and protect him. If you don't protect your brother, they'll take him away from you and he needs you. He'll never survive by himself. The two of you need to stay together. Can you do that for Mommy?'

"I remember sitting there as she stared at me, begging me to promise her. Damn it, I was only ten years old," I said as I sat up.

Ian pulled me into his chest and held my head against him. "Shh...it's okay. You never broke your promise to her and you still haven't. You're getting Stephen the help he needs. She'd be so proud of you for the way you took care of him all these years."

"That's the reason my aunt wanted nothing to do with either of us. But she was so desperate for money to feed her drug addiction."

I broke free from his embrace and stared into his eyes, which reminded me so much of the blue ocean water. "Now you know. You know everything and the reason why I'm not broken, just shattered."

I swore I saw a tear in Ian's eye when he turned his head and looked away. "Come on. I'm taking you back to your place to pack an overnight bag. You're staying at my house tonight. I don't think you should be alone."

I didn't argue with him because I didn't want to be alone. "I have to call Jordyn and let her know that I won't be in tomorrow," I said as we walked across the grass.

"I already talked to her and I told her you won't be in the rest of the week."

"Ian, why the hell would you do that? I'm going to get fired."

The corners of his mouth curved up as he looked at me. "No, you're not. You're going to quit. But that's something we'll talk about when we get back to my place."

Chapter 12

I was soaking in the luxurious tub that I'd grown to love since I first came to Ian's house. As I was taking in the lavender-scented bubbles, there was a light knock on the door.

"Rory, can I come in?"

"Ian, I'm taking a bath. No!"

"I'm assuming you're covered in bubbles and, anyway, we've done things and I've seen you, so there's nothing to be embarrassed about."

Oh my God, he did this every time I was taking a bath. *Why couldn't he ever wait until I was done?* I scooted myself down so I was fully covered up to my neck in bubbles.

"Come in."

He opened the door and gave me that cocky smile. "I want to talk to you," he said as he took a seat on the toilet.

"It can't wait until I'm out of the tub?"

"No. You know I'm an impatient man. So when I want to talk, I want to talk *now*, no matter the circumstances."

I just looked at him and shook my head. "What do you want to talk about?"

"You quitting your job and coming to work for me as my assistant."

Where the hell did that come from? "Why would you do that?" I asked in confusion.

"Because I think you'd make a good assistant and I need one. My other assistant just quit. You'd be working here, from the house. I will pay you very well in salary, medical benefits, and vacation time. You'll find that I'm a very generous man." He smiled.

I glared at him, trying to figure out what his plan was. "Listen, Rory, you can't work in a coffee house the rest of your life, and I'm offering you one hell of a deal. Now, sit up and I'll wash your back for you."

"No! I'm fine."

Ian sighed. "Rory, I've fondled your breasts. I've had my fingers inside you and I gave you an amazing orgasm. You don't need to hide from me and there's nothing to be embarrassed about."

Ugh, he was right, but for some reason, I still didn't want him to see me. I slowly sat all the way up and brought my knees to my chest.

"That's a good girl," he said as he took the sponge from the hook and the shower gel from the shelf.

He started rubbing my back in a soft, circular motion. I closed my eyes because that ache was back. The ache that begged for his touch.

"I would just need you to do some paperwork for me. You know how to use a computer. Can you type?" he asked.

"Yes, I can type."

"Good. I'll need you to type up some contracts, run some errands, handle some appointments, and there may be the need for you to travel with me sometimes."

Why did I have a feeling this was going to involve more than just office work? I needed the money and I definitely needed the medical benefits. "How much do you pay your assistants?" I asked casually.

"I would pay you $2,000 a week."

I gasped. "What?!" I exclaimed.

Ian chuckled as he continued across my shoulders. "This is Malibu, Rory."

I was lucky if I made that in three months. Two thousand dollars a week was like gold to me. That was a ridiculous amount to pay someone with no experience.

"So, let me get this straight. You're going to pay me $2,000 a week to be your assistant, with no experience?"

Ian leaned in closer and lightly began kissing my neck. "You have some experience, so I don't mind, and when I get done training you, you'll have more experience than you'll know what to do with," he whispered.

"So, sex is required as part of the job?"

I could feel his teeth lightly scrape against my skin as he smiled. "No, there's no sex involved. It's purely business. Sex is for after business hours."

He was killing me, as every nerve in my body was on alert. The tingling sensation, the ache, his touch; all were sending me right over the edge. Ian stopped washing my back and looked at me. He positioned himself so he was in front of me. He held up the sponge and, with a smile, he said, "Put your knees down so I can wash the front of you."

"The deal was my back, Ian."

"Put your knees down," he said in an authoritative voice. "Please." He smiled.

I slowly put my knees down into the water and sat there with my breasts fully exposed to him. He looked at them and then at me with a seductive look in his eye. He took the shower gel and poured some more onto the sponge. I took in a sharp breath when he began stroking my breasts with it.

"Relax and enjoy it, Rory."

I turned my head and looked at the marble wall. I wanted to look at him, but I couldn't. He took his other hand and, with the slightest touch of his finger on my chin, he turned my head so I was staring at him. He leaned in and softly brushed his lips against mine. His kiss was light, seductive, and I wanted to come right on the spot. I was so turned on that I wanted to pull him into the bathtub. He smiled as he licked my bottom lip and put the sponge down. He got up and grabbed the large towel that was sitting on the counter. Opening it up, he held it in front of me and told me to get out.

"Just hand me the towel, Ian."

"No. Now, get out of the tub."

"No, I won't. You give me the towel and leave."

"Rory, I'll tell you one last time to get out of the tub. You're being absolutely ridiculous. Now do as I ask!" he commanded in a sharp tone.

I wasn't liking his attitude and I didn't appreciate him taking that tone with me. He kind of scared me when he spoke like that. I sighed as I stood up and stepped out of the tub. He walked over to me and wrapped the towel around me, holding it tightly around my body. He pulled me into him as he wrapped his arms around me. I could feel his erection.

"Do you feel how hard you got me? I hate letting this hard-on go to waste and I know you want it inside you. Have you made your decision yet?"

He had me in his hold. His whispering voice and hot breath in my ear hypnotized me.

"Yes, I've made my decision, and I'll do what you want."

I felt him let out a sigh of relief. "Thank you and I promise you won't regret it," he said as he kissed my neck. He broke our embrace and led me to the bedroom.

"Why don't you get into your pajamas and get some sleep. We need to get up early to go for a run before we head to the hospital, and I want you to think about my job proposal. Remember, I'm an impatient man and I want an answer ASAP," he said as he moved to the door.

"Just one more thing," I said. Ian turned around and looked at me. "I won't move back here."

His glare burned through me when I said that. He opened the door and left without saying a word.

****

I was up all night, thinking and worrying about Stephen, but he wasn't the only one on my mind. I couldn't stop thinking about Ian. *Could this man be husband material? Could I change him?* There was still so much I didn't know about him and yet I told him my deepest secrets. I threw back the covers, put on my running clothes, and headed downstairs to meet Ian.

"Good morning, Charles." I smiled.

"Good morning, Rory. It's good to see you. I've missed your smiling face here in the mornings."

"Thanks, I've missed you too. Where's Ian? We have a running date."

Charles looked at me in confusion. "Mr. Beckman is back from his trip and Ian went running with him. They left about ten minutes ago."

"Who is Mr. Beckman?" I asked in a pissed off tone.

"Andrew Beckman, Ian's best friend."

I took a bottle of water from the refrigerator. "That was nice of him to ditch me like that and not even tell me. I guess I'm not going running now, because I'll just feel like an ass if I run into the two of them."

"You can always use the gym downstairs," Charles said.

I knitted my eyebrows as I looked at him. "There's a gym downstairs?"

"You didn't know that?" he asked.

"No. I didn't know that."

"I'll take you to it. Follow me."

I followed Charles down the stairs that were located to the side of the laundry room. I just assumed it was the basement. When I reached the final step, I gasped. It was a full-on gym.

"Are you kidding me? Why didn't Ian ever tell me about this?"

"I'm not sure. Maybe he just assumed you knew."

"Thank you, Charles. I'll just do my workout here." I smiled.

I looked around at all the equipment. He had everything. Hanging in the middle of the room was a punching bag. Perfect. I found some cotton hand wraps and wrapped my hands before putting on the gloves. They were a little big, but I could manage them. Once my hands were wrapped and my gloves were on, I stepped in front of the punching bag and lightly tapped it. Moving from side to side, I started with several jabs and then cross punches. *Jab. Jab. Cross punch. Side kick. Jab. Jab. Cross punch. Round kick.*

"Wow," a male voice said.

After my last round kick, I turned around and saw Ian and his friend, Andrew, staring at me. Andrew started clapping.

"That was hot," he said.

"Rory, what the hell are you doing?" Ian asked with irritation.

"I'm just doing a little workout since I was stood up for our run this morning," I said as I removed the gloves.

"I'm sorry. That was my fault. I stole Ian away. By the way, I'm Andrew." He smiled as he walked up to me and held out his hand.

I would've shook it, but my hands were so sweaty and still taped. I looked at him and smiled. "Hi, sorry, my hands are—"

"Andrew, this is Rory Sinclair," Ian interrupted. "You better go shower. We need to leave in a bit."

The tone of his voice had a hint of anger in it. *What the hell did he have to be mad about? Am I not allowed to use his gym?* I felt better anyways because I pretended that bag was him. I was still pissed at him for standing me up, though. I glared at him and then looked at Andrew and smiled.

"It was nice to meet you," I said as I walked up the stairs and took a shower.

I wrapped the large white towel around me and opened the bathroom door. I jumped when I saw Ian sitting on the edge of the bed.

"What the hell, Ian?" I said as I stood there and looked at him.

"What the fuck were you doing and where did you learn that?"

"I was working out. We had a date, remember?"

"We didn't have a date. We were going to run together. Don't you dare get the two confused," he snapped.

Was he serious? "Okay, fine. You stood me up. I went downstairs to let you know I was ready and you were gone."

"So. Andrew called last night and he'd just gotten back from his month-long trip to Europe and he asked if I wanted to go running this morning so we could catch up."

"So? You think that it's acceptable that you just leave me and don't say a word?"

"I don't owe you any explanations, Rory. I hadn't seen my friend in a month. I see you every day."

Can you say "fucking asshole"? "So, you don't see anything wrong with what you did?"

"No, I don't. Now explain to me how you knew how to use that punching bag."

"Can I get dressed, please?" I asked with a raised voice.

"Fine. I'll meet you downstairs. You can explain it to me on the way to the hospital."

The hell I will. As soon as he walked out of the room, I grabbed my phone from the nightstand and called a cab. There was no way I was going anywhere with him. I quickly got dressed and threw my hair up. I quietly tiptoed down the stairs and looked around. I didn't see Ian, but Charles was in the hallway. I brought my finger up to my mouth, signaling him to be quiet.

"Where is he?" I whispered.

"He's out on the patio, waiting for you," Charles whispered back.

"Good, let him wait."

Charles smiled and gave me a wink as he walked back to the kitchen and I walked out the front door. The cab dropped me off in front of the hospital. Before I could open the door, someone opened it for me. I looked out and saw Ian standing there. *Shit. Shit. Shit.* I stepped out of the cab and walked straight towards the door.

"STOP!" he exclaimed.

I stopped and took in a deep breath. He closed the cab door and walked up behind me while clutching onto my hip with his hand. "Paybacks, Rory. Is that what this is?" he mumbled in my ear as his hot breath on my skin alerted every sense in my aching body.

"It sucks to be kept waiting. Doesn't it?" I said as I stared straight ahead and walked through the doors.

"I did nothing wrong," he spoke.

"I don't want to talk about it anymore," I replied as I walked into Stephen's room.

"Rory!" Stephen said with excitement.

"Hi, Stephen." I smiled as I walked over and kissed his head. I took a hold of his hand and sat down on the edge of the bed. "Remember yesterday when I was here and we talked about you going to that special place where you'll be taken care of?"

"Yeah," he said as he looked down.

"I want you to tell me how you feel about that?"

"I don't want to go. I want to go home with you. I want to live with you like we used to."

Tears welled in my eyes at the sound of his pleading voice. I needed to stay strong. I needed to be strong; not for myself, but for Stephen.

"I know you do, Stephen. Remember how we'd lie in the grass at night and look up at the stars? I'd tell you my dreams and you'd tell me yours?"

"Yeah, I remember."

"Do you remember what your dream was?"

"To get better and get the voices out of my head."

"That's right. And this place where you're going to be living, they're going to help you with that. I want you to think about this as the beginning of your dreams coming true." I smiled softly. "The doctors are going to take away the voices and help you to get better."

"Okay, Rory. If you say so, then I'll go."

I reached over and hugged him. Dr. Michaels walked in and asked us if were ready to go. Stephen sat down in the wheelchair and I held his hand as Ian pushed him out of the hospital. We met one of the nurses from Hudson Rock outside and she climbed into the limo with us. When we arrived at Hudson Rock, we were greeted by a group of people who introduced themselves to Stephen. They were trying to make him as comfortable as possible. It was time for me to say goodbye as I hugged him tight.

"I'll come visit you every Thursday, Stephen. You'll be safe here."

"I'll look forward to Thursdays."

"I'll see you later, okay?" I said as tears started to fall.

"No tears, Rory. My dreams are going to come true now." He smiled.

Sandi Lynn

I kissed him on the cheek and turned away. I heard him call Ian's name.

"Take care of my sister while I'm in here. Okay, buddy? She needs taking care of."

I looked over at Ian as he smiled at Stephen and nodded his hand. "Don't worry. Rory will be well taken care of."

I walked outside and climbed into the limo as I wiped the tears from my face. Ian opened the door and climbed in next to me. He took my hand and brought it up to his soft lips.

"He's going to be okay."

"I know and I just want to go home. I want to be alone for a while."

"Are you sure?" Ian asked. "You can stay with me and I'll leave you alone for as long as you need."

"No, I want to go to my home."

Ian sighed and told Joshua to drive us there.

Chapter 13

I spent the next few days locked up in my tiny apartment. The only time I stepped out was when Adalynn took me to her OB/GYN so I could get on birth control. Ian called me a couple of times, but I didn't answer. I sent him a text message that said when I was ready, I'd call him. My whole life had changed. Now that Stephen was safe at Hudson Rock, it was time to get *my* life together. For the first time in my life, I was no longer in charge of taking care of someone else. It was my turn to take care of me. I thought a lot about taking the job as Ian's assistant. I needed the money and the health benefits, not to mention all the other little perks of being his assistant. I had already fallen for him and his charm, knowing what kind of man he was and how he treated women. I missed him, even though it was my choice not to see him.

I opened up my laptop and googled him. There was picture from two nights ago of him and some woman at a dinner party. He was smiling at her as she was at him. The caption above the picture read: '*Could She Be the One?*' I felt sick and my heart started racing. He was obviously still seeing other women. I guess I was the stupid and naïve one who thought that he was only interested in me.

I walked next door to Java Hut and had a long talk with Jordyn. I told her that I appreciated everything she'd done for me, and I explained to her about my life and what had happened with Stephen. We sat at the table for three hours and she listened intently to every word I said. I told her that I needed to start new and that Ian had offered me a job. She told me that I'd be fucking crazy if I didn't accept it. I felt better knowing that she wasn't mad at me for bailing on her. I left Java Hut and walked back to my apartment to find Ian sitting on the steps.

"Ian? What are you doing here?" I asked.

"I need an answer, Rory. I'm not playing any more games with you. Are you going to accept my job offer?"

"I was actually just going to call you."

"Really? And why's that?"

"To tell you that I accept your offer."

A big smile graced his face as he stood up from the steps. "Rory, that's great."

I walked by him on the step and unlocked the door to my apartment. "I have rules, Mr. Braxton."

"Is that so, Miss Sinclair?"

I needed to use the bathroom, so I told him that I'd be right back. When I came out, I saw him looking at my computer. I'd left the article up. *Shit.*

"Are you stalking me, Rory?"

"No. Why would you ask that?"

He looked at me with knitted eyebrows and turned my computer around, pointing to the picture.

"Oh that. I was on the computer and I saw a blurb with your name, so I clicked it. No big deal."

"Are you jealous?"

"No, not at all. Would you like to explain to me what that's about?"

"No. I don't feel that I have to."

Oh boy. This was not going to be easy. "Do you want me to work for you, Ian? Yes or no?"

"Of course I do. If I didn't, I wouldn't have asked you in the first place."

My stomach was churning and my heart picked up a faster pace. "Then I will accept your offer under my terms."

"Okay, what are your terms?" he asked as the corners of his mouth curved up.

"Our relationship is strictly business. There will be no flirting of any kind and no sex. I'm your business assistant. Not your personal assistant. There's a difference, and if you don't know what that difference is, then I suggest you look it up and become familiar with it."

He studied me as he stood there with a smirk on his face. He walked over to where I was standing and placed his finger on my chin. "You will have sex with me; that I can guarantee, Miss Sinclair."

Goddamnit. "Who is she, Ian? The woman in the picture."

"Like I said before, I don't need to explain myself to you," he said as he kissed the tip of my nose. "Now, I'm happy you decided to accept the job. I have to go and arrange a couple of things. I'll be back here later, so don't go anywhere." He smiled as he kissed me on the forehead, walked to the door, and stopped. "By the way, did you get on birth control yet?"

"I believe that's none of your business, Mr. Braxton."

His mouth curved up into that sexy smile that drove me insane. "I'll take that as a yes." He winked as he walked out the door.

I shook my head and went and sat on the couch. I picked up my phone and dialed Adalynn.

"Hello," she answered.

"I took the job."

"Good for you. Now all you have to do is keep Ian on a tight leash."

"I have a feeling it's going to be the other way around," I said.

"Only if you let it, Rory. Remember, you're taking your life back. Don't let anyone stop you from doing it."

"Thanks, Adalynn. I knew I could count on you."

"You're welcome. We'll talk later. I'm on my way to a meeting."

I lay down on the couch and closed my eyes. I must've fallen asleep because I was woken up by Ian running his hand down my face and his soft lips brushing against mine.

"You looked so peaceful."

"I can't believe I fell asleep," I said as I sat up.

"Come here. I want to show you something outside." He smiled.

Ian took my hand and helped me up from the couch. I put on my flip-flops and walked outside. Sitting at the curb was a white BMW convertible.

"What do you think?" he asked.

"It's beautiful, Ian. I didn't take you for a white car kind of guy."

"It's not for me. It's for you." He smiled. "This is your company car."

"Shut the fuck up!" I exclaimed.

Ian chuckled. "I take it that means you like it?"

"I can't, Ian. I can't drive this car."

"You do know how to drive, right?"

"Yes, I know how to drive, silly." I smiled.

"Then what's the problem?" he asked in confusion.

"It's too fancy. I don't belong in a car like this."

Ian took my arms and put them around his neck as he put his hands on my hips. "Stop putting yourself down. You do belong in a car like this, and you'll look sexy as hell driving it. The company car is just one of many perks."

"Thank you, Ian," I said as I kissed him.

"You're welcome." He smiled.

We walked back to my apartment and Ian shut the door. He had that look in his eye. The same look he had in the limo. As he slowly made his way to me, I kept backing up until my back was against the wall. His smile grew wider.

"Just the way I like it; right up against the wall," he said as he grabbed my arms and pinned them over my head with one hand.

He was strong and so sexy. He tilted my head to the side as he began kissing my neck. "Did you get on the pill?" he asked in between kisses.

"Yes," I answered breathlessly.

"When can I fuck you?" he whispered.

"Three days, safely."

"Fuck. I still have to wait?"

His tongue traveled from my neck to my earlobe and down my jawline. He pushed his knee in between my legs and spread them as his hand moved up my skirt and to the edge of my panties.

"Oh, baby, you're so wet again," he said as his mouth crashed into mine.

He didn't waste any time ripping the side of my panties and plunging two fingers inside me as I was lifted slightly off the ground. He was like an animal; a beast out of control.

"You're so tight. I can't wait until my cock feels how tight you are. God, Rory, I can't stop wanting you. There's a part of me right now that just wants to put on a condom and fuck you senseless."

I was so turned on by him that I didn't care. I wanted him inside me. "Ian, just put the damn condom on and fuck me, please."

He let go of my wrists and instantly, his hand went up my shirt, pulling down my bra as he fingered my hard nipple. I reached for his pants and unzipped them as his erection was dying to be released. He grabbed my hand and stopped me.

"Let me make you come first and then I want you to suck me off."

My body went from hot to flames when he said that.

"I want you to look at me as you come. Don't take your eyes off of me. Do you understand me?"

I nodded my head because I understood perfectly. His scent engulfed me as he stood in front of me, with his fingers inside, alternating between circles and a steady in and out movement. The pressure was building and he could tell.

"Good girl, you're almost there," he said as he took his thumb and slowly rubbed my clit with it.

The moaning sounds that came from my body surprised me. I stared into Ian's eyes as my legs started to tighten and the pressure built up to the point of no return.

"Don't take your eyes off of me," he commanded.

I bit down on my bottom lip as I clasped his shoulders and my body shook. I released myself all over him.

"Christ, Rory. That was so fucking hot. I need to be inside you. Shit. I'll wait, baby. It'll be worth it. But make no mistake that in three days, no matter what's going on, I'm fucking you all night long. So you better be prepared to spend the night, because I'm not letting you leave."

I took in a sharp breath because, I swore, I just had another orgasm. I nodded my head because the word *yes* wouldn't come out of my mouth. He had me hypnotized. I was so lost in him at that moment that I couldn't see or think straight. Ian took his finger and ran it lightly across my lips. I took his finger in my mouth, tasting what he desired. He closed his eyes and let out a low hiss as he took down his pants and pushed me on my knees. I wrapped my hand around the base of his cock and wrapped my lips around his sensitive tip.

"Fuck, Rory. A few sucks and I'll be coming," he moaned.

He placed his hands on each side of my head and, with a bobbing motion, I ran my tongue around his cock as I took his entire length in my mouth. I reached under and gently stroked his balls as his stomach contracted and he moved his hips back and forth.

"Sweet Jesus, Rory. Oh God, don't stop," he said as his breathing became rapid.

One last thrust into my mouth and he immediately pulled out, taking his throbbing cock in his hand and spilling his pleasure all over. It was just about the sexiest thing I'd ever seen. The look on his face, the sounds from within. I had a feeling that once he was inside me, I'd never be the same again.

I stood up and ran to the bathroom and grabbed a towel. I handed it to him and he smiled at me. He cleaned himself up, tucked himself back in his pants, and walked over to the sink and washed his hands. I sat down on the couch and watched him as he dried his hands. He walked over and sat down next to me.

"You." He smiled as he shook his finger in front of me.

I grabbed it with my hand and held it still. "What?" I giggled.

"For someone who only had sex twice in her life, you sure as hell know how to give a blow job. You were amazing."

Knowing that I'd satisfied him and he enjoyed it gave me the confidence I needed. *Thank you, Google and porn.* I didn't want to tell him I'd researched it, so I just smiled and said thank you.

"You never told me where you learned to punch the punching bag like that," he said as he ran his fingers through my hair.

"There was one in the barn behind my aunt's house. My aunt had this guy friend who came over the house quite often. Okay, he was her drug dealer. Anyway, for a drug dealer, he was a nice guy. He saw me in the barn one day, punching like crazy and all wrong and he taught me the proper way to punch and kick. I needed to be physically strong in case Stephen came after me. I just didn't expect him to knife me from behind. I practiced every day, and whenever the drug dealer came over and brought my aunt her drugs, he would make me show him my progress and then he'd teach me some new moves."

"He sounds like a very nice drug dealer." Ian smiled.

"He actually was a nice guy."

"Well, we should get going."

I looked at Ian in confusion. "Where are we going?"

"Back to my house. So, pack a light bag because you're staying the night."

"No, I'm not."

"Yes, you are, Rory, and it's not up for discussion."

"Ian, no."

"Rory, yes. How do you expect me to get home?"

"Call a cab!" I exclaimed.

"I don't do cabs. Come on. You have to be at my house early anyway. I promise you we can go running in the morning. Unless you'd rather go down to the gym and use that punching bag again. I was totally turned on watching you do that."

I sighed as I stared at him. He pouted and made me laugh. "Damn you, Braxton," I said as I playfully hit his chest.

He grabbed my hand and, with a wide grin, he said, "So you like it rough, eh? I'll have to remember that. Now let's go," he said as he kissed my lips.

"One question. What does one wear as the business assistant to Mr. Ian Braxton?"

"You'll find out when we get back to the house."

"Huh?" I said.

He grabbed my hand and helped me from the couch.

Chapter 14

I rolled over and smiled as I looked out the window at the sunrise over the ocean waters. As I lay there for a few moments, I heard a soft knock on the door.

"Come in."

Ian stood in the doorway and smiled at me. He looked incredibly sexy in his black sweat pants and black t-shirt, which clung to every definition his upper body had.

"You're not out of bed yet?" he asked as he walked over and sat down on the edge. I sat up and stared at him as he took a hold of my hand.

"I sort of fell back asleep. That nightmare last night drained me again."

"Your first duty as my assistant today is to call Dr. Neil. I thought maybe once Stephen was found and you knew he was safe, the nightmares would've stopped."

"They've always been there. I can't remember a night when I didn't have them, except when I was drugged up for two days after you found me."

Ian smiled as he brought his hand up to my face. "We'll figure this out and get rid of those nightmares for good. Now, get dressed. We have a run to go for before we start our day."

I stepped out of bed and threw on my yoga pants and tank top. When I went outside to meet Ian, he was standing by the water with his hands on his hips. Even the back of him was sexy, and I could sit and stare at him and his body all day.

"Hey, I think you're falling behind, buddy!" I yelled as I ran past him.

"No fair." He smiled as he ran and caught up to me.

I slowed down my pace and we ran together. I was curious to know more about Andrew, so I asked Ian about him.

"Tell me about Andrew," I said.

"Why do you want to know about him?" he asked as he looked at me.

"He's your best friend, and I want to know about your friends. Is something wrong with that?"

"No, I guess not. Andrew and I have been friends since we were thirteen years old. We're like brothers. His dad died a few years back and left him his entire estate and business."

"What about his mom?" I asked.

"He doesn't see her very often. His parents divorced when he was sixteen and his mom started dating some guy that was twenty years younger than she was. As soon as his dad found out, he took her out of his will and left her with nothing."

"Have you ever thought about looking for your mom?"

Ian suddenly stopped, and when he looked at me, anger consumed his eyes. "Why the fuck would you bring her up?" he asked in an angry tone.

"I'm sorry, Ian. I just wondered."

"Well, stop wondering and don't mention it again. It was a one-time deal, me talking about her to you that night and it won't happen again," he snapped.

"You're right, it won't happen again," I said as I ran ahead of him.

I finally saw the anger that consumed him about his mother, and it frightened me. The rest of the run was silent as we headed back to the house. I took a shower, changed into my business clothes, and walked down the stairs. Ian was walking through the foyer when he glanced up and immediately stopped in his tracks.

"You look amazing, Rory. The business look really suits you." He smiled.

Thank you, asshole, is what I wanted to say. "Thank you."

"Follow me to my study. I have something to show you," he said.

We walked to his study, and I went over to the new cherry wood desk that sat against the sidewall from Ian's desk.

"This is your desk. I've supplied you with everything you'll need and the computer is fully loaded with all the software you'll be using."

I looked at Ian and twisted my face. "There's that adorable look again. Now, what?" He smiled.

"You never had an assistant work from home, have you?" I asked.

Ian put his hands in his pocket and casually walked over to his desk. "What makes you think that?"

"Because this desk wasn't here the last time I was in your study and I don't recall ever seeing another female in the house besides your maids and sex partners."

Ian sighed and looked down at his desk. "Please don't refer to those women as my sex partners, and you're right, there was no assistant."

"So you lied to me?" I asked.

Ian stepped away from his desk and walked over to me. He put his hands on my hips as he tried to explain to me what I'd asked him.

"Technically, no. I'd been planning on hiring someone all along. You came along and I thought you were perfect. End of discussion," he said as he kissed my lips.

"Excuse me, Mr. Braxton, but I do believe we're on company time. I would hate to think that you kiss all of your female employees on the lips."

Ian chuckled. "Only the special ones." He winked. "I do have to head to the office. I have some contracts here that need to be typed up. You'll find the program on the computer. If you have any questions, just call me or Adalynn. She knows my software and she could probably help you."

"You never told me that you're partners with her at *Prim*."

"Should I have? I didn't really think about it," he said.

"No, I guess not." I sighed.

Ian smiled and left his study. I sat down in the plush black office chair and opened the first file for the contracts that needed to be typed up. I turned on the computer and a picture of the most amazing flowers filled the screen. I smiled because he remembered how much I loved flowers. As I became familiar with the program, and started typing the contracts, an hour had passed, and Mandy, one of Ian's maids, knocked lightly on the study door.

"Come in, Mandy."

"I brought you some coffee, Miss Sinclair, and a chocolate chip muffin. Charles made them per the request of Mr. Braxton."

"Thank you, Mandy, and please call me Rory. Tell Charles I said thank you."

"I will." She smiled.

Mandy was a cute girl. She looked to be about mid-twenties with short black hair and green eyes that resembled cat eyes. She was very attractive. As I finished up the contracts, I ate my muffin and drank my coffee. The day went by pretty fast as I sat on the computer all day, studying the software that was loaded in the computer. Ian sent me a couple of text messages, asking me to make some phone calls for him. I got up from my desk just as Mandy walked in with a beautiful arrangement of flowers.

"These just arrived for you, Rory."

"Oh my gosh. They're beautiful." I smiled as I took them from her and set them on the desk.

There was an envelope that was sticking out from the top, so I pulled out the card that was inside.

Sandi Lynn

For a beautiful assistant.

Welcome to Braxton Development.

Best, Ian

My smile widened as I took note of the word "beautiful" he had called me again. I stuck my nose in the flowers and took in their amazing scent, then picked up my phone to send Ian a text message.

"Do you always call your assistants beautiful? Thank you very much for the flowers."

"No, because I only have one assistant who's beautiful and you're welcome. 2 more days!"

After my work was finished, I left Ian's study and walked to the kitchen. I stopped dead in my tracks when I saw Ian's father, Richard, sitting at the table.

"Well, well, I thought you moved out," he said.

I walked over to the refrigerator and took out a bottle of water before replying to him.

"I did move out, Richard. I'm working as Ian's assistant. Today's my first day."

He looked at me and knitted his eyebrows while giving me a sinister look. "Really? My son hired you?"

Remain calm. He's nothing. You've handled far worse. "Yes, Ian did hire me. Now if you'll excuse me, I have work to do." I smiled as I began to walk out of the kitchen.

"You're not excused, little lady. Get back here!" he exclaimed.

I slowly turned around and stared at the so-called man before me. He got up from his chair and walked over to me.

"How old are you?"

"Twenty-three," I replied.

"You're just a baby. No wonder why my son is keeping you around. If it's money you want, name your price."

His words were unbelievable to me, and I felt like a ticking time bomb ready to explode any second.

"I don't have a price, Richard. Ian was kind enough to take me in and help me out. He's given me a chance to start my life over, and I will always be indebted to him for that."

"You poor, naïve little girl. My son will break you. When he tires of you, which he will, he'll break your spirit and then he'll go on with his life as if you never existed."

"Dad of the year, right? You taught him well. You should be so proud," I said.

"Rory! That's enough!" Ian yelled.

I quickly turned around to find Ian standing there with anger displayed all over his face. "What the hell do you think you're doing?"

I couldn't answer him because it was apparent that he walked in on what I said, and he didn't hear the rest of the conversation. I shook my head and stormed past him, bumping into his shoulder as I walked by. As I went down to the beach to try and calm down, I was burning mad at the way that man talked to me and also at how Ian walked in and yelled at me without hearing what his father had said.

"He's an asshole; what can I say?" Ian said as he walked up behind me.

"Yeah, well, you didn't hear the things he said to me."

"Then tell me, Rory," he whispered as he put his hands on my shoulders.

"He told me to name my price."

I wasn't about to tell him what his father had said about him. So I just left it at that.

Ian's hands lightly squeezed my shoulders. "I'm sorry. He's just looking out for me. He doesn't trust you because he thinks all women are after my money."

"I don't care about your money. But I will tell you this: you better set him straight or I will quit being your assistant and you won't ever see me again."

He wrapped his arms around me and pulled me back. "I know you don't give a shit about my money and don't talk crazy. You aren't going anywhere. Two more days," he said as he lightly kissed my neck.

I couldn't help but laugh. "Do you know how many times you've said that today?"

"Yes. Can you tell how impatient I am?" he said as he kissed my head.

I brought my hands up to his arms, which held me tightly. "Thank you again for the beautiful flowers."

"You're welcome. I'm having dinner with Andrew tonight so I have to get ready to leave. Are you going to be okay?"

"I'm fine. I'm going to head home anyway. Enjoy your dinner," I said as I broke from his grip and started to walk away.

"You can spend the night again," he said.

I didn't respond. I just put my hand up and waved. Grabbing my purse from Ian's study, I got into my new car and drove away.

Chapter 15

I was up all night, thinking about Ian. He plagued my every thought, my every dream, and completely invaded my existence. There wasn't a second that I wasn't thinking about him. I threw on some sweats and drove to Ian's house to change for work. As I walked through the door, Andrew was walking down the stairs with two women following behind him.

"Morning, Rory," he said with a wide grin.

"Tell Ian thanks for last night." The woman with the long black hair winked.

"Morning, Andrew," I replied as I walked past him up the stairs.

My stomach was twisted in knots at the thought that Ian was with one of those women last night. I shook my head as I rummaged through the closet, pulling out a short, black skirt and a fuchsia-colored shirt. I headed downstairs and, as I walked into the kitchen, Charles handed me a cup of coffee. Andrew was sitting at the table, eating eggs.

"Hey, sunshine, you're looking good." He smiled.

"Is Ian out for a run?" I asked.

"Yeah, but I don't know how after last night. That boy has to be exhausted. He probably only got a couple of hours of sleep."

"Well, I'm glad the two of you had fun," I said with a smirk. "Now, if you'll excuse me, I have some work to do."

I was bothered by the fact that Andrew was so smug. I got the impression that he didn't like me very much. So far, I was not impressed by the people in Ian's life, with the exception of Adalynn. I walked into the study and sat down at my desk. I looked at the flowers that were displayed beautifully and smiled as I took in their scent. There were some more contracts sitting on the desk that needed to be typed up. I turned on the computer and got to work. A while later, Ian walked in with a smile on his face.

"Good morning, beautiful," he said as he walked over and kissed me on the head.

"Morning," I replied without even looking at him.

"Uh oh, what did I do now?" he asked.

I figured I better play it cool because I was in no mood for an argument.

"Nothing. Why would you ask me that?" I said as I looked up at him.

"Just the way you said 'morning.' I got the feeling that you were pissed off at me."

"No. I was just concentrating on getting these contracts done. Why would I be pissed off at you? I haven't seen you since yesterday." I smiled.

"Just making sure. Anyway, I have a few things I need to give you and go over with you today."

He opened his desk drawer and pulled out a bankbook and card. "I opened up a bank account for you in your name only. Your checks will get direct deposited in there. Here's your bankcard to use. I told you that you'd be getting health insurance, so I've added you to my plan and your medical card should be coming soon. Since I won't be needing you every day, I've decided that you'll have Tuesdays and Thursdays off as well as the weekends, unless I need you to travel with me. Sound good?"

"Thank you, Ian. It sounds great."

He shot me that sexy smile and sat down at his desk. I turned back to my computer and resumed what I was doing. I didn't want things to be awkward, especially after what he did for me, so I asked him how his night was. I wanted to see how much he would tell me, if anything.

"How was your evening last night with Andrew?"

"It was good. We had a great time."

I bet you did. "I was surprised to see him here this morning."

"He had too much to drink last night and his car was here, so I just told him to stay."

"He seems like a really nice guy," I lied.

"He is. Like I told you before, we're like brothers."

I didn't say another word because I didn't want him to start to get suspicious.

"How was your evening?" he asked.

"It was good. I watched a couple of movies and then tried to get some sleep."

"Did you have the nightmares again?"

"I sure did. In fact, if you'll excuse me, I'm going to call Dr. Neil and set up an appointment."

"That's a good idea, Rory."

I took my phone from my desk and stepped into the guest bathroom that was next to the study. I felt like I couldn't breathe, and I needed to get out of there. I sat down on the toilet and called Dr. Neil's office. I told the receptionist who I was and that Ian had spoken to Dr. Neil already. She set my appointment for later that afternoon. After I collected myself, I walked back into Ian's study.

"Well?"

"I have an appointment this afternoon."

"Good. I think it'll be good for you. Now, come here for a moment," he said as he held out his arms.

I walked over to him and he pulled me onto his lap. "One more day," he whispered as he traced my lips with his finger. "One more day and I'll be inside you, fucking you, and giving you the most pleasure you've ever felt. And you'll be giving me the most pleasure as well." He smiled.

The pit of my stomach fell deeper. The thought of those women walking down the stairs crept into my mind. I brought my hand up to his face and gave him a fake smile.

"After your appointment with Amanda, I'm taking you somewhere for the night. Because once the clock strikes midnight, you're mine," he whispered as he kissed my lips.

"I thought I accepted this job on my terms, and my terms clearly stated that there was no flirting or kissing during work hours."

"Fuck your terms. You're here and you're too hard to resist."

Damn it. Damn him. Damn it all to hell. Why does he do this to me? Why does he have such a hold on me? "Where are we going?" I asked, as I was curious to know where he planned on taking me.

"My yacht. You don't get seasick, do you?"

"I don't know. I've never been on a boat before. I guess we'll find out."

"You'll be fine and I have some medication on board in case you do get sick."

"I didn't know you had a yacht. You never mentioned it before."

"I guess there wasn't the need to."

"Is there anything else you may not feel the need to tell me?" I wanted to see if he would talk more about last night.

"No. I don't think so. Is something bothering you, Rory?"

"Not at all. I'm just wondering what else will pop up that you didn't think to mention." I smiled.

He lifted me from his lap and set me on the edge of his desk. "One day, I'm going to take you right here on top of my desk," he said with seduction.

"It better be after work hours, Mr. Braxton."

"Oh no, it *will* be during work hours, Miss Sinclair. I have a tendency to break all the rules."

He smiled, kissed me on the head, and told me he had a meeting to get to. "Good luck at your appointment, and I'll see you back here later for our night together." He winked.

Fuck. Fuck. Fuck. Suddenly, I didn't care about him being with another woman last night. He wanted *me,* and he wanted *me* bad. Nobody had ever wanted me, and for him to come along and tell me how beautiful I was and pay me so much attention; of course, I was going to fall head over heels for him. This was one area that I needed to talk to Dr. Neil about. I hopped off the desk, went back to my seat, and finished up the contracts. I went upstairs to the bedroom to see what I could pack for tonight. The thought of being on a yacht with Ian excited me. Just the two of us, out in the open ocean, without any distractions. I would have him all to myself and that made me happy.

****

"It's nice to meet you, Rory. Please have a seat."

"Thank you, Dr. Neil. I appreciate you being able to fit me in today."

Her office was beautifully decorated. It was made up of beiges with burgundy accents. I took a seat on the leather couch while Dr. Neil sat in the leather chair across from me.

"Why don't you tell me what's going on," she said.

I began telling her about my childhood and Stephen. We were in deep conversation, and before I knew it, our time was up and our session was over.

"We have a lot of ground to cover, Rory. I would like to see you at least two days a week."

"Thank you, Dr. Neil. I think that would be okay."

"Good. Now I don't want you to worry because we're going to get those nightmares to stop. Would you like me to prescribe you a sleeping pill?"

"No. I don't think that'll be necessary. I'd rather not start taking medication."

She smiled at me as she walked me to the door. "I'll see you in a couple of days"

I walked out of her office, feeling pretty good. Even though I had told Ian about my past, it felt different when I talked to Dr. Neil. I pulled my phone out of my purse when I got into the car and sent Ian a text message.

"My appointment just ended. Going to stop by my apartment to pick up a few things. I'll be over soon."

"See you soon. A few more hours left."

When I pulled up to my apartment, I noticed there was a piece of paper taped to the door. It was a notice from the city that the building was being shut down for safety issues, and I needed to find a place to stay until further notice. *Shit. Shit. Shit. Are you kidding me?* I ripped the paper off the door and walked inside. I looked at my phone and dialed Ian.

"Hey, is everything okay?" he asked when he answered.

"You're never going to believe what I came home to," I said, distraught.

"Rory, calm down. What happened?"

"My building is being shut down for safety issues, and I have to move out until further notice."

"Is that all? You had me scared something bad happened."

"Ian, this is serious! What the hell am I going to do?"

"You'll stay with me until it's okay for you to go back. It's only temporary."

Ian was right. I always had a room at his house and this was only temporary. "Okay, I'll see you soon," I said as I hung up the phone.

I grabbed the big duffel bag and started packing it with everything I thought I'd need. I grabbed my laptop, put it in the car, and drove to Ian's house. As soon as I pulled up, Ian walked out and grabbed my bag from the backseat.

"Welcome to my home, Miss Sinclair. I hope you enjoy your stay and that your needs are fully satisfied."

"Shut up." I laughed.

Ian chuckled and took my bag upstairs. I followed behind. When I entered the room, there were five bathing suits, all bikinis, spread out on the bed.

"What's all this?" I said as I walked over and picked up the black one first.

"Some new bathing suits for you to choose from. I really don't think you're going to need them, but just in case."

"You think of everything. Thank you, Ian."

He smiled softly as he grabbed my hand and brought it up to his lips. "You're welcome. We leave in about ten minutes. I'll meet you downstairs."

****

I stood in front of the docked yacht and stared at it as Ian walked ahead of me.

"Rory, are you okay?" he asked as he turned and walked back to where I was standing.

"I'm fine. I've never seen a yacht before and I just can't believe it. It's amazing, Ian."

He chuckled and grabbed my hand. "Come on; wait until you see the inside."

We stepped onto the yacht, and I felt like I was entering a whole new world. I couldn't help but stare at the fine furnishings and beautiful woodwork.

"I could live here," I said.

"I'm glad you like it."

A man dressed in all white came to the living area and took our bags. "Good evening, Mr. Braxton."

"Good evening, Roland. This is Miss Sinclair."

"Very good to meet you, Miss Sinclair." He smiled as he bowed slightly.

He took our bags and walked away. I looked around and tried to take it all in, but it was difficult. I felt like I was in a dream and that I was going to wake up any second. Moments later, another man, also dressed in white and wearing a chef's hat, told Ian that dinner was about to be served. Ian took my hand and led me up to the top floor of the deck where a table was elegantly set for two. Sitting in the middle of the table were beautifully lit candles that flickered in the night air.

"Ian, I—"

"It's beautiful, isn't it?" he asked as he pulled out my chair for me.

"Beautiful isn't the word for it," I said as tears sprang to my eyes.

"We're going to start with a wonderful dinner and then we'll have a couple of drinks on the lower deck while we stare at the night ocean," he said as he sat down.

We enjoyed a wonderful dinner. It was probably the best food I'd ever had in my life. When we were finished, Ian took my hand, grabbed the bottle of wine, and led me to the deck below to some lounge chairs that sat facing the ocean. The crew told Ian that everything was set and then he dismissed them. We set sail and it was just the two of us on board. I could get used to this real fast. Ian came back and wrapped a sweater around my bare shoulders.

"Thank you." I smiled.

"You're welcome." He smiled back as he sat down in the chair next to me.

"How did you come to have all of this?" I asked him as I took a sip of my wine.

"I guess you can say I'm a smart businessman. I get that from my father."

He had to go and mention his father. The thought of that man burned my skin. I would've been happy if I never had to hear about him again. Ian got up from his seat, walked over to a small table, and picked up a remote. Suddenly, "Unchained Melody" started to play. He walked over to me with a smile on his face as he held out his hand.

"Would you like to dance, Miss Sinclair?"

I removed the sweater from my shoulders as I took his hand and he led me to the middle of the deck. We began to dance to the song that played when we shared our first dance together. I hated to say it, but that song would be forever etched into my heart. Ian and I stared into each other's eyes before he leaned in and softly teased my lips. He pulled me closer as I teased his lips back. I watched him slowly close his eyes as he pulled me into him, wrapping his arms tightly around me as we swayed back and forth to the slow melody. The song ended and Ian looked at his watch. A smile graced his face.

"It's after midnight," he said as he picked me up and carried me down to the bedroom.

Chapter 16

I wrapped my arms around him and took in his scent. Excitement and nerves shot throughout my body. This was it. It was finally happening. My heart was rapidly beating as he put me down in front of the bed and his fingers deftly took a hold of the bottom of my sundress, lifting it over my head and throwing it on the floor. He took a step back and slowly shook his head as I stood there in nothing but my white lacy thong and matching push-up bra. He studied me. His eyes moved up and down every inch of me and his hunger became real.

"You are so fucking beautiful and you drive me crazy. I want you to slowly take off your bra."

I did as he asked and reached behind me to unhook it. I held the cups over my breasts as I slowly took down each strap before letting it hit the floor. He gasped.

"Perfect. You're so perfect. Now, slowly take off your thong and toss it at me."

As I hooked my thumbs into the strings, I slowly shimmied out of the thong, trying to make it look as sexy as possible for him. He growled.

I stood there before him as his eyes scanned me, taking note of every inch of my bare skin. I tossed him my thong and, when he caught it, he felt the crotch with his thumb, feeling the wetness that was made because of him. He tossed my thong to the side and unbuttoned his shirt, letting it drop to the floor as he slid it off his muscular shoulders. I took in a sharp breath as his perfectly tight and chiseled abs were staring me in the face. Ian unbuckled his belt and took it off. He undid the top button of his pants, but left them on as he slowly walked towards me with a ravenous look in his eye. When he approached me, his finger instantly plunged into me. I gasped, closing my eyes and letting out a soft moan as he inserted another finger inside me and worked my sensitive flesh articulately. The palm of his hand rested on the back of my neck as he brought his mouth to mine, licking and nipping my lips before kissing me passionately. My body was on high alert as the warm sensation pooled between my legs.

"Fuck, Rory. You keep getting wetter and wetter. I need to taste you. I need my mouth on your pussy, but first I want you to come."

I just about convulsed when he said that. He expertly moved his fingers in and out of me while he slowly rubbed my aching clit in circles with his thumb. I groaned as the tension built up and yelled out his name as my body exploded like never before.

"That's right, baby. Let it all go. I want to feel every ounce of juice you have inside you."

As soon as my body went limp in his arms, he gently laid me back on the bed. He scooted me up so my head was on the pillow and his tongue slid its way to my right breast and his other hand caressed my left. His mouth wrapped around my puckered nipple and a soft groan escaped his lips. He moved his mouth to the other nipple as he lightly took it between his teeth. I threw my head back and moaned. I was aching for him to tear me up inside.

"Ian," I whispered as my hands ran through his hair.

"Tell me how much you love it, sweetheart," he whispered as his tongue slid down my torso and to my sensitive clit.

"I love it, Ian," I whispered.

As his mouth engulfed me, his hands reached up and latched onto my breasts, kneading them and pinching my nipples. Bolts of lightning flashed throughout my head as Ian's tongue flicked fast and furious at my clit. My body tightened as he pushed me to the brink of another amazing orgasm. His tongue licked its way up my sensitive area, to my torso, over my breasts, and finally to my mouth where he forcefully pushed his tongue inside, making me taste what he'd done to me. His strong body hovered over me. His eyes gazed into mine as his mouth curved into a sexy smile.

"Are you ready, sweetheart, for what I'm about to give you?"

I nodded my head. "Yes, I want you inside me, now."

I could feel his hard cock between my thighs, teasing me and waiting for the perfect moment to strike.

"Tell me how bad you want it," he said.

With a heavy breath, I whispered, "I want you so bad. I need to feel you inside me."

"That's my girl." He smiled as I felt his tip pushing its way inside me. "Jesus Christ, sweetheart, you're tighter than I thought. Oh God, you're so fucking tight. You feel so good," he moaned as he pushed further inside me. His carnal groans were enough to make me come. Each pleasurable sound he let out aroused me even more, and the fact that *I* made him feel so good excited me. His thrust became harder, and finally, he was deep inside me. He thrust in and out of me a few times before he started to move his hips in a circular motion, hitting every sensitive nerve inside me.

"Fuck, you're so beautiful," he said with a ragged breath before bringing his mouth to my puckered nipple.

I wrapped my legs around him and pulled him down on me. He fell deeper inside and let out a loud groan as he pounded into me; hard, fast, and bringing me ecstasy. I tightened myself around him.

"That's it, baby. I want you to look at me when I come inside you."

He raised himself up so he was hovering over me. He placed one hand on the bed and the other on the side of my face, making sure that I stared straight into his eyes as we both came. He pounded into me like a wild beast, sending my body straight into oblivion. I had no shame and screamed his name as my body shuddered beneath him and my nails dug into his back. He gave one last thrust and spilled his come inside me, slowing his thrusting as he pushed out every last drop. Sweat dripped from his forehead as he kissed me breathlessly.

"That was perfect." He smiled as he stared into my eyes.

He pulled out of me, rolled over, and grabbed some tissues from the nightstand and handed them to me. My body felt like jelly.

"Are you okay, sweetheart?" he asked as he propped himself up on his elbow and traced my breast with his finger.

"I'm fine. In fact, I've never been better." I smiled as I ran the back of my hand down his face.

With the lightest movement, he brushed his hand over my scar. "Are you sure I didn't hurt you?"

"Ian, you didn't hurt me. The only thing you did was make me feel amazing."

"Thank you for doing this. I loved fucking you without a condom on."

I smiled softly and he positioned himself so he was on his back. He put his arm around me and pulled me into him. "I think we should get some sleep now, because when we wake up, I'm going to need to fuck you again."

"Is that so?" I smiled as I lifted up my head and looked at him.

"Yes. I really feel the need to pin you down and fuck you again right now."

"Then what are you waiting for?" I smiled.

"Seriously? You're up for it again?"

"Yes. But if you don't mind, I'd like to get on top."

"Fuck, yes, sweetheart; get up here!" He smiled as he pulled me on top of him.

****

I smiled as I felt the soft tips of fingers stroking my lips. I opened my eyes to find Ian leaning over me and smiling.

"Good morning."

"Good morning," I said as I stretched.

"You know what?" he asked.

"What?"

"You didn't have a nightmare last night."

I smiled as he leaned closer and brushed his lips against mine. "That's because I was in bliss after our night together. There was too much happiness to think bad things."

"Let's go get some breakfast. I don't know about you, but I've worked up quite an appetite." He winked.

Ian got up from the bed and handed me my silk robe. "Just wear this and nothing underneath. I want to be able to see your nipples get hard when I look at you, and I want easy access for when I need to fuck anywhere on this boat."

I took the robe from him and put it on. He led me to the kitchen and asked me to get the fruit cups out of the fridge while he cooked us some eggs. I couldn't help but stare at him from behind. His broad, muscular frame made me weak, and the way his pajama bottoms sat low on his hips sent an ache down below that made me want him again. I walked up behind him and lightly ran my finger across the definition of his back. I heard him gasp.

"If you're trying to get me hard, you're doing a damn good job."

"I'm sorry. I just couldn't resist," I said as I lightly kissed his back and asked him where the spoons were.

I glanced over to my left and saw a black baby grand piano sitting in the corner. Smiling, I walked over to it and sat down. With my finger, I pressed a couple of keys. Ian turned his head and looked at me. I positioned my hands on the keys and began playing "Prelude No. 1 in C Major" by Johann Sebastian Bach. The minute my fingers touched the keys, I went to a world that

I hadn't visited in a long time. A world where there was no pain, no humiliation, and no fear. An escape from the reality of the hell that was my life.

"What the hell, Rory," Ian said as he stood next to the piano and watched me.

I finished my song and he asked me to play another as he sat down beside me. I played "Somewhere over the Rainbow." I deftly pressed the keys of ivory white and charcoal black with my slender fingers, and swayed back and forth as I let the music take over my soul. As I finished and played the last note, I looked over at Ian, who was staring at me intently.

"My God, where did you learn to play like that and why didn't you ever tell me you played the piano?" he asked.

"I first learned to play when I had to transfer elementary schools when Stephen and I went to live with my aunt. There was a piano in the music room, and one day after music class let out, I sat down at it and pressed each key, one at a time. I'll never forget the sound. It was like magic as far as I was concerned. My music teacher was Mr. Brand, and he knew I was the new kid and didn't have any friends. I guess he could tell by the expression on my face how happy it made me to press the keys and hear the sounds that came from it. He told me that if I stayed after school every day for two hours, he'd teach me how to play. He'd give me an hour worth of instruction and then an hour of practice."

"Didn't your aunt wonder where you were?"

I smiled softly. "She believed that school got out when I told her it did. She was too high and didn't care enough to check it out. Stephen stayed with me every day and did his homework. The music helped him to relax and he said it kept the voices quiet. On the weekends, I'd go to the music store and sit at one of the pianos and start playing."

"They allowed that?"

"Not really, but once I started playing, they didn't say too much. I think they enjoyed it or felt sorry for me. When I was in junior high and high school, I asked if I could join band, but play the school's piano as my instrument, and they said yes. Again, I think they felt sorry for me."

Ian put his arm around me and pulled me into him, gently kissing the side of my head. "I'm in awe right now because I just can't believe how beautifully you play."

"The piano was my escape from this reality into one that was much better."

"Does your aunt know you play?"

"No. I never mentioned it. I had to stop playing after I graduated because I no longer had access to a piano. God, what I would've given to have one."

"Come on; let's go eat some breakfast. I'm sure our eggs are stone cold."

"Just pop them in the microwave to warm them up."

"That's disgusting." He smiled.

We got up from the bench, grabbed the food, and Ian led me up on deck. The bright sun in the sky, the light wave that caressed my face, and the blue ocean water were just about the most perfect things I'd ever seen.

"Oh, Ian. It's amazing up here."

"I knew you'd like it. That's why I brought you on the boat," he said as his lips kissed my bare shoulder.

We sat down at the table and ate breakfast; just the two of us, alone, in the middle of the ocean. It was perfect, he was perfect, and God help me because I'd already fallen in love with him. I wanted him to open up more about himself.

"Tell me about your childhood," I blurted out.

Ian looked at me and, instead of the anger in his eyes that I thought I'd see, he gave me a small smile.

"You already know my mom left and my dad raised me as a single parent. There's nothing else to really tell you, Rory."

There was a lot more to tell me, but he just refused to. "Didn't you find it odd that your dad never remarried?"

Ian leaned back in his chair. "Nah, he never found anyone worthy, I guess."

He was lying, because I knew exactly what kind of man Richard Braxton was. I didn't want to ruin our time together, and I knew if I kept pressing, he'd get pissed. I got up from my chair and leaned on the railing of the boat. Ian walked up behind me. His hands cupped my bare ass from underneath my short, silk robe.

"Your ass is amazing," he growled as he squeezed it.

I leaned my head back on his chest and looked up at him and he leaned down and kissed me. "I think I'm going to fuck you right up against this railing," he said as his hand reached in front of me and slowly untied my robe.

His hands moved up to my breasts, fondling them and pinching my erect nipples, close to sending me on my way to an orgasm. I moaned as he slid the robe off my shoulders and let it fall to the floor. We were in the middle of nowhere, and we were the only boat in sight, so I didn't mind that I was completely naked in broad daylight. I reached my hand back and stroked his hard cock through the lightweight fabric of his pajama pants. He let out a groan as he plunged two fingers inside me without even a moment of hesitation.

"You're so wet. I love how wet you get with me. You have no idea what a turn on that is," he whispered as his teeth scraped along my shoulder.

My fingers grasped at his waistband. I couldn't wait any longer. I needed to feel him inside me. He removed his fingers from me and took down his pants, stepping out of them and kicking them across the deck.

"Hold onto the railing tight, sweetheart, because I'm going to take you on a ride you'll never forget."

His fingers swept across my slick area one last time to make sure I was wet enough and ready for him. Ian wrapped one arm tightly around my waist as he thrust inside me from behind. Our bodies were connected as mine was pressed up against the railing. He moved in and out of me at a fast pace, pounding into me as if his life depended on it. His skillful finger made its way down and caressed my wet clit, sending me over the edge.

"Ah, that's right, sweetheart; come for me. I want to hear you scream my name when you do. Can you do that for me?"

I was breathless. My heart was rapidly beating as the pools of warmth between my thighs and the tightening of my body took over. One final hard thrust and he had sent me into pure intoxication. Ian and I let out each other's name as we came simultaneously. His groan became louder as he slowed his pace, making sure that he poured every last drop of his come inside me. I could feel the swift beating of his heart as his chest was pressed against my back. Ian buried his face into my neck.

"Have I told you lately how amazing you feel?" he whispered.

"Yes, but keep telling me." I smiled.

Ian pulled out of me and turned me around. His smile was bright and his eyes were dancing. He leaned in and kissed me as his hands cupped the sides of my face. "I need to turn the boat around so we're back tomorrow morning. Tomorrow's Thursday; you have your visitation with Stephen."

"I know and I can't wait to see him. I hope he's okay."

"I'm sure he's fine," he said as he kissed my head.

We spent the rest of the day soaking up the sun, drinking a few cocktails, and having more sex than I'd ever imagined. I was in Heaven. There was no other word to call it. That was the day that Ian Braxton changed my life forever.

Chapter 17

I woke up and Ian wasn't in bed. I lay there, thinking about this day. Thinking about what it meant. Its pure existence; my and Stephen's existence. A day that was special for everyone else but me. A day that was meant to be celebrated, but never was.

Ian walked in the room with a smile on his face, bringing me a cup of coffee.

"Good morning," he said.

"Good morning." I smiled as he leaned over and kissed me.

"We'll be docking soon."

"Okay. I'll get dressed."

My phone was sitting on the dresser and it began to chime. Ian looked at me.

"Who would be sending you a message this early in the morning?" he asked.

"I don't know; maybe it's Adalynn. Can you hand me my phone, please?"

Ian walked over to the dresser and picked it up. He looked at it and then stopped and stared at me.

"What? Who's it from?"

"It's from your friend, Jordyn. She's wishing you a happy birthday. Is today your birthday, Rory?" he asked sternly.

I looked down at the sheet that I had covering my breasts. "Yes."

"For fuck's sake, why didn't you tell me?" he yelled.

He had no right to start yelling at me. I threw back the sheet and got out of bed. "What did you want me say, Ian? Hey, guess what, it's my birthday! Let's go celebrate my shit life," I yelled back as I grabbed my thong from the floor and put it on.

"Yes, you should have told me!" he spat.

"Why? What difference would it have made? My birthday is nothing. It hasn't been acknowledged since I was ten years old!" I hollered as I put my bra on.

Ian walked over and took a hold of my arm. He spun me around and pulled me into him. "It means something to me," he whispered. "I'm sorry for yelling at you. It's just that we spent this time together and to find out from a text that it's your birthday, it upset me."

I broke our embrace and placed my hand on his chest. "I've gotten used to my birthday being another ordinary day. It's no big deal, Ian. So, please, drop it."

"The hell I will. It's your birthday and I always help my friends celebrate their birthdays. We're going to celebrate tonight, okay?" He smiled as he ran his finger down my cheek.

His warm smile, his seductive eyes staring at me, and the simple touch of his finger on my skin made it impossible to refuse him. "Fine, we'll celebrate tonight. Now, if you'll excuse me, I need to finish getting ready."

Ian smiled and turned to walk out of the room. "Oh, by the way," I said. "Do you think that we could stop at the store on the way home so I can pick up an iPod for Stephen?"

"We sure can." He winked.

I read my text message from Jordyn and responded.

"Thank you, and how did you know it was my birthday?"

"It's on your application. When I saw the date, I put it in my calendar on my phone. Do you have plans today?"

"Actually, Ian and I are doing something."

"That's good. Ollie and I want to take you out to celebrate. How about tomorrow night?"

"Tomorrow night will work."

"Great! We'll figure something out and I'll text you with the details."

"Thank you, Jordyn."

"Happy Birthday, Rory."

When I finished getting dressed, I went up on deck to find Ian leaning over the railing and staring out into the ocean. He looked like he was in deep thought. I didn't want to disturb him because something told me he didn't want to be. Don't ask me how I knew that. It was just a feeling I had. I went back downstairs and popped a bagel in the toaster. As I was in the refrigerator, getting the cream cheese, I felt strong arms wrap around my waist.

"Go sit down and let me get that for you. It's your birthday, after all."

"Ian, I can make a bagel."

"It's not a request, Rory; it's a command."

I rolled my eyes as he lifted me up and turned me around, away from the refrigerator. I went and sat down at the table.

"Jordyn and Ollie are taking me out tomorrow night to celebrate my birthday."

"Is that so? Where are you going? Just a quiet dinner, perhaps?"

"I don't know. She said she and Ollie will talk about it and she'll text me with the details."

"We'll see," Ian said.

That struck me as odd when he said that. *What the hell did he mean by it?* "What do you mean, 'we'll see'?" I asked.

He walked over to the table, set my bagel down in front of me, and kissed me on the head. "We'll see. That's what I mean." He smiled as he walked away.

I sat there while I took a bite of my bagel. If he thought that he was stopping me from going out with my friends when he consistently did it, he had another thing coming. We weren't in a relationship and he didn't control me. I'd spent my life being controlled by people, and I wouldn't ever let it happen again.

I heard Ian yell my name as I went up on deck. We had docked, and his crew was standing on the side of the dock, waiting for us. Ian grabbed my hand and led me off the boat and over to the limo. One of his crew members grabbed our bags and set them in the trunk, which Joshua already had open.

"Joshua, we need to make a stop at the Apple Store so Miss Sinclair can pick something up, and today's her birthday."

"Sure thing." He smiled. "Happy Birthday, Rory."

Smiling, I thanked him as we climbed into the limo. "I wish I could go with you to see Stephen, but I have some business things to take care of since I've been gone," Ian said as he kissed my hand.

"It's okay. Don't worry about it."

Joshua dropped us off in front of the Apple Store. Ian and I walked in and I picked out an iPod. Ian told the sales clerk just to put it on his account. I told him no and that I was paying for it. He shushed me and then grabbed my hand and hurried me out of the store before I caused a big scene. The minute the limo door shut, Ian crashed his mouth into mine.

"What was that for?" I smiled.

"You turned me on when you started arguing with me. I couldn't get you out of that store fast enough. If you only knew the things I want to do to you right now," he said.

I sort of had an idea and I was pretty sure it had to do with that room. He still hadn't mentioned it to me. Now I was wondering, since we had sex, if he'd take me there.

We pulled up to the house and Ian and I went our separate ways. I went up to my room and downloaded a bunch of songs on Stephen's iPod; a majority of them being classical music.

"Hey," Ian said as he slowly opened the door and stepped inside the room.

"Hey. I just finished putting the music on here for Stephen." I smiled.

"Come here."

I pushed the laptop to the side and walked over to Ian and right into his arms. "Happy birthday, Rory," he said as he hugged me.

He held my face in his hands and kissed me passionately. "I have to go now, but I'll be back later. Say hi to Stephen for me."

"I will, and thank you." I smiled.

****

I got into my car, punched in the address to Hudson Rock in my GPS, and drove away. I couldn't help but think of Ian and our past two days together. God, he was amazing and breathtaking. Not only did he steal my love, he stole my soul. I knew I meant something to him. I could tell by the way he touched me. I was completely head over heels for Ian Braxton, and when the time was right, I was going to let him know.

As I walked through the doors of Hudson Rock, one of the clerks escorted me to the visiting room and handed me a Ziploc bag to put my keys in. She asked what was in the bag and I told her it was an iPod for Stephen. She nodded her head and let me through the door. Stephen saw me and a huge smile splayed across his face. I walked over to where he was standing and wrapped my arms around him.

"Happy Birthday, Rory," he said.

"Happy Birthday, Stephen. Let me look at you," I said as I broke our embrace. "You look good, really good."

"Thanks, sis. I'm starting to feel better. Come on; let's go outside."

Stephen led me outside to a large courtyard that was off to the side of the visitors' room. There were two security guards standing watch on each side of the courtyard, which was filled with trees, flowers, and small wrought-iron tables and chairs.

"Happy Birthday, Stephen." I smiled as I handed him the bag.

"Aw, Rory, you shouldn't have done that."

"Just open it. I think you'll like it."

Stephen took the tissue paper out of the bag and pulled out the box that held his iPod. The smile on his face was pure bliss. He looked at me with happiness in his eyes.

"I can't believe it. I can't believe you bought me this."

"I put a bunch of your favorite songs on there."

He plugged the earphones in, turned on the iPod, and listened as the music started to spill into his ears. Nothing made me happier than seeing my brother like this. He seemed to be calm and content. He was a week into his new medication and in group therapy. I looked at him with a sadness in my eyes. I hated seeing him in this place and I hated not being able to take care of him myself. He was my twin and we had a bond and connection stronger than any other.

"Don't be sad, Rory. I'm okay. I'm finally getting the help I should've gotten years ago. I don't want you to worry about me," he said as he placed his hand on mine. "You're finally getting the life you deserve. That Ian guy seems to really like you."

"We're friends." I smiled.

"Are you spending your birthday with him?"

"Yeah. We're going to do something tonight."

An announcement came over the speakers that visiting hours were over. We both stood up and I hugged my brother as tightly as I could.

"Enjoy your music, Stephen."

"Happy Birthday, Rory. Thank you," he said as he kissed my head.

"I'll see you next week. Behave yourself." I smiled.

He smiled back, and I walked out of the visiting room. When I reached my car, my phone chimed. I pulled it from my purse and there was a text message from Ian.

"When you get home, I want you to get all dolled up because I'm taking you to dinner. Wear one of the dresses in your closet."

I smiled as I read it because I loved the fact that he referred to his house as "home." *Did I finally have a home? Could Ian's home become mine?*

"I can't wait," I replied.

When I walked through the door, I headed straight for my closet to pick the dress I wanted to wear. I pulled out a beautiful champagne-colored, A-line, strapless dress that was covered in beautiful beads. I tried it on and turned as I looked at myself in the mirror. It was perfect. A little short, but perfect. I laid it down on the bed while I stepped into the shower. I couldn't wait to see Ian and spend the night with him. My mind kept wondering if he would want me to stay with him in his bedroom. It would only make sense. *Why would we stay in separate rooms?*

I decided to curl my hair and pin it all up so it sat on top of my head, with some curls cascading down. I wasn't sure if I could pull it off, but once I was done, it turned out nice. Once I was done with my makeup, I stepped into my dress and grabbed the champagne-colored peep-toed shoes with four-inch heels. As I took one final look at myself in the full-length mirror, there was a knock on the door.

"Can I come in?" Ian asked.

Nervousness started to shoot throughout my body because I didn't know what Ian would think. I was scared that he wouldn't like the way I did my hair or he wouldn't like the dress on me.

"Yes, you may," I replied.

He opened the door and, as he was walking in, he stopped dead in his tracks.

"Well?" I smiled.

"You're—you're absolutely stunning. Rory, I—"

"It's okay, Ian. You don't have to say anything."

He walked over to me, shaking his head as he took my hand and held it up, twirling me around. "You look so beautiful."

"Thank you." I smiled.

The look in his eyes was one of pure hunger. I could tell he wanted to devour me right on the spot as much as I wanted to devour him in that sexy suit he was wearing. "Jesus Christ, Rory, you have me hard."

I let out a soft laugh as I kissed him lightly on the lips.

"I have something for you," he said as he reached into his suit pocket and pulled out a small box. "Happy Birthday."

I was elated, but nervous. The last person to give me a birthday present was my mom. I was scared to take it from him.

"Go ahead, Rory. It's okay." He smiled.

I took the box from his hand and slowly lifted the top. I gasped when I saw what was inside and tears started to fill my eyes.

"Do you like it?" Ian asked.

"It's beautiful," I said with shaking hands.

Inside the box was a silver necklace in the shape of a key with a few diamonds on the blade. The bow of the key was a diamond heart with another heart that sat in the middle. It was the most beautiful necklace I'd ever seen. Ian took the box from my hand and removed the necklace. He held it up to me and asked me to turn around so he could put it on me.

"There," he said as he turned me around and had me look in the mirror. "It looks beautiful around your neck."

I took the key in between my finger and thumb and stared at it. "Thank you, but you shouldn't have, Ian."

"Of course, I should've. It's your birthday and you're my friend. I always give my friends gifts on their birthdays," he said as his teeth lightly scraped across my neck. "I'm so hard for you right now, but Joshua is waiting for us, so we better get going."

Ian put his hand on the small of my back and we walked down to the limo. Joshua smiled as he opened the door for me. "You look very pretty, Rory."

"Thank you, Joshua." I smiled.

"I sure hope that wasn't you flirting with Miss Sinclair," Ian spoke.

"Shut up, Ian." Joshua smiled.

We climbed into the back of the limo and headed to the restaurant. Ian put up the privacy window and leaned over, stroking my bare shoulder with his fingers and making the hairs all over my body stand straight up.

"Am I exciting you by touching you like this?" he asked.

"Yes, and you know you are."

He moved closer and trailed my neck with his lips. His clean shaven scent was alluring and his warm breath on my skin was enough to arouse me. He didn't have to touch me. I would get wet just by his scent. His fingers trailed down my dress until he reached in between my thighs, where pools of warmth had already started to gather. Slowly, his hand inched up until he reached the edge of my panties.

"Just how I like it." He smiled as he gently kissed my lips, referring to how wet I already was for him. "Do you trust me, Rory?" he asked in a whisper.

"Yes," I answered reverently.

"Good, because I'm going to do something to you that will give you great pleasure and I don't want you to be scared."

He didn't want me to be scared, yet he just scared me with what he said. I didn't know how to react, but I didn't want to disappoint him, so I agreed.

He reached over and grabbed a small ice cube from the ice bucket. I gulped. *What was he going to do with that?* When he looked at me, he must've seen the fear in my eyes.

"I promise you, sweetheart, you'll love this. Okay?" he asked.

I nodded my head as he took the ice cube and put it in his mouth. He sucked on it for a minute and then kissed me. His tongue was so cold and exhilarating as he transferred the ice into my mouth. I could feel it getting smaller as I slipped it back into his mouth. He smiled as he took it and stroked my face.

"Take your panties off," he commanded.

Oh shit. Now, I knew where he was going with that ice cube and suddenly I wasn't so sure about this anymore. He sensed it when I hesitated.

"You said you trusted me, and I won't disappoint you. I promise."

I lifted my ass up and took down my panties. Ian drew in a sharp breath when he saw them fall to my ankles. He got down on the floor, lifted my leg, removed my shoes and panties, and put my foot on his shoulder. His hands lifted up my dress so my bare ass was resting against the soft leather. He took the ice cube from his mouth and slowly moved his hand to my aching pussy. When the ice cube touched my clit, I jumped. Ian placed his hand firmly on my leg to hold me in place.

"It's only going to feel weird for a few seconds, sweetheart. I promise."

He moved the ice cube in small circles around my clit while plunging his finger inside me. A light moan escaped me as Ian watched my face.

"Are you enjoying this? I can stop if you want me to."

"No, don't stop."

My body was in a frenzy and an orgasm was coming. My breathing became rapid as my muscles tightened and Ian pushed me over the edge in exhilaration and until my orgasm was over. He sat back up on the seat and kissed me passionately, letting my body rest for a few minutes. He broke our kiss and grabbed another ice cube. He put it in his mouth and kissed me while injecting two fingers inside me. He waited until the ice cube became smaller and then he got back on the floor, putting his head between my legs. His cold tongue flicked my clit and then his mouth consumed the entire aching area, sucking and tantalizing me. He rubbed the ice cube around my clit before inserting it inside me. His hand was holding me down while the finger on his other hand was inside me and his tongue was circling my clit. The sensation between hot and cold was exhilarating and sending spasms throughout my body.

"Fuck, the ice cube melted and I need to be inside you. You're so hot and dripping wet," he said with a heated breath as he sat up and quickly took down his pants. "Get on top, now!" he commanded.

I positioned myself on top of him, my knees resting against the back of the seat as I gently slid him inside me. I could feel the melted ice cube, mixed with my juices, pouring out of me and onto him. He grabbed my hips and held me up as he thrust in and out of me at a rapid pace, rocking my body and sending me straight into another orgasm as I rode him back and forth.

"Christ. Don't stop, Rory. Keep fucking me, baby, I'm about to come."

My body was overcharged as bright lights flashed across my eyes and his pleasure surged inside me. Ian let out several sexy moans before wrapping his arms around me and holding me. I sat there, safe in his arms, as our heart rates began to slow. He pulled back and smiled at me.

"Are you okay?"

"No. I'm—"

"Fantastic?" he chuckled.

"Yes. Fantastic is a good word."

"I told you that you could trust me."

"I never doubted you for a second."

Ian smiled as I climbed off of him. We cleaned up just in time as Joshua pulled up to the restaurant.

Chapter 18

"Look at you. You're glowing." Ian smiled as he took a drink of his martini.

"Can you blame me?" I smiled.

"No, I can't." He chuckled. "How was your visit with Stephen?"

I picked up my wine glass and swirled the liquid around. "It went good. He really seems to be doing well and he's optimistic."

"What did he think of the iPod?"

"He loved it." I smiled. "He was so happy when he saw the classical music on there."

The waiter set down our plates of filet mignon and lobster. I had ordered the filet, and Ian had chosen the lobster. I looked at him and smiled as I took a bite.

"What's that look for?" he asked.

"Do you always do that in your limo?"

"Do what? Fuck women with ice cubes?"

"Yes."

"No, you're the first," he said as he held up his fork. "Why do you ask?"

I shrugged my shoulders. "I don't know. I was curious."

The ringing of Ian's phone interrupted us as he pulled it out of his pocket and held his finger up. The conversation only lasted a few seconds with Ian saying "Okay, and thank you." I assumed it was a business call.

"Sorry about that," he said. "Now, back to you wondering if I always fuck women in the back of my limo. Why were you curious?"

"I don't know. I just was."

I never should have brought it up. But I took comfort in knowing that I was the only woman he'd done that with in the back of his limo. But then again, why me?

Ian poured some more wine into my glass as he started to speak. "Your plans for tomorrow night with Jordyn and Ollie have been canceled."

"What? Why?"

"Because I'm throwing you a birthday party tomorrow night and they'll be at my house."

"A party? No, Ian, I'm not comfortable with that. I don't like to be the center of attention."

He chuckled. "You don't seem to mind it when you're the center of my attention."

I cocked my head and narrowed my eyebrows. "That's different."

"Well, it's too late. I wanted to do it tonight, but since you're so stubborn and didn't bother to mention that it was your birthday, there was no time. I've already made the arrangements and the party is scheduled for tomorrow evening at eight. Oh, and by the way, Adalynn is pissed at you for not telling her it was your birthday," he smirked.

Just as he said that, my phone chimed with a text from Adalynn.

"Boo on you for not telling your friend it's your birthday! Happy Birthday and we need to talk. I want to hear all about your boat trip with Ian. Love you."

I smiled as I replied, *"We have lots to talk about, lol. Thank you for the birthday wishes. I'll see you tomorrow at the party. Love you back."*

"Oh good, he told you. We'll have to sneak off and have a little girlfriend time. I'm dying to know what happened."

As I looked up from my phone, I noticed Ian staring at me. "It was a text from Adalynn wishing me a happy birthday."

We finished up our dinner and walked back to the limo. I would never look at that limo the same again.

When we walked into the house, it was dark. Ian reached over and flipped the light switch in the foyer. I went to go up the stairs and Ian stopped me.

"Where are you going?"

"I was going to put my purse away."

"You can do that later. I want you to come into the living room with me."

He grabbed my hand, and as we walked into the living room, he turned on one of the lamps. I shrieked when I looked over and saw a beautiful, dark cherry wood baby grand piano sitting in the corner. I covered my mouth with my hand, for I was in complete shock.

"Are you all right?" Ian laughed.

I turned my head, hand still covering my mouth, and looked at him. "What? When? Oh my God, Ian."

"The necklace symbolizes that you'll always have a home here and the piano so you'll always have an escape when you need it."

I threw my arms around him and wrapped my legs around his waist. As I crashed my mouth into his, he let out a moan. "Thank you. Thank you. Thank you," I said with each kiss.

"You're welcome." He laughed.

He held onto me tightly as his hands pushed my dress up above my waist. He looked down and then back up at me with seductive eyes.

"I'm going to need to fuck you now, right here, in front of the fireplace."

"You can fuck me anywhere you want." I smiled.

That was all it took for him to let out a low growl and carry me over by the fireplace and lay me down.

****

The next morning, I awoke to a strong arm wrapped tightly around me. I looked at the clock and it was 5:15 a.m. I was a little surprised that Ian brought me to this bedroom instead of his. I carefully lifted his arm and crawled out from underneath. I didn't want to wake him because he looked so peaceful sleeping, and the alarm was going off in fifteen minutes for our run. I was feeling a little sore down below, compliments of Mr. Ian Braxton.

"Where are you going?" he asked quietly.

"To use the bathroom, if you don't mind," I said as I turned around and saw that he was staring at me.

"Can we just lie here and fuck as our morning exercise instead of going running?"

As tantalizing as the thought sounded, there was no way I was going to have sex with him again right now. "No, we need to run. It's been a few days," I replied.

"Are you okay, Rory?"

"Yeah, why?" I yelled from the bathroom.

"You're walking funny. Are you sore down there?"

I flushed the toilet and walked out of the bathroom, pinching my thumb and finger together. "Maybe just a little."

"Come here," he said as he held out his arms.

I climbed back into bed and laid my head on his chest. He wrapped his arms around me and kissed the top of my head. There was nothing in this world that made me feel safer than his strong chest and strong arms.

"I'm sorry."

"It's okay. Don't worry about it. I'll be fine."

"I do like knowing that I was the cause of it, though."

I lightly smacked him on the chest just as the alarm went off.

"Are you going to be okay to run?" he asked.

"I'll be fine. Go get changed so we can go."

Ian got up from the bed, pulled on his pajama bottoms, and walked out of the room. I changed into my running clothes and headed downstairs.

"Good morning, Charles," I said happily.

"Good morning, Rory, and happy belated birthday. When you and Ian get back from your run, I'm making you a special breakfast." He smiled.

"Charles, you don't have to do that."

"I know I don't. I want to." He winked.

Ian came downstairs and we both headed out the door for our daily run. It was starting to get cool in the mornings. Fall was settling in and you could really feel the drop in the morning temperature. As we were running side by side, Ian looked over at me and asked a question.

"Is there one place in the world that you've always dreamed of seeing?"

"Yes, anywhere but Indiana." I laughed.

Ian chuckled. "I'm serious."

"I've always wanted to go and see the Eiffel Tower in Paris. I remember when I was a little girl that my mom received a postcard with the Eiffel Tower on it from one of her friends that had to move there because her husband got transferred. She put it up on the refrigerator and I stared at it every day. So yeah, that's one specific place I've always dreamed of seeing."

Ian didn't say anything; he just stared straight ahead as we kept running. When we arrived back to the house, Ian and I sat down at the dining room table and waited for breakfast to be served. It smelled wonderful and I was starving. Mandy brought us a fruit cup to start.

"I see that I'm just in time for a grand breakfast." Adalynn smiled as she walked over and kissed Ian's cheek and then mine.

"Good morning, Adalynn. Perfect timing as usual," Ian said.

"Hi, Adalynn." I smiled.

She took a seat across from me and pointed her finger. "I'm still mad at you, missy."

Ian chuckled as he looked at me.

"And as for you, mister, don't think it's a coincidence. You know I'm a sucker for Charles' cooking."

Ian nodded his head as he bit into a strawberry. Mandy set a plate in front of me of something that I wasn't quite sure of. It looked like a rolled up pancake with fruit inside. I picked up my fork and knife and looked at it as Mandy served Ian and Adalynn.

"Rory, it's a crepe." Ian smiled.

"A what?" I asked as I looked at him.

"Honey, just taste it. Trust me; you'll die when you do," Adalynn said.

I took a bite and it melted in my mouth. It was probably the best thing I'd ever had, except for the earth-shattering orgasms Ian gave me. "Oh my God, this is delicious."

"Told ya." Adalynn winked.

"Rory, I'm giving you the day off," Ian said.

"Why?"

"Because the caterers are going to be in and out and so is the party planner. You can resume work on Monday."

"Are you sure, Ian?"

"I'm positive, sweetheart," he said as he got up from the table.

Adalynn looked at me and smiled. "Spill! How was it?"

"It was amazing. Absolutely fucking amazing!" I exclaimed as I got up and grabbed her hand. "Come with me upstairs."

I told Adalynn to wait for me while I took a quick shower. When I walked back into the bedroom, she was admiring the necklace that Ian gave me.

"Did he give you this?" she asked.

"Yes. Isn't it gorgeous? He told me that the key represents that I'll always have a place to stay here."

"I get the feeling you were hoping it meant more."

"I'm falling in love with him," I said as I looked down.

"Oh, Rory. What did I tell you?"

"I know. But I can't help feeling what I feel."

"Have you ever been in love before?"

"No."

"Sweet, Jesus. Ian is not the person who should be your first love."

I knew what Adalynn was getting at. She warned me and I didn't listen. "I can't help it. He's an amazing person, and I know deep down he has feelings for me," I said as I lightly applied some makeup.

"Ian Braxton has never had a romantic feeling about anyone in his life."

"He bought me something else. I'll show you after I blow dry my hair."

Once my hair was done, I led Adalynn to the baby grand piano.

"Wow, this is beautiful," she said as she ran her finger along it.

"Have you heard her play?" Ian smiled as he walked out from his study.

"You can play the piano?" Adalynn asked.

I nodded my head as I sat down and began to play. Adalynn stared at me in disbelief and then looked at Ian.

"I know. It gets me hard every time." He winked as he walked away.

Adalynn sat down on the bench next to me. Once I was finished, her big eyes and wide smile stared at me. "That was fucking incredible. You have to teach me to play someday."

"I will." I laughed.

"Okay, doll, I have to get to the office. I'll see you tonight for your birthday party. It's going to be fun," she said as she kissed me on the cheek and left.

I sighed at the thought of my party. There had never been a party to celebrate me. No sweet sixteen, no graduation, nothing. My aunt didn't even come to my and Stephen's graduation from high school. I was nervous about this party, and I prayed to God that Ian didn't invite his father.

****

The house was chaotic between the caterers, florist, and the party planner. The party was being held outside in Ian's gigantic and beautiful backyard. White tents with white lights were being set up, flowers were being arranged in vases, and tables were being set up with linens. I couldn't believe what I was seeing. Ian wouldn't have gone to all this trouble if he didn't have feelings for me. He came home and walked straight to where I was standing in the backyard.

"Looks great." He smiled as he looked around.

I hooked my arm around his and laid my head on his shoulder. "It looks amazing. Thank you, Ian, but it wasn't necessary."

"It was. You should have a great birthday party. You deserve it," he spoke as his lips touched my head. "I'm going to go shower and get changed. I suggest you do the same so you're ready when the guests start arriving."

We walked back into the house. He went to his room and I went to mine. After my shower, I wrapped a towel around me and walked over to my closet, searching for the perfect dress to wear. I turned on some classical music and listened while I put on my makeup and did my hair. I slipped into a chiffon black strapless dress and a pair of black heels. As I walked downed the stairs, Ian was walking through the foyer when he stopped and looked at me.

"You look beautiful, Rory."

"Thank you." I smiled as I walked up to him. "You're looking pretty sexy yourself in that suit."

He couldn't look any sexier if he tried. The way he wore his black suit with a white shirt underneath that was left partially unbuttoned, showing a hint of his taut chest, made me want to forget the party and just make love to him all night, not to mention the scent of Ralph Lauren that poured from him seduced me. Ian smile and walked me to the back and handed me a glass of wine.

"Here, this will calm your nerves."

"How do you know I'm nervous?" I asked.

"I can tell. You have the same look on your face that you always get when you're nervous." He smiled.

I took a sip of wine and then a deep breath as guests started to arrive. The only people I would know at my own birthday party were Adalynn, Daniel, Ollie, and Jordyn. Ian introduced me to the guests as they arrived. There were a lot of beautiful women and it made me uncomfortable. A few of them I recognized from when Ian brought them home at night. I was talking to Adalynn when a boisterous voice echoed through the yard. I turned my head to see Andrew standing by the door, asking where the birthday girl was. I took in a deep breath and walked over to him.

"Look at how pretty you are." He smiled as he kissed me on both cheeks. "Happy Birthday, Rory." He leaned in to hug me and whispered in my ear, "Don't think that Ian doing this for you means something." He winked and smiled at me before walking away.

There was something about him that bothered me. I watched him as he walked over to Ian and the two of them hugged.

"Bros before hos. Isn't that the expression they use?" Adalynn said as she stood next to me and watched Ian and Andrew.

"There's something about Andrew that screams 'watch your back,'" I said.

"Andrew's not that bad. He's very protective of Ian. They're like brothers."

"I don't think he likes me."

"I'm sure he does, Rory. His problem is jealousy. I'm sure he's thinking you're going to steal Ian away from him."

"That's weird," I said.

"Men are weird." She laughed.

"Rory!" I heard Jordyn exclaim.

I turned around and she and Ollie were behind me. I hugged and thanked them for coming.

"Oh my God, look at this party!" she exclaimed. "This is so amazing."

"Thanks. Ian outdid himself, didn't he?" I smiled.

"He sure did," Ollie replied.

As the night progressed, I felt uncomfortable, especially with the way Andrew kept his eye on me. Adalynn handed me a Mai Tai as I watched Ian talking and laughing with those women.

"You can't let it get to you. You'll drive yourself crazy," she said.

"How can I not? Look at the way he's acting with them. It's disgusting."

"That's how Ian is, Rory. I warned you about him. I wouldn't give those little hussies a second thought."

"It's not that easy, knowing that he fucked them all."

"Oh God, I hope you're not thinking that way about me," she said with concerned eyes.

"Of course not. You and Ian haven't slept together in a couple of years. That's different. These bitches were here not too long ago."

"Well, good, because I would hate for you to think of me like that."

The alcohol made its way down and the effects riveted throughout my body. I was feeling great as I took another drink from the waiter when he walked by. I walked over to where Ian and Andrew were standing with the women. I came up from behind and wrapped my arms around Ian's waist.

"Hey, sexy." I smiled.

Ian put his hands on my arms, turned around, and looked at me. "Are you enjoying your party?" he asked as he removed my arms from his waist.

"I am," I said as I faked a smile and looked at the women who were ruining my party. "Thank you, ladies, for coming." I couldn't tell if they were actually smiling at me or if it was just their permanent plastic look. I walked away feeling like an idiot and grabbed a glass of wine from a passing waiter. I heard Ian's voice call everyone's attention and was caught off guard when he called me over to where he was standing.

"I want to thank all of you for coming to Rory's birthday party tonight. I know it was a bit of short notice, but I had only found out yesterday that it was her birthday and, as her friend, I thought it would be a good idea to throw her a party so she could get to know you, since she's new in town."

That's great. He really had to go and say that? I stood there, drowning in alcohol, feeling like I was going to fall over with all of Ian's friends staring at me, judging me, and probably thinking the worst about me. I could feel Andrew's scorching glare, and I didn't even need to look at him. Ian announced it was time to sing as Charles wheeled out a beautiful three-tiered birthday cake that was decorated in pink. It was beautifully lit with twenty-four burning candles and it was the most beautiful cake I'd ever seen. Tears sprang to my eyes as everyone sang "Happy Birthday," and I blew out the candles.

"Rory, would you like to say a few words to your guests?" Ian asked.

"Of course." I smiled. "I would like to thank you all for coming and celebrating my birthday with me. I look forward to getting to know each of you better." I then turned my attention to Ian. "Ian, thank you for this wonderful party and for everything you've done for me. You've been a great friend and I want you to know that I appreciate it," I said as I kissed his cheek.

I had the feeling earlier in the evening that he didn't want to show any affection out in public, especially in front of all his friends. It was fine to hold me, kiss me, and fuck me behind closed doors where no one could see. This night had started to open my eyes a bit and I wasn't happy with what I saw. I held up my glass as everyone clapped, and Charles cut into the cake.

Chapter 19

"Holy shit," I whined as I tried to open my eyes. I put my hand on my forehead to try and stop the excessive pounding. I rolled over and stared at the perfectly made side of the bed. I didn't remember a thing about last night after I blew out my candles. It was obvious that Ian didn't sleep with me last night. I looked over at the clock and saw that it was noon. When I sat up, the room spun and I reeked of alcohol. The smell was making me nauseous as I stumbled into the bathroom and turned on the shower. As I sat on the shower floor, the hot water poured down on me. I scrubbed my body with some magnolia-scented shower gel and then washed my hair. I was feeling somewhat better except for the pounding going on in my head. I headed down to the kitchen and looked at the empty coffee pot. *Shit.*

"Good afternoon, Rory. Are you looking for coffee?"

"Yes, Charles. I need it now." I sighed as I rested my arms across the counter.

"I'll make you a pot. Shall I make it extra strong?"

"Please, Charles."

He walked over to the cupboard and took out a bottle of pills. He shook two of them in his hand and handed them to me with a glass of water.

"Take these and you'll start feeling like your old self again real soon."

"What are these?" I asked as I looked at them.

"Hangover pills. Ian brought them back with him from Indonesia. They aren't sold here in the United States."

I shoved the pills in my mouth and chased them down with water. I sat down at the table and put my head down. Just as I closed my eyes, I head Ian's voice.

"Did you give her the pills, Charles?" he asked as he walked into the kitchen.

"She just took them," he replied.

"Are you okay?" Ian said as he rubbed my back.

"No."

"Maybe you shouldn't have drunk so much last night."

I didn't respond. He obviously didn't realize that he was the cause of my drinking binge. "Leave me alone, Ian."

"That's exactly what you said last night when I was carrying you upstairs to bed, after I picked you up from the beach where you passed out."

I slowly lifted my head and with one open eye, I looked at him. "I passed out?"

"You sure did."

Charles set my coffee on the table and I immediately grabbed it. "Thank you, Charles."

"You're welcome, Rory. I hope you feel better soon."

I looked at Ian as I took a sip of the hot, strong black coffee. "When I woke up this morning, the other side of the bed was still made. You didn't stay with me last night?"

"No. You were too drunk and, to be honest, you smelled."

Asshole. I couldn't believe he'd just said that. "Thanks, Ian," I said with knitted eyebrows.

"Sorry, sweetheart, but it's the truth." He grinned.

"Are we doing anything today?" I asked like an idiot, having no clue where the hell those words even came from.

Ian looked at me and cocked his head. "We aren't, but Andrew and I are. He's on his way over and we're going to play some golf and then go out for dinner."

"Have fun." I smiled as I got up from the table.

"Where are you going?"

"Upstairs. Enjoy your day and I'll see you later," I said as I walked away.

The pills started to work their magic. My head was beginning to clear and I wasn't feeling sick anymore. I shuddered at the thought of Ian and Andrew going out. Somehow, women were always involved. I went back downstairs. Ian wasn't around. I sat down at the piano and started playing Beethoven's "Moonlight Sonata." It was the first song that came to mind because I always found it sad, and since I was in that frame of mind, it seemed like the right song to play. I finished that song and went right into "Fur Elise." I closed my eyes and played, hitting each key as if it was my last breath. A single tear fell down my cheek as I immersed myself in the melody. Another tear fell, and then another. I was so lost in my sad world that I didn't even notice Ian standing at the piano, staring at me. When I opened my eyes and saw him, I immediately stopped playing. He didn't say anything. He just stared at me as if he so badly wanted to say something, but couldn't. I wiped my eyes and got up from the bench.

"I thought you left," I said as I walked past him.

Ian reached out and lightly grabbed my arm. "Why are you crying?"

I wouldn't turn around and look at him. I looked down at the ground as I replied. "That song always makes me cry. No big deal," I said as his grip softened, and I walked away.

****

I lay down on the couch and fell asleep. My mind wandered back to that house. The house where I spent the last thirteen years of my life. Images of my aunt haunted my dreams. The men she brought home, the alcohol she drank, and the drugs she put into her body had a tight grip on my mind and I couldn't escape from it.

"Rory, wake up. You're having a nightmare."

My eyes flew open at the sound of Ian's voice. I looked at him as I sat up and threw my arms around him. He softly rubbed my back, telling me that it was okay. No, it wasn't okay. It would never be okay. My past would always haunt me and I needed to figure out how to stop it.

"What time is it?" I asked.

"Eight o'clock."

"Why are you home already?"

Ian looked at me strangely before he replied, "Why would you ask that?"

"I don't know. I'm sorry. I'm just not thinking clearly right now."

"Have you eaten dinner?" he asked as he pushed a strand of my hair behind my ear.

"No."

"Come on; let me make you something." He smiled.

"I'm not hungry. In fact, I'm just going to go work out for a little bit," I said as I started to get up from the couch.

Ian grabbed the back of my pants and stopped me. He placed his hands on my hips as his thumbs hooked into the waistband of my pants and panties and he took them down. He pulled me onto him. "Would you like a workout partner? I have some new moves to show you," he said as his lips touched mine.

That was all he had to do to pull me back in and forget about everything else. I didn't resist him when his fingers pulled my shirt over my head. He reached behind me as his fingers unhooked my bra, sending shivers throughout my body. He took my breasts in his hands as he stared at me, giving me that look of hunger. The look that screamed, *I'm going to devour every inch of you.* He leaned forward and took my nipple in his mouth as my hands raked through his hair. I let out a moan at his powerful sucking and nipping that ignited the fire between my legs. I pulled his shirt up as he lifted his arms and tossed it to the side.

"Wrap your legs around me and hold on," he whispered.

He picked me up and carried me up the stairs. As soon as we got in the hallway, he held me up by my ass, pressing my back against the wall. His eyes gazed into mine. Once I undid his belt, I unbuttoned his pants and took them halfway down, releasing his throbbing cock. He held me up by one hand and his other took his pants down all the way. His finger played around my slick area as he gasped.

"You're ready to be fucked and I can't wait any longer."

He pushed into me and I let out a moan. "That's right, sweetheart. Let me know how much you love it when I fuck you."

I licked his lips as he thrust into me, deeper and harder with each one, hitting the right spot that sent my body into pure bliss. His body was tightening and I could feel him getting ready to explode.

"Fuck, sweetheart, you're coming and you're making me come," he said, exasperated, as his last forceful thrust took me.

I dropped my head on his as he held me in place, squeezing my ass as he poured every last drop into me. "That was amazing, Rory," he said with an exhausted breath. "I'm going to put you down for a minute so I can take my pants off."

I unwrapped my legs and he gently lowered me down. As soon as he stepped out of his pants, he smiled and told me to wrap my legs around him again. I did what he asked as he held me up and kissed me. He carried me to the bedroom and gently laid me down on the bed, falling onto me as he continued to explore my lips. He broke our kiss and rolled off of me. A few things had been started to bother me. Why he never took me into his bed and why he never mentioned that room. I rested my head on his chest as he brought his arm around me.

"What's in that other room, down the hall?" I asked.

"It's just another guest room," he replied.

"Why do you keep the door locked?" I couldn't help it; I had to ask.

"There's some private things I keep in there."

"What kind of private things?"

"Nothing you need to worry about, Rory."

"Really, because I've seen you take women into that room."

"Is that so?" he asked. "Do you want to start an argument, Rory? Because I can guarantee you'll lose."

A nerve inside my body went ballistic when he said that. I sat up and looked at him in disbelief. I turned away and climbed out of bed, grabbing my workout clothes from the drawer.

"Where the hell are you going?"

"Avoiding an argument that you can guarantee I'll lose and to do what I should've done instead of letting you fuck me: work out."

"Too late, Rory. The argument already started," he yelled as I walked out the door.

"Fuck you, Ian," I screamed from the hallway.

I headed downstairs to the gym. I finished putting on my clothes and wrapped my hands. I put on the boxing gloves and stood in front of the punching bag. *Jab. Jab. Punch.* My mind went back to the days when my aunt's drug dealer taught me how to punch the bag properly.

"Focus all your energy into your hands. Let it build and then focus on the bag."

Jab. Cross punch. Punch. Punch. Round kick.

"How long do you plan on staying down here?" Ian asked.

I couldn't believe he had the nerve to come down and talk to me after what he said. "I don't know." *Punch. Punch.*

"Suit yourself. I'm not playing games," he said as he turned and walked away.

"I'm not either," I yelled.

About an hour later, I finished my workout and went up to my room. Ian wasn't in there. I looked down the hall at his bedroom. His door was shut, but I could see the light shining from underneath the door. I took a shower to wash off the sweat I built up from the workout, and when I was finished, I climbed into bed. I didn't want to sleep alone. I had gotten used to Ian holding me at night. When I was with him, I didn't have the nightmare. I took my phone from the nightstand and sent him a text message.

"You suck."

"So do you."

"I'm sorry," I wrote.

"Apology accepted."

Seriously? Was he not going to apologize to me for what he said?

"You're not going to apologize to me?"

"For what? I said nothing wrong."

"I take my apology back."

"You can't."

"I just did. Goodnight."

He didn't reply back. I turned off the light and rolled on my side. I tucked my hands underneath my pillow and closed my eyes. Later that night, I awoke and felt his arm around me. I looked at the clock and it was four a.m. I didn't hear him come in the room or climb into bed, but I was happy he was there. I slowly rolled over and cuddled into him. He kissed the top of my head and I drifted back to sleep.

****

The morning air was cold when Ian and I stepped outside for our run. We didn't talk about last night. I guess we both kind of silently called it a truce and moved on.

"I'm surprised you wanted to run this morning after your vigorous workout last night," Ian said.

"There's nothing like a good run in the fresh open air."

"True." He smiled.

I couldn't let it go. I needed to tell him that I saw the room and I knew what was in there. "I was in the room, Ian. The door was unlocked. I was looking for you the night you left. I thought it was your bedroom, so I turned the knob and walked in. I'm sorry, but I just had to tell you."

Ian stared straight ahead as we ran and cleared his throat before he began to speak. "What did you think when you saw it?"

"I don't know. At first, I was freaked out a bit, but it's your business, not mine. The only problem I have is wondering why you never took me in there."

He turned his head and looked at me. "Do you want me to take you in there? Do you want me to do those things to you?"

"I don't know," I said.

"I don't want you in that room. If I did, I would've taken you there. I can't and don't want to explain to you about that room. I have no desire to do those kinds of things with you."

That's nice. Was that supposed to be a compliment? I couldn't help but wonder.

"I like what we have, Rory."

"What do we have, Ian?" my big mouth spit out.

"A close friendship," he replied.

"Like you and Adalynn?"

"Sure, you could say that."

"Nothing else?"

He stopped in the sand and I stopped with him. He looked at me and put his hands on each side of my face. "I told you there would be nothing else, remember? We talked about this."

"I remember," I said as I looked down.

He lifted my chin with his finger. "Let's not make this complicated."

I couldn't do anything but agree with him because I wasn't going to fight with him again. This was what Adalynn had warned me of, and I knew full well what I was getting myself into. My name is Rory Sinclair, and I'm Ian Braxton's friend with benefits.

"No complication here," I said as I began running.

My feelings were hurt and I just wanted to collapse on the sand and cry. I felt like a call girl. Ian Braxton's own personal call girl. *Is that what I've resorted to now? Is that what I've let myself become?*

Chapter 20

I walked down to the kitchen, grabbed a cup of coffee, and headed straight to Ian's study to start the day. I hadn't seen him since we had sex last night and, when I woke up this morning, he was gone. I was still bothered by the fact that he hadn't taken me to his bed, but that was another argument I was saving for later. When I walked into the study, I noticed a yellow post-it on the computer screen.

"I had to go to the office early for a meeting. I'll be back later. Revise the contracts I left and then I need you to drop them off to Adalynn at Prim. Talk soon ~ xo Ian."

My phone beeped, reminding me that I had an appointment with Dr. Neil this evening. I dismissed the alert and began working on the contract revisions. Mandy was kind enough to bring me in a fruit cup and a chocolate chip muffin.

"Umm, Miss Sinclair, I just thought you should know that Mr. Braxton's father is on his way over to pick up some papers."

I sighed and rolled my eyes. "Thank you, Mandy, for the warning. I can't stand that man."

Mandy let out a sigh of relief and put her hand on her chest. "Oh good, because I can't stand him either. Can I tell you something privately?"

"Of course you can, Mandy. You can tell me anything."

"Mr. Braxton's father is always grabbing me and hitting my butt, and he says things to me."

I looked at her with knitted eyebrows. "What does he say to you?"

I could tell she was nervous by the way she was wringing her hands. "He says he wants to take me to bed and have sex with me, but he doesn't say it like that. It's much dirtier."

I sat there, shaking my head, and then I got up and hugged her. "You are to ignore that pig and don't even look his way."

"I try to hide every time he comes around, but sometimes I can't."

"Have you told Ian about this?" I asked.

"No, and please, Miss Sinclair, don't tell him. He'll fire me and I need this job so bad. I'm a single mom and I need to provide for my daughter."

My heart sank. I didn't know Mandy was a mother. "I didn't know you had a child. How old is she?"

"She's two."

"What about her father?"

"He took off when he found out I was pregnant. I don't know where he is," she said as she looked down.

"Don't worry. I won't tell Ian about it. Mandy, please call me Rory. We're friends and you don't need to call me Miss Sinclair."

A smile graced her face when I said that. Just as she was about to walk out the door, she stopped and turned around.

"I'm really glad you're here, and I'm happy you're doing so much better. I was here the night Mr. Braxton brought you home."

I gave her a smile and she left the study. I finished up the contract revisions and, as I was sending a text message to Adalynn, Richard came blowing in.

"Well, well, well. Good morning, Rory."

"Good morning, Richard." I smiled. "What can I do for you?"

"Since you asked, you can start by giving me a blow job."

Calm. Deep breath. Handle him. "Oh, Richard, I'm sorry, but I don't blow old men with wrinkly dicks."

"You stupid trashy little bitch," he said as he glared at me.

"Now, if you'll excuse me, I have things to do. Get what you need and leave," I said as I walked out of the office.

I went upstairs to my room to grab my purse. I fumbled through it, trying to find my keys. As I was walking downstairs, I saw Richard talking to Mandy. She looked uncomfortable. As he was talking to her, she kept backing up until her back was against the wall. Richard took her hands and lifted them over her head.

"Let her go, NOW!" I commanded.

"Don't you have somewhere you have to be, little girl?" he smirked.

"I said 'let her go.'"

"Who the fuck do you think you are?" he said as he let go of Mandy's arms and turned towards me.

"Richard, please, just leave."

"Not until you tell me who you think you are," he said as he inched closer to me.

I took off my heels and tossed them to the side. I gave him a seductive look before grabbing his balls and pushing him up against the wall. He let out a yell and Mandy stood there in shock.

"I'll tell you who the fuck I am. My name is Rory Sinclair and I come from a family of crazies. My brother is a schizophrenic who's locked up over at Hudson Rock Psychiatric Hospital. Did I mention that my brother is also my twin? So I guess that makes me a schizophrenic too," I spat as I tightened the grip on his balls. "You will never speak to or look at Mandy again. Do you understand me? Because if I so much as even see you walking near her, I'll rip these babies off. Do you understand me?" I yelled.

"YES!"

"Oh, and that also goes for me or any other female in this house. I wouldn't tell Ian about this if I were you. You'd just make yourself look stupid," I said as I let go of him and walked over to where my shoes were.

"You're a fucking crazy bitch. You're fucking crazy!"

"I know. It runs in the family." I smiled. "Now, if you've gotten what you came here to get, then you need to leave."

Richard walked out the door and Mandy hugged me. "Thank you. Thank you so much, Rory."

****

The thought of Richard burned through me all the way to *Prim*. He was such a vile and disgusting human being. I rode the elevator up to the eleventh floor where *Prim* was located. As I walked through the large, glass double doors, the receptionist showed me to Adalynn's office. When I walked in, I saw a very handsome man sitting in the chair across from her desk.

"Rory! Welcome to *Prim*!" Adalynn said excitedly as she walked over and hugged me.

"Hello, Miss Sinclair." He winked.

"Hello, Mr. Braxton." I smiled.

I handed Adalynn the folder with the contracts in it and sat down next to Ian.

"I didn't know you were going to be here," I said to him.

"I was in the neighborhood, so I thought I'd drop in and see how things were going. I just invited Adalynn and Daniel over for Thanksgiving."

"Shit. That's this week, isn't it?"

If Ian was having Thanksgiving at his house, that meant Andrew and Richard would be there. Oh God, there was no way I could deal with the two of them, especially after what had just happened with Richard.

"You are going to be there, right?" Adalynn asked me.

"Of course she is. She lives there. Where else would she go?" Ian replied.

I didn't want to talk about Thanksgiving. Holidays were not a pleasant subject for me. I looked at my phone and saw the time.

"I have to go. I have an appointment with Dr. Neil," I said as I got up from my seat.

Ian followed me out of Adalynn's office and into the elevators. "Are you okay?" he asked.

"I'm fine."

He pushed the stop button on the panel and the elevator came to a halt. I should've seen this coming. "Let me guess. We're going to have sex in the elevator."

"You're a smart woman. I knew I hired you for a reason." He smiled. "I'm already hard and I bet you're already wet," he whispered as he leaned over and kissed my neck. His hand wasted no time traveling up my skirt as his fingers pushed my thong to the side.

"I knew it. I knew you were wet. I bet you were thinking about it too, weren't you?"

"Thinking about what?" I asked breathlessly as his fingers moved inside me and his hot tongue took over my neck.

"About me fucking you in this elevator. I've thought about it since you walked into the office."

I wasn't going to lie; the thought did cross my mind as I rode up to Adalynn's office. "Yes," I whispered.

He had his hold on me again and I couldn't break free. "I thought so. You're so hot, sweetheart. I can't wait to get my cock inside you," he said as I unbuckled his belt and unzipped his pants.

I took them down and stroked his erection, gliding my thumb over his slick head. He moaned.

"Turn around, put your hands on the wall, and bend over," he said as his hands first took down my thong and then pushed my skirt over my waist. "Fuck, look at that perfect ass," he said as he lightly slapped it.

He pushed into me hard and moved in and out at a rapid pace while his hands had a tight grip on my hips. The pressure was building, my body was tightening, and I was ready to explode.

"That's it, sweetheart."

I let out a moan with each thrust and Ian put his hand over my mouth. That turned me on even more as my body shuddered with pleasure. His thrusting slowed as he released himself inside me.

"Ah, you feel so damn good," he whispered as his last thrust stayed deep inside me.

We stayed like that for a moment and then Ian pulled out of me, pulled up his pants, and handed me my thong. After I put it on and pulled down my skirt, he pulled me close to him and kissed me as he hit the button. The elevator jerked and then started going down. He looked at me and smiled as he ran his finger down my cheek. When the doors opened, Ian put his hand on the small of my back and we walked out of the building.

"I'll see you when you get home and I'll have Charles cook us dinner," he said as he kissed me on the cheek.

"See you at home." I smiled.

Home. He'd see me at home. The sound of that coming from him was bittersweet. I loved living there with him, but it also hurt more times than not. I drove to Dr. Neil's office and was instantly seen when I arrived.

"I need to discuss Ian, Dr. Neil."

"Okay, what's going on?"

"I'm in love with him and he doesn't feel the same way. He told me yesterday that he's happy with our friendship the way it is and not to complicate things."

Dr. Neil tilted her head and looked at me with empathy. "Only you can make the decision if that's how you want to keep things. If you do, then you're opening yourself up to extreme heartache down the road. If you don't, then you need to move on and start rebuilding your life, without Ian. I'm not sure a man like Ian Braxton can change."

"The nightmares don't exist when Ian is with me at night. When he's not, they come back."

"Ian saved your life. He gave you safety. He took care of you and saw that you had everything you needed. From what you've told me, you've never experienced safety. You've lived pretty much in fear since your mother died. Ian takes that fear from you when he's around, and when he's not, you go back to that place of pain. Let me ask you something. Have you ever confronted your aunt about your feelings and how you felt growing up in her house?"

"No," I whispered as I shook my head.

"In order to move on from the past, you need to confront it."

****

When I walked into the house, the first thing I did was change into comfortable clothes. I walked to the kitchen and saw Ian sitting on the patio. I stepped outside and sat in the lounge chair next to him. As he handed me a glass of wine, he smiled.

"How did your appointment go?"

"It went good. Dr. Neil told me that I need to face my past in order for the nightmares to stop. She suggested that I go back to Indiana and put closure on it."

"Then we'll leave tomorrow," he said.

"Tomorrow? Are you crazy? And what's this 'we' business?"

Ian chuckled. "The sooner the better. The holidays are coming up and you need to put all this behind you. Plus, I'm going with you. There's no way you're going back to that place by yourself. I won't allow it."

"You won't allow it? I do believe this is *my* life, Ian, and *I'm* the one who's in control of my life."

Hell, I didn't even know where those words came from, but I was proud of myself for saying them. Ian stared at me. He was giving me the "I'm trying to figure you out" look.

"Rory, please let me accompany you back to Indiana so you don't have to go alone. It would make me feel better knowing that I was there with you."

I smiled at him as I got up from my chair and sat on his lap. I wrapped my arms around his neck and lightly kissed his cheek. "Thank you for offering, Ian. I would love for you to come with me."

"Why do you have to make things so difficult?" he smirked. "I'll call my father's pilot and tell him that we're leaving tomorrow morning, and we'll fly back on Wednesday."

"You father has his own plane?"

"Yes, and it's very nice. You'll like it." He smiled as he kissed the tip of my nose. "Let's go eat. Charles made us a nice dinner."

As we walked into the dining room, Mandy was setting the food on the table. She looked over at me and smiled. I winked at her.

"What was that for?" Ian asked.

"What was what for?"

"Why did you wink at Mandy?"

"She had a problem earlier and I helped her resolve it," I said as I folded my napkin in my lap.

"Don't get involved with help, Rory."

"Ian, do you even know anything about her? Do you even know what goes on in your own house?"

"Why would I care anything about her? She's my maid. She's here to do a job and that's it."

His stone cold heart was rearing its ugly head again. I couldn't believe he'd just said that.

"She's a single mom. She has a two-year-old daughter."

"Where's the dad?" he asked.

"He took off when he found out she was pregnant."

"Smart man."

My eyes widened when he said that and I had a feeling a whole new side of Ian was about to emerge that I wasn't going to like. Did I comment and run the absolute risk of starting a huge argument or did I let it go? I opted for commenting.

"How could you say that? He left that poor girl pregnant and alone to raise their baby by herself while he took the easy way out."

Ian sighed. "Then maybe she should've been more careful."

Oh, shit. I knew he didn't just say that. It takes two people to make a baby.

"Why is it up to the woman to be careful? What about the guy? A woman doesn't get pregnant by herself, Ian."

"Listen, Rory, I'm not arguing about this with you. It's stupid. Okay, she's a single mom. I pay her well, so she shouldn't have too much trouble paying the bills."

"Give her a raise," I blurted out.

Ian wiped his mouth on his napkin and looked at me. "No, I'm not giving her a raise."

"For the bullshit she had to put up with concerning your father, I think she deserves one."

"What are you talking about?"

Shit. I didn't mean to say that.

"What are you talking about?" Ian asked again. "You know, Rory, you've had an issue with my father from the first day you met him and I don't understand why, but it's really starting to piss me off."

Breathe. Breathe. Okay, this time, the breathing wasn't working, and I was all fired up.

"Piss you off?!" I exclaimed as I got up from the table and pointed my finger at him. "Your father asked me to give him a blow job this morning and then he had Mandy pinned up against the wall. So, the only one who should be pissed off here is me! Not you, Ian, because you don't get to be pissed off. You can go fuck yourself because I'm done here. You've defended that disgusting pig one too many times."

I stormed up the stairs and slammed the bedroom door. Tears started to fill my eyes and I was so burning mad that I couldn't think or see straight. I needed to take to heart what Dr. Neil said about Ian. I paced back and forth across the room. A while later, the door opened and Ian stood there, staring at me. "Why are you pacing back and forth?" he asked.

"Get out, Ian. I don't want to see you."

"I called my father and he admitted that he did those things."

I stopped dead in my tracks and turned to him. "Of course you called him, because my word wasn't good enough."

"What did you do him?" he asked as he stepped inside the room and shut the door.

"Nothing. Why?"

"He said you're a crazy bitch and I need to kick you out of my house before you hurt someone." He smiled. "What did you do or say to him?"

"Did you ask him yourself?"

"Yes. But he just said that you're crazy and he wouldn't tell me anything else."

I walked over and sat down on the bed. "I just grabbed him by his balls and told him that I'd rip them off if he ever looked my way or Mandy's way again."

Ian busted out laughing. "Are you serious? I would've given anything to see that," he said as he walked over to the bed and sat down next to me. He put his arm around me and pulled me into him.

"I'm sorry, Rory. My dad has some serious issues and it all started when my mom left. I told him that he's to apologize to you and Mandy on Thanksgiving."

"What did he say to that?"

"He said he didn't want to talk about it right now and that he probably won't be coming for Thanksgiving."

"I'm sorry, Ian."

"Don't be. It's his problem, not ours. I'll have a talk with Mandy tomorrow."

"She didn't want you to know. She's afraid that you'll fire her."

"Why would I do that?" he asked.

"Maybe because you intimidate people."

Ian sighed and pulled away. "Do I intimidate you?"

"No. You just irritate me."

"Is that so?" he asked as he pushed me back on the bed and started tickling me.

I wiggled around, trying to make him stop. Finally, he did and he looked into my eyes as he ran his finger along my face. We stared at each other for a moment before he leaned down and softly brushed his lips against mine. We didn't just have sex that night. We made love. It was beautiful and I knew Ian felt something more.

Chapter 21

Hollis, Indiana. The town where I spent the last thirteen and a half years of my life in pure misery. To come back to this place caused me pain and anxiety. Ian rented a car and we drove to my aunt's house. As we pulled onto the street, I started to get extremely nervous and my chest felt like it was tightening.

"It's right here," I said as I pointed to the white vinyl house on the right. The fall air was a lot cooler here than in Malibu.

Ian pulled up to curb and grabbed my hand. "You're strong, Rory. This place made you strong, so there's nothing here that can hurt you anymore."

I smiled at him and we both got out of the car. I could see the look of disgust on Ian's face as we walked towards the door. I lightly knocked and was shocked when I saw Shane open the door.

"Rory?"

"Hi, Shane."

"It's good to see you, girl. Get in here." He smiled as he hugged me.

"Ian, this is Shane, my aunt's drug dealer. Shane, this is Ian. He's a friend."

Against Ian's better judgment, they shook hands. The house was a mess. Shit was lying around everywhere.

"Where's Aunt Nancy?" I asked.

"She just ran to the store. She'll be back soon. What are you doing here?" he asked.

"I came to put some closure on my past. My therapist said that I needed to. You know, the therapist I have to see because of the fucked up life Nancy provided for me."

Shane didn't say anything as he walked to the refrigerator and grabbed a beer. "You want one?" he asked Ian and me. We both said no. "Nancy told me that Stephen attacked you. Is that true?"

"Yes," I said as I lifted up my shirt and showed him the scar. "He caught me off guard. Came at me from behind."

"I'm sorry, Rory."

"Yeah, me too, Shane. He's in a psychiatric hospital, getting the help he needs."

"That's good. That's real good. That boy needs it."

"Why are you here?" I asked.

"I'm living here now. My house caught on fire about a month ago and Nancy was kind enough to take me in."

"Yeah, I bet she was. Let me guess; the house fire had something to do with you cooking up some crystal meth, didn't it?"

"I suppose you could say that," he sighed.

I walked to the room that Stephen and I shared. When I opened the door, everything was still exactly the way I left it.

Ian walked in behind me and looked around. I was embarrassed to have brought him here and I shouldn't have agreed to it.

"Is this where you slept?" he asked as he pointed to the mattress on the floor.

"Yeah," I said as I turned around and walked out.

I looked out the kitchen window at the barn that sat in the back. The place I would go to and escape.

"You were always a good kid, Rory," Shane said as he walked up behind me. "Is that your boyfriend?" he asked.

"No, he's just a friend. He saved my life."

"Have you been practicing those moves I've taught you?"

"She sure has," Ian spoke.

The door opened and Nancy stopped when she saw me. "Rory, what are you doing here?" she asked nervously.

For the first time in my life, I wasn't afraid of her anymore. "I'm here to put closure on my past. You know; the one you fucked up," I spat.

"Stephen's not here, is he?"

Shane walked over, took the bags from her hands, and set them on the table as she walked inside.

"No, Stephen's not here. He's locked away in a psychiatric hospital in California."

"Good, that's where he should be," she said.

My emotions were running rampant and the hate that I thought I had buried came rushing back to me as I looked at her.

"Who's this?" she asked as she pointed to Ian.

"This is Ian. Ian, this is my Aunt Nancy."

The two of them said hello and Nancy walked to the refrigerator and grabbed a beer. That was all the house reeked of: stale beer and cigarettes. It was a smell that I would never forget.

"I know damn well you didn't come here to say hi. So say what's on your mind and then you can get going."

I couldn't say anything to her. I just stood there and stared at her, shaking my head. "I hope you rot in hell. Come on, Ian; let's go," I said as I walked to the door.

"I'm sorry," she said.

I stopped as soon as she said that. Nancy had never been sorry about anything in her life. I turned around and glared at her. "You're sorry? Sorry for what?" I asked as I slowly approached her. "Sorry for ruining mine and Stephen's lives? Sorry for not being there for us and letting us raise ourselves? Sorry for never celebrating our birthdays, Christmas, or any other holiday that all the other families celebrated? Sorry for what!" I screamed.

At that point, I was shaking and Ian walked over and clasped my shoulders. She looked at me with those stone cold eyes. The eyes that had the same look in them every single day. She wouldn't say a word. I shook my head and turned away.

"Your daddy. He was my life until your mom got drunk one night and slept with him."

Instantly, I felt sick to my stomach. "Rory?" Ian said.

I wouldn't turn around and look at her when I spoke. "You know who my father is?" I asked with a shaking voice.

"Why do you think you didn't meet me until you were seven years old? When your mom told me that she was pregnant, we didn't speak for seven years. You and Stephen are the spitting image of him. That's why I didn't want you because every time I looked at the two of you, it was a reminder of how you ruined my life. What did I ever do that was so bad to deserve that?"

I didn't hesitate to whip my body around as fast as I could when she said that. "Did it ever fucking occur to you that it wasn't about you? That it was about two poor innocent children that lost their mother and had nowhere to go."

Tears started to pour down her face. "I just couldn't. I couldn't be a mother to you. I hated everything you represented."

"Nancy, that's enough," Shane said.

"What's my father's name?" I asked. She didn't answer me. I lunged towards her and Ian grabbed my arms. "What's his name?!" I screamed.

"Jimmy O'Rourke. His name is Jimmy O'Rourke."

"Do you know where he lives?"

"No. After he found out your momma was pregnant, he took off. He told me he was sorry and he left. I have no idea where he went. He was the love of my life."

"Really? The love of your life slept with your sister and got her pregnant and then took off. What kind of real man does that?"

"Rory, we better go, sweetheart," Ian said. "I think you've heard enough."

"You'll never see me or Stephen again. Goodbye, Aunt Nancy. Have a nice life."

I walked out the door and climbed into the rental car. Ian started the car and pulled out of the driveway. I needed to hold it together. No more pain. No more hurt. No more past.

"You need to find us a hotel, Ian. Like now."

"Okay," he said.

"Seriously. This is no time to be fancy. Just pull into the first hotel you see."

"But, Rory—"

"There's no buts, Ian. Just fucking find a hotel, now!" I snapped.

"Oh thank God," Ian whispered as he pulled into the Hyatt Regency.

He parked the car, grabbed our bags, and helped me out. "I saw a Holiday Inn Express a few miles back," I said.

"I'm sorry, Rory, but I'm not staying at a Holiday Inn."

We walked inside the hotel and one tear fell. The clerk handed Ian the key and we took the elevator up to the top floor. Ian found our room and slid in the key. He opened the door and when I stepped inside, another tear fell. I was losing control.

"Rory, are you okay?" Ian asked.

The sound of the hotel door shutting was the detonator that set off the tear bomb inside me. I sat down on the edge of the bed and cupped my face in my hands as the sobbing began.

"Come here, sweetheart," Ian said as he wrapped his arms around me.

"I hate her, Ian."

"I know, and she's an easy woman to hate. I'm sorry you had to hear the things she said. It's over now," he said as he kissed the top of my head.

My tears started to slow down and I looked up at Ian. He smiled softly at me as he wiped the tears from my face. "Do you feel somewhat better now?" he asked. "I'm going to start a bath for you."

While Ian was starting the bath water, I twisted my hair up in a clip and took off my makeup. I got undressed and Ian held my hand while I climbed down into the tub.

"What scent is this?" I asked as I smelled the bubbles.

"I'm not sure. It was sitting on the shelf." Ian grabbed the bottle of bubble bath and looked at it. "It's cherry vanilla."

"I like it." I smiled.

"Well, then, I'll make sure to buy a few bottles before we leave." He winked.

I brought my knees up to my chest as Ian washed my back. "Tonight is all about you, Rory. We'll do whatever you want. Name it."

"That's sweet, Ian, but I just want to stay in."

"Okay. We can do that. We'll order in room service and rent movies."

"Really?"

"Of course. We'll have quiet evening in," he said as he lifted my chin and gave me a kiss. "Finish up your bath, and I'll go order us a bottle of wine."

I didn't want to stay in the tub anymore. I just wanted to lie on the bed in Ian's arms. I stepped out and put on my pajama shorts and tank top. I climbed on the king-sized bed where Ian was looking over the dinner menu. I snuggled up next to him and we looked at it together.

"What sounds good?" he asked.

"Let's eat burgers, fries, and a coke."

"I already ordered the wine," he said.

"We can drink it later."

"Do you like cheese on your burger?" Ian smiled.

"Yes," I replied.

Ian dialed the number for room service and ordered two cheeseburgers, fries, and two cokes. After he hung up the phone, he wrapped his arms around me and we both sank down into each other. Being wrapped up in his arms took my pain away. I didn't think about anything but him and the moment we were sharing. I could picture this always. I could picture us always. I knew that deep down, he felt the same way I did and he needed me just as much as I needed him. I just had to figure out a way to reach him. Room service arrived with our food and the bottle of wine Ian ordered. He rolled the cart to the middle of the room and took the tops off the silver trays. He looked at me and smiled as he picked up one plate and handed it to me on the bed.

"Your gourmet burger, Miss Sinclair," he said in a sexy accent.

I took it from him with a smile and positioned it on my lap. Ian brought his plate over to the bed, climbed next to me, and turned on the TV.

"What do you want to watch?" he asked.

"I don't care. Pick something," I said as I took a bite of my burger.

"Okay. Let's see what they have in the way of porn."

"Ian!" I laughed as I smacked his arm.

"I'm just teasing." He chuckled.

He turned to the movie channels and the movie *Friends with Benefits* was just starting.

"I love Justin Timberlake," I said.

"Do you want to watch this? I kind of like the title," he smirked.

Of course he did. "Sure." I smiled.

Ian reached over and took a fry from my plate. "Hey," I said as I smacked his hand.

"I'm all out."

"You ate all those already?" I smiled.

"I was hungry. What can I say?"

I took a fry from my plate and put it in his mouth. Ian put his arm around me and I snuggled into him while we finished watching the movie.

****

It was good to be back in Malibu and at Ian's house. When we arrived home, Adalynn was in the kitchen, talking with Charles.

"Oh goodie, you two are back. How was your trip?" she asked me.

"Eventful, to say the least."

Ian walked over and kissed Adalynn on the cheek. "Are you bombarding Charles with requests for Thanksgiving dinner tomorrow?" he asked.

"You know me, Ian. I have to have my mother's special cranberry nut bread."

"Then why don't you make it yourself?"

Adalynn waved her hand in the air. "You know I don't bake. The last time I attempted to bake it, the bread was completely flat and tasted like pure yeast."

"I can make it for you," I said.

"Don't be silly, Rory. Charles will bake it. Right, Charles?"

"Of course I will," Charles replied.

"No, I'm serious. I want to help," I said as I looked down.

Ian walked over to me and put his hands on my hips. "What's wrong?"

"The last time I celebrated Thanksgiving with a home cooked meal was the last one before my mom died. She and I would go shopping together every year and then, on Thanksgiving morning, we'd cook. After she died, there wasn't any more turkey or potatoes. Nancy didn't believe in Thanksgiving because she said she had nothing to be thankful for, so she would just stay in bed all day and shoot herself up. Once I was old enough and worked, I would take Stephen to this little diner that was opened every Thanksgiving for the truckers that were passing through town and we'd order the turkey dinner. So, for me to help Charles out tomorrow would mean the world to me."

A tear dropped from Adalynn's eye as she walked over and hugged me. "I'm so sorry."

"Charles, it looks like you're going to have some help tomorrow," Ian said.

"I'm looking forward to it, Rory." Charles smiled.

Adalynn left and Ian went to his study. After Charles and I discussed the events of tomorrow morning, I walked into the study and Ian hung up the phone.

"I tried to get Stephen out for tomorrow so he could have dinner with us, but the doctor said it was too soon and wouldn't be a good idea. They're having a lunch with all the works, so I thought we could go for a while and you could spend some time with him before the guests arrive here."

"That would be great." I smiled as I leaned against the doorway. "Thank you for thinking of him."

"No problem. Andrew called and we're going out in a bit," he said as he got up from his chair.

"Oh. Where are you going?"

"Out to dinner. I'll be back later."

"Maybe I'll call Jordyn and see if she and Ollie want to do something," I said as I turned around and walked into the living room.

"Like what?" Ian asked as he followed me.

"I don't know. Maybe go to a club or something."

"Why do you have to go and do that? Why can't you just stay here and read or watch a movie or something?"

Was he serious? "No, I don't feel like staying in. I'm going out," I said as I walked up the stairs and sent Jordyn a text.

I went to my room and Ian followed me in. "Seriously, Rory. Stay home."

I turned around and looked at him in confusion. It was okay for him always to go out with that douchebag Andrew, but if I wanted to go out with my friend, he had a problem with it. No, this wasn't okay anymore.

"So, let me get this straight; you want me to sit around this house while you go out with your best friend again."

"Damn it, Rory. You act like we're a fucking couple or something. This is the exact reason why I don't do relationships."

The fire inside reared its ugly flames as I stood there and glared at him. "We aren't a couple, and you can't tell me what

I can and can't do, Ian." That was it; once I started, I couldn't stop. "Who the hell do you think you are?" I asked as I pointed my finger at him. "You've made it very clear what our relationship is, and what I do when you're not fucking me is none of your business."

I could see the anger in his eyes as he stared at me. "Fine, Rory. You said it. It's none of my business what you do, just like it's none of your business what I do. Go out with your friends. I don't care," he said as he looked at his watch. "I have to go get ready. Have fun tonight. But when you get into trouble, don't call me."

"Fuck you!" I yelled as he walked out and slammed the door.

I sat on the edge of my bed in tears. My phone beeped with a text message from Jordyn.

"I'm sorry, Rory, but Ollie and I are staying in tonight. We're both sick with the flu."

"I hope you two feel better before tomorrow. Get some rest."

Great. There was no way I was staying in this house alone tonight, so I called Adalynn to see if she was doing anything.

"Hello," she answered.

"Hi," I said with a sad tone. "Do you want to hang out tonight? Ian is going out with douchebag Andrew and I'm not sitting here alone."

Adalynn laughed loudly into the phone. "I'm sorry, Rory. But douchebag Andrew is brilliant. Anyway, Daniel and I are going to dinner. You are more than welcome to come with."

I didn't want to be a third wheel and disrupt their dinner plans. "It's okay, Adalynn; you and Daniel have a great dinner. I'll see you tomorrow."

"Are you sure?" she asked.

"I'm sure. Have fun," I said as I hung up.

I sighed and got up from the bed. I walked down to the kitchen to get a bottle of water. When I turned around, Ian had just walked in. Goddamn it, his scent was amazing. He looked amazing and, at that moment, I hated him for going out looking and smelling like that. I looked away when he looked at me and headed towards the stairs.

"Have a good night," he said as he put his hand on the door handle.

"You too," I said as I put my hand up while walking up the stairs.

"Don't worry. I fully intend to," he replied.

I flinched when I heard the door shut. I stopped when I reached the top of the stairs and sat down with my back against the wall. I ran my hand through my hair and pressed my palm against my forehead. As I sat there, feeling sorry for myself and angrier than hell, I heard the door open. I looked over and saw Adalynn and Daniel standing in the foyer.

"Why are you sitting there like that?" she asked.

"What are you doing here?"

"Daniel and I are picking you up for dinner. It's not even an option for you to tell us no, so go freshen up because I'm starving."

"Hi, Rory." Daniel smiled and waved.

"Hi, Daniel." I smiled back. "Adalynn, I'm not hungry."

"Nonsense. Did something happen between you and Ian?"

"Yeah."

She walked up the stairs and took a hold of my arm. "Come on, up you go. You're coming with us."

I knew if I didn't go, she'd hound me to death. The one thing I noticed was that Adalynn always got her way.

"Fine, just let me go brush my hair and I'll tell you all about it in the car."

****

We arrived at the restaurant and were promptly seated in a corner booth. The waitress brought our drinks and took our food order. As Adalynn, Daniel, and I were talking, I heard a familiar voice and laugh. I stopped sipping my cosmopolitan and froze.

"Are you okay, sweetie?" Adalynn asked.

"That voice. That's Andrew's voice," I said as I slowly turned my head and looked behind me.

"Oh no," Adalynn said as she looked where I was looking.

Sitting at a table with Andrew, were Ian and two beautiful twin brunette women. Instantly, I felt sick to my stomach and it was getting hard to breathe.

"Rory, calm down," Adalynn said. "We don't know the situation."

"The situation? They are both on dates with those women. Look at how Ian is smiling at her and leaning closer to her. He lied to me. He told me it was him and Andrew," I said as tears sprang to my eyes.

"You know, I'm getting really sick of him," Adalynn spat as she got up from the booth.

"Where are you going?" I said as I grabbed her wrist.

"To say hi, darling." She smiled.

Adalynn walked over to the table and talked to Ian and Andrew.

"Duck down, Rory," Daniel said. "They're looking over here," he said as he smiled and gave a small wave to them.

A few moments later, Adalynn came back to the table. "Well, wasn't that pleasant."

"What happened?"

"Nothing much. I asked Ian where you were and he said he didn't know and that you mentioned something about going out with Jordyn. So I asked the bastard why he didn't bring you to dinner. He didn't answer me. Those two women are Andrew's cousins from out of town. They're here for the holiday, so Andrew decided to take them to dinner."

"I bet he did, and I bet Ian has fucked both of them too. I'm so sorry, Adalynn and Daniel, but I have to get out of here because I feel like I'm going to lose it any second."

The thing that sucked was that I would have to pass their table to get out of the restaurant. While I was contemplating my escape, the waitress came over and set down our food.

"Excuse me, but is there another way out of this restaurant besides the front?"

She looked at me like I was crazy. "There's the back way through the kitchen, but customers aren't allowed back there."

"Listen, just show me. I have to get out of here, but I can't pass that table over there with those two men and women."

The waitress glanced over at the table and then at me. "Is one of those guys your boyfriend?"

"Yes," I lied.

"Is he cheating on you, sweetie?" she asked.

Oh my God, why couldn't she just show me the way to the kitchen?

"Hold on." She winked.

Uh oh. I didn't like the way she said that. Daniel kept an eye on the table and the waitress. He busted out laughing and told me to turn around quickly. The waitress had spilled drinks all over Ian and Andrew. They both looked pissed as they got up from their seats and went to the bathroom. The waitress walked over to our table and smiled.

"Okay, sweetie, you can go out the front now." She winked again.

"Oh, you're good," Adalynn said as she reached in her purse, pulled out a fifty-dollar bill, and handed it to her.

"You two stay and finish your dinner. I'll call a cab. I meant it. Stay!" I exclaimed.

Adalynn stood up and hugged me. "I'll see you tomorrow," she pouted.

I smiled at her and Daniel, and walked out of the restaurant. There was a cab coming down the street, so I put up my hand and he stopped. I climbed in and gave him Ian's address.

When I arrived home, I changed my clothes and headed down to the beach. I sat down in the sand to do some serious thinking. I kept going over and over in my head the things Ian said earlier about relationships. Maybe I was being selfish and only wanted to keep him to myself for the night or maybe it was because I was so in love with him and I didn't trust him. His reputation was pretty bad when it came to women, and he'd made it very clear that we were not in a relationship. I picked up a stick that was next to me and started drawing in the sand. A few moments later, I heard a voice behind me.

"You stayed home."

I took in a deep breath. "Yeah. Ollie and Jordyn are sick with the flu. Why are you back so early?"

Ian walked over and sat down next to me. "The waitress at the restaurant we were at spilled drinks on me and Andrew. Needless to say, I was soaked. So, we called it a night and I came home and changed."

"Wow, what a bad waitress," I said as I laughed hysterically inside.

"Yeah. She didn't get a tip." He smiled. "You'll never guess who I ran into there."

"Who?"

"Adalynn and Daniel. She asked where you were."

I waited for him to tell me about Andrew's cousins, because maybe, just maybe, I'd be able to let it go, but he didn't.

"Well, I'm sorry you got drinks spilled on you, but I'm really tired, so I'm going to head upstairs," I said as I got up.

Ian grabbed my hand. "Do you want some company?"

I looked down into his amazing eyes. "No, I don't," I said with a small smile and walked away.

Since I was already mad at him and we really weren't on good terms at the moment, I decided to add a little fuel to the fire. It was better to bring it up now and get it over with. Before I reached the patio, I stopped.

"Why is it that you've never taken me to your bed?" I asked.

"I can take you there now," he replied.

Okay, so me and my big mouth. I couldn't help it. I wanted to hurt him like he hurt me earlier. The only difference was that I don't know if Ian Braxton could feel hurt.

"Maybe you should've brought home one of those brunettes you were with tonight. I'm sure that she would've loved your bed."

"STOP!" he yelled.

I just shook my head and walked up the stairs. I knew it was only a matter of time before he busted through the bedroom door. I went into the bathroom and locked the door. One. Two. Three.

"Rory! Are you in there?" he shouted as he shook the door handle.

"If you don't mind, I'm going to the bathroom, Ian."

"Hurry up! I'll be waiting on the bed."

I rolled my eyes as I sat on the counter with my feet on the toilet. I didn't want to go out there and face him. *Shit.* I never should've said anything. Well, I was going to have to face him sooner or later. I unlocked the door and stepped into the bedroom. Ian was sitting on the edge of the bed with his elbows resting on his knees and his hands folded.

"Adalynn texted you, didn't she?"

Fuck. I couldn't lie to him when it involved Adalynn. I had no choice; I had to tell him the truth.

"No, I was there. I was at the restaurant with Adalynn and Daniel."

"What? No you weren't. I didn't see you and I waved to Daniel."

"That's because I ducked down into the booth," I said as I pulled out my nightshirt from the drawer.

"Are you serious? Why the hell didn't you come over and say something?"

"Like what, Ian? Oh hi, who are these whores you're with?"

"Rory, stop. Those girls were Andrew's cousins."

"Did you know they were going?"

Ian looked down before he answered my question. "Yes, I knew they were going."

"Why didn't you tell me?"

"Because, it's none of your concern, Rory. Like I said earlier, we aren't a couple. I'm sorry, sweetheart, if that hurts you, but I can't help it."

I gnawed at my bottom lip as his words shot through my heart. My eyes started to fill with tears and my breathing became restricted.

"I'm sorry, Ian. You're right. I'm sorry."

The words just came out my mouth. I was apologizing to him for killing me. I needed to think things through. I couldn't just up and leave like I was about to. I needed to think. Ian got up from the bed and wrapped his arms around me.

"It's okay, sweetheart," he said as he rubbed his hand up and down my back. "Come on; I'll take you to my bed," he said as he kissed my head.

As I broke our embrace, I looked at him. "No, Ian. Not tonight."

"Are you sure? I'm already getting hard."

He was slowly killing me. I put my hand on his chest. "Then I suggest you either play with yourself or call one of your other girls, because this girl isn't having sex with you tonight."

"Okay, fine. I'll just go masturbate, then," he said as he headed towards the door.

"Seriously, it's okay if you want to call one of the other girls over."

Ian shook his head and walked out the door. I jumped when I heard his bedroom door slam.

Chapter 22

I was up all night. I couldn't run the risk of having a nightmare because I didn't want Ian coming in to rescue me. I didn't want to see him *period* and now it was Thanksgiving morning. How stupid was I to think that this Thanksgiving was going to be different. I walked into the kitchen and Charles handed me an apron.

"Good morning, Rory. Happy Thanksgiving." He smiled.

"Happy Thanksgiving, Charles," I said as I tied the apron around my waist.

He handed me the recipe for the cranberry nut bread and I began to gather the ingredients. A few moments later, Ian walked into the kitchen. He walked over and gave me a kiss on the cheek.

"Happy Thanksgiving."

"Happy Thanksgiving," I replied.

"No nightmare last night?" he asked.

"I didn't sleep. So no," I said as I mixed the bread batter.

"You didn't sleep at all?"

"No. See these," I said as I put the spoon down and pointed to the bags underneath my eyes.

"I'm sorry," he said.

"Sorry for what? That I didn't get any sleep or sorry for what you said?"

"Now I'm sorry for even saying sorry," he said as he walked out of the kitchen.

"Oh, by the way, you don't need to come with me to visit Stephen. I'm going by myself," I shouted.

"Good, have fun."

Asshole.

I put the bread in the oven and went upstairs to get ready to go and see Stephen. Even though Ian hurt me, I felt horrible for the two of us fighting on Thanksgiving. *Shit.* I let my conscience get the best of me. After I finished getting dressed, I went to find Ian. The smell of turkey started to infiltrate throughout the house as I walked down the stairs. I found him sitting in his study.

"Hey," I said as I stood in the doorway.

"Is there something you need, Rory? I'm busy."

"It's Thanksgiving. What could you possibly be busy with?"

"I'm busy, Rory. What do you want?" he said in a stern tone.

"I just wanted to apologize. So, I'm sorry about last night and this morning," I said as I turned around and started to walk away.

"Come here," he said.

I turned around and looked at him as he sat behind his desk, staring at me with eyes that were pleading with me to come closer.

"Please."

My face gave away a smile as I walked over to him and he stood up. He wrapped his arms around me and held me tightly as he sighed.

"I'm sorry too."

"I don't want any tension or bad feelings today. It's Thanksgiving and I want it to be perfect," I said.

"Me too," he said as he broke our embrace. "I would like to go with you to see Stephen, if you don't mind." He smiled.

"I would like that." I smiled back as I kissed the tip of his nose.

A couple of hours later, when we arrived home after our visit with Stephen, Ian poured me a glass of wine and we walked into the living room.

"I'm sorry, but I really hope your dad doesn't show up. I'm nervous about seeing him."

Ian let out a light chuckle. "Don't be. I think after your little talk, he's the one who's nervous."

The door opened and Andrew walked in. "Happy Thanksgiving!" he shouted.

My stomach dropped at the sound of his voice. He smiled as he walked over and hugged me. "You look gorgeous, Rory."

"Thank you, Andrew."

Ian and he shook hands before Andrew went over to the bar and poured himself a drink. I excused myself and went into the

Sandi Lynn

kitchen. A few moments later, Adalynn and Daniel strolled through the door.

"It smells amazing in here!" she exclaimed as she walked into the kitchen. "How are you, sweetie?" she asked as she gave me a light hug.

"I'm okay. Ian and I got into a huge fight last night after he came home. I let it slip that I was with you at the restaurant, and that I saw the women he was with."

"Ouch. What did he say?"

"He pretty much told me it was none of my business and that we're not a couple, so I need to stop acting like we are."

"Bastard. Would you like me to castrate him for you?" She smiled.

"Thanks for the offer, but then *I* would suffer." I winked.

We walked to the living room, where everyone was gathered around talking. The door opened and Richard and his date walked in. She was young, tall, toothpick thin, and she had burgundy hair. She went by the name of Arianna. Richard glared at me before introducing her.

"Ari, this is Rory. She's Ian's houseguest."

"Hello." She smiled as she lightly stuck out her hand.

Ian walked over to me and whispered, "Be nice. I guess he changed his mind."

"It's nice to meet you, Arianna. Happy Thanksgiving," I said with the biggest fake smile I've ever displayed.

She giggled and Adalynn walked over and whispered in my ear, "Jesus. You have to be kidding me."

Since we were in the company of guests, I decided that I would stay away from Ian so I didn't embarrass him. Mandy walked into the room and announced that dinner was ready. Before we sat down, Daniel pulled me to the side and told me he was proposing to Adalynn tonight. He asked me if I could play the piano. I smiled and told him that I would be honored. I didn't know quite where to sit at the table. I didn't want to take the chance of stepping over any boundaries by sitting next to Ian. So, to make it less awkward, I went into the kitchen to get the bread I made.

"What are you doing in here?" Ian asked as he came up from behind.

"Just getting the cranberry nut bread."

"Sweetheart, I have people who are serving. You don't need to do that. Now, come on." He smiled.

"But I want to. I made it and I want to put it on the table."

"You're too cute," he said as he kissed me on lips.

We walked back to the dining room and Ian pulled out my chair. The chair that I always sat in for breakfast, lunch, and dinner. The chair that sat by his.

"Thank you." I smiled.

****

Dinner was amazing. Charles really outdid himself with the food. We gathered into the living room for drinks.

"Rory, Adalynn tells me you can play the piano," Daniel said.

I knew that was my queue. "Yes, I can play."

"Why don't you play something for us? I would love to hear it."

Ian looked over at me from the bar and smiled. I sat down at the piano, took in a deep breath, placed my hands on the keys, and began playing "Endless Love." Everyone stopped talking and looked at me. Daniel walked over to the bar where Adalynn was talking to Ian, took her hand, and led her to the middle of the room. He said a few beautiful romantic words and then got down on one knee and asked her to marry him. Tears welled in my eyes as I played. Adalynn was in shock as she cupped her hand over her mouth and said yes. I looked over at Ian and he was staring at the two of them smiling. Everyone clapped and whistled after she said yes. Daniel picked her up and spun her around. It was so romantic and Adalynn was totally caught off guard. After I finished the song, I got up and walked over to her.

"Congratulations." I smiled as I hugged her.

"Thank you. You knew, didn't you?"

"Daniel just told me before dinner because he asked me to play the piano."

"The song was beautiful, Rory. Thank you."

Ian walked up, shook Daniel's hand, and then hugged and kissed Adalynn.

"I'm really happy for the both of you," he said.

"Thanks, friend. Maybe you should try it." Adalynn winked.

"Nah, I'm good. I'm not marriage material."

My heart instantly broke. *Why?* I already knew how he was. But to hear the words again shot bolts of lightning through my heart. I didn't know how much longer I would be able to go on like this. I excused myself and walked into the kitchen. As I was cutting a slice of apple pie, Andrew walked up behind me. He put his hands on my hips and whispered in my ear.

"Hey, gorgeous."

What the hell was he doing? "Hey," I said nervously.

"You know, I've been admiring you all night and I just want you to know how beautiful I think you are."

My heart felt like it was going to jump out of my chest; not out of excitement, but out of fear. "Thank you. Now if you'll excuse me, I have to go say goodbye to Adalynn and Daniel."

His grip tightened on my hips as he leaned in closer. His hot breath traveling from my ear down to my neck was making me sick. "I think you want me to fuck you. If you're worried about Ian, don't be. We share women all the time and you're no different."

Don't break. Stay strong. "Actually, Andrew, I don't want you anywhere near me. So, I'll say it one last time. Please let go of me so I can say goodbye to my friends and I won't tell Ian about this."

Andrew laughed as he released me. "Are you kidding me, Rory? Ian wouldn't give a shit if I were to fuck you. We're like brothers; we share everything and everyone. If you think that he's in love with you or something, you're crazy. He's only using you because of your fine ass. It's all he wants, at least for now, until he gets tired of it and moves on to a new hot ass."

"You're right. I am crazy. Crazy for not drop kicking you right here in this kitchen. Now get the fuck out of my way," I said as pushed him back and stormed out of the kitchen.

I was shaking and I needed to control myself. I went into the bathroom by Ian's study and locked the door. I sat down on the toilet as the tears began to fall. Suddenly, there was knock on the door.

"Rory, are you okay?" Ian said.

"Yeah, I'm fine. I'll be out in a minute."

"Adalynn and Daniel are leaving now."

"Okay, tell them to hold on and I'll be out in a minute."

I looked at myself in the mirror and wiped my eyes. I opened the door and walked to the foyer to say goodbye to Adalynn and Daniel.

"Congratulations again. I'm so happy for the both of you."

"Thank you, Rory. Let's do lunch. I'll call you," Adalynn said while she hugged me.

I gave Daniel a hug and the both of them left. Richard and Arianna left before they did, but Andrew decided he was going to stay a while longer. I walked into the living room and looked at him while he sat on the couch.

"Don't you have some whore you need to go fuck?" I said.

The corners of his mouth curved upwards as he replied, "I tried. She turned me down."

Ian walked into the room just as I was getting ready to walk out. "What are you two talking about?" he asked.

"I was just telling Rory how pretty she looks."

Ian smiled as he looked at me. "Yes, she does look very pretty."

The smug look on Andrew's face was making me ill. "If you'll excuse me, I'm going to head up to my room."

I started the water for a bath. I just wanted to lie back, relax, and not think about Ian or Andrew. As I climbed in and closed my eyes, Ian knocked on the door. *Are you serious?*

"Rory, are you taking a bath?" he asked.

"Yes, Ian, I am."

"I'm coming in."

"Sorry, but the door's locked. I'll talk to you when I get out."

The door opened. I opened one eye and looked at Ian standing in the doorway.

"I can open any door." He shrugged.

"Why aren't you downstairs with Andrew?" I asked.

"He just left. He got a call from someone and said he had to go. You know, we've never taken a bath together."

"I know. I like to take my baths alone."

"I think I can change your mind about that," he said as he started to undress.

"Seriously, I don't want you in the bathtub with me."

Before I knew it, he was completely naked and looking hotter than hell. His body was a wonderland and I couldn't help but to want more of it.

"Scoot up so I can climb in behind you."

I did, and he climbed in, wrapping his arms around me and pulling me into him.

"See, now isn't this nice?" He smiled as he kissed my cheek.

I could feel him getting hard beneath me. "Did you have a nice Thanksgiving?" he asked as he grabbed the loofah sponge and began rubbing it in circles on my shoulder.

"Yes, it was wonderful, and I'm so happy for Adalynn and Daniel."

"Me too. They're great together. I wanted to talk to you about something."

"What is it?"

"A friend of mine and his wife are flying in this weekend and I usually entertain them while they're here. There's a business deal we're working on, and we've been friends for a long time. I was hoping that you'd like to join us for dinner."

"Sure, I'll join you." I smiled.

"We usually go golfing too, so maybe you and his wife can do some shopping or whatever."

"Sure. Sounds fun."

"Great. Now, turn around. I'm so hard for you. I've been wanting you so badly all day."

I turned around like he asked and we had amazing sex. As I lay in bed and with Ian's arms wrapped around me, my mind wouldn't stop thinking about Andrew and the things he said about him and Ian sharing women. I could feel myself retreating, just like I used to when I was a child. I was slipping back into that world of loneliness and it scared me. I was beginning to become emotionally withdrawn. I wanted more out of this relationship. I wanted him to love me like I loved him. I needed him to want more from me than just sex. A tear fell from my eye as I slowly closed them both and finally fell asleep.

Chapter 23

We were taking Ian's friends out tonight for dinner and dancing. I was still amazed that Ian wanted me to join them. I'd been emotionally withdrawn the past couple of days and I could tell Ian sensed it. He asked me if anything was bothering me and I lied and told him no. If I did discuss my feelings with him, it would end in a terrible argument and I wasn't up for that yet. We still had sex every day, sometimes twice, which made it harder on me because of the emotional attachment. Every day I spent with Ian, I fell deeper and deeper in love with him.

"They're here," Ian said as he knocked on my door.

"Okay, I'll be down in a second."

I looked at myself one last time in the mirror and walked down the stairs with a smile.

"Rory, I would like you to meet Connor and Ellery Black."

Holy shit. He was hot.

"Connor and Ellery, this is my houseguest, Rory Sinclair."

Houseguest. Nice. He couldn't introduce me as his friend? No, I was his houseguest.

Connor held out his hand and, with a smile, he told me how nice it was to meet me. I turned to Ellery and the two of us lightly hugged. She was amazingly beautiful and the two of them looked stunning together. We climbed in the back of Ian's limo and headed to the restaurant. Ellery and I chatted while Connor and Ian were discussing business. Connor was interested in a piece of property that he said would be perfect for an art gallery.

"Do the two of you have any children?" I asked her.

"We have a daughter who's six months old. Her name is Julia."

I smiled as Ellery pulled out her phone and showed me pictures of her. She was adorable and I couldn't help but be a little envious. When we arrived at the restaurant, Connor helped Ellery out of the limo and Ian just stood there. That was odd because he always helped me out of the limo. I noticed Ellery gave him a strange look and then looked at me. The two of them walked hand in hand inside the restaurant while Ian walked next to me. Once we were promptly seated, I ordered a cosmopolitan. The four of us talked and enjoyed a nice dinner. I excused myself and Ellery followed me into the bathroom.

"Are you all right, Rory?" she asked as she touched up her lipstick.

"Yeah, I'm fine."

"Ian's a pretty special guy."

"Pretty special asshole," I accidentally let slip out.

"I've known Ian for a couple of years and you're the first woman he's ever brought to dinner." She smiled.

"Really?"

"Really."

"He reminds me a lot of how Connor used to be when we first met. We can talk about that tomorrow. The men are going golfing and I think maybe the two of us should go shopping. Julia can come with us and we'll have a great time."

"Julia's here?"

"She's back at the hotel with our manny, Mason."

"I would love to meet her." I smiled.

Ellery smiled back and we went back to our table. The four of us talked a bit more and then called it a night. We dropped Connor and Ellery off at their hotel.

"They're a great couple," I said to Ian.

"Yes, they are. They're probably two of the nicest people I've ever met," he said as he put his arm around me and tried to pull me closer. I resisted. "What's wrong with you?"

"Nothing. I'm just tired."

He hadn't shown any type of affection towards me all night and then the minute Connor and Ellery got out of the limo, he wanted to touch me.

"Why are you so tired? Are you feeling okay?"

"Yes, I'm feeling fine."

Ian removed his arm from me and sighed. As Joshua pulled up to the house, Ian climbed out and held out his hand.

"Oh, *now* you want to help me out of the limo?"

"What the hell is that supposed to mean?" he snapped.

"At the restaurant, you didn't help me at all. You just stood there."

"I did? I didn't realize."

I smacked his hand out of the way and got out myself. I just wanted to go to sleep.

"Wow, Rory. You have issues," he said as he followed me up the stairs.

"Don't come into my room," I spat as I slammed the door in his face.

"You need to talk to me, Rory, and tell me what's going on with you. If you're upset, you need to talk to me about it."

I stood in my room in silence. "Fine, Rory. Suit yourself," he said as he slammed his door.

****

The next morning, Ian didn't say a word to me. Connor and Ellery came over and the men left to go golfing. Joshua drove Ellery and me around for the day.

"She's so adorable, Ellery," I said as I held Julia.

"Thank you. She's our entire world. Why don't you tell me what's going on with Ian? I noticed that the two of you weren't speaking."

"I'm sorry. Things with Ian are complicated and I don't know how much more I can take," I said as we walked into a little boutique.

"Ian is a complicated man. Like I told you last night, he reminds me a lot of how Connor was when we first met."

"Really?" I said as I looked through the racks.

"Yes. Let me guess. You're in love with him, aren't you?" Ellery asked me.

"Yes, I am."

"Have you told him?"

Julia started to whine and Ellery took her from me. "No. He keeps saying he doesn't do relationships. I feel like his own personal call girl."

"Aw, sweetie. You need to tell him how you feel. If you don't, you'll keep arguing. When Connor finally admitted to me that he was in love with me, it changed everything. We've had our ups and downs and we struggled to get where we are today, but it was all worth it because it strengthened our relationship and made us realize that we couldn't live without each other."

"What the two of you have is rare," I said.

"No, it's not. Two people who truly love each other can have it too. I noticed the way Ian looked at you last night. I saw something in him that I'd never seen before. If it was truly meant to be for the two of you, then it will happen. Unfortunately, sometimes we have to make them see what they'd lose if we were gone."

"Really?"

"You've heard the saying, 'Sometimes you don't know what you've got until it's gone,' right?"

I nodded my head. "Yes, I've heard it."

"I believe that sometimes people need to open their eyes and see what's standing in front of them and how it could be gone in an instant."

"You're right. Maybe I'll talk to him tonight. Thanks, Ellery." I smiled.

"You're welcome, sweetie. Don't worry; everything will work out if it's meant to be. Fate has a strange way of throwing two people together."

We got in the limo and went back to the house. Ian and Connor were already back from their golf game and were sitting on the patio, having some drinks.

"Well, you're finally back. Did the two of you have fun?" Connor asked as he got up from his seat, kissed Ellery on the lips, and took Julia from her arms.

"We had a great time." She smiled.

Ian looked at me and then looked down. I had a headache, so I walked into the kitchen and grabbed the bottle of ibuprofen from the cabinet. I shook two pills into my hand and chased them down with a bottle of water. When I walked back out to the patio, Connor and Ellery were gone and Ian was holding Julia. I stopped and stared at him. Seeing him holding a baby was just about as sexy as him being naked.

"She's adorable. Isn't she?" I said.

"Yeah, she's pretty cute."

"Where are Connor and Ellery?"

"They went down to the beach for a minute. Connor just handed her to me."

Julia started to fuss and I could tell Ian became nervous. "Here, take her," he said as he handed her over to me.

I took her and, instantly, she stopped fussing. She looked at me and put her hand on my face. Ian stared at me and with a smile he said, "You're a natural with babies."

Connor and Ellery walked back up to the patio and Ellery took Julia inside. Their plane was leaving soon and they had to get back to the hotel and fetch Mason. Ian and Connor shook hands and lightly hugged. Apparently, they had sealed their business deal on the golf course. I hugged Connor and Ellery goodbye, gave Julia a kiss, and they left. Ellery was kind of enough to give me her phone number and told me to call her if I just wanted to talk or if I ever needed anything. I had just made two new friends. Too bad they lived in New York.

I went up to my room and Ian followed me. "I think we need to talk about last night," he said.

I guessed this was as good a time as any to let it all out. "Yeah, you're right. We do."

Ian walked up to me and ran the back of his hand down my cheek. "What's going on with you lately? You seem distant, like you were when I first brought you here."

I didn't know what to say. Actually, I did, but I didn't know how to say it. My stomach was twisted in knots and I felt like I was going to vomit. This was it. The words I was about to say were going to either make us or break us and I had a feeling it was going to break us.

"I love you, Ian."

He looked at me and then turned around and ran his hands through his hair. "No, you don't, Rory. You just think you do."

"You're wrong, Ian," I said as I grabbed his arm. "I'm in love with you."

"You're in love with what I've done for you, not me."

Now I was pissed. *Who the hell was he to deny me my feelings for him?* "No, I appreciate what you've done for me, but I'm in love with you, Ian Braxton. I'm in love with you as a person. Sure, you piss me off sometimes, but I still love you. I want *us*. I want *us* to be something special to each other."

He turned around and looked at me. "You're loving the wrong person because I'm not in love with you."

Those words. Those six, god awful words. I felt like I'd been stabbed all over again. In fact, the pain I just felt was worse than that.

"I don't believe you," I said as a tear fell from my eye. "How can you stand there and say that to me? What are you so afraid of?"

"I'm not afraid of anything. It's just how I feel. I'm sorry if I've hurt you. It's the last thing I want to do, but you're being ridiculous."

"I'm ridiculous because I told you that I loved you? You saved me and you made me fall in love with you. You took my soul and you stole my heart. I'm a human being and I have feelings."

Ian looked away from me and slowly shook his head. "Maybe I was the fool for thinking that you wouldn't fall in love with me. I told you before that this is me. This is how I am and you can either accept it or—"

"Or what, Ian?!" I yelled. "I think this has something to do with your mother leaving you as a child."

The rage in his eyes grew even more as he turned and looked at me. I could see the fire behind the color. "Don't you ever bring my mother up again! This has nothing to do with her."

"Really? Because you want to hear what I think?"

"NO! Actually, I don't."

"Well, too bad. I think you're scared to love anyone. You won't let anyone in because you're afraid they'll leave you, like she did."

"Bullshit. You know nothing, Rory. So spare me your stupid little insights because you don't know what the hell you're talking about!"

"You've let your father poison you all these years with his view of women since your mother left. Did it ever occur to you that she left for a reason?"

"I'm warning you, Rory. Stop right now. Just because I don't love you, doesn't mean you have to bring my mother into this," he said with sadness.

I couldn't hold it together anymore. Hearing him say that he didn't love me was a thousand knives through my heart.

"I want the truth. When I woke up after you brought me here, you said that you saved my life and that you did something for me and I would have to do something for you. Is that when you decided you wanted to have sex with me without using a condom? I need the truth, Ian. Tell me the fucking truth!" I yelled.

He looked at me with such sadness as he whispered no. "I'm sorry, Rory," he said as he took a step closer to me. I never meant to—"

"Stop," I said as I put up my hand. "Don't come any closer to me, please." I couldn't take any more of his bullshit. The way he manipulated me with his touch, his kiss, and his words.

"I can't give you what you want. I wish I could, but I can't," he said.

At that moment, I realized that I couldn't do this anymore. I couldn't be his friend with benefits, his call girl, or whatever the hell I was to him. The tears were now flowing uncontrollably.

"Sweetheart, please," he said.

I put my finger up. "I am not your sweetheart," I said through gritted teeth.

"I'm sorry, Rory," he said as he walked out and shut the door.

I couldn't breathe. It felt like a ton of bricks was sitting on my chest. I got down on the floor and crawled into the corner. I curled into a ball and silently cried. After about an hour, I went into the bathroom and looked at myself in the mirror. My mascara-stained eyes were red and swollen and my face had streaks going down it. I washed my face and sat down on the bed. My head was pounding and I just wanted to sleep. I had to make a plan to leave. I picked up my phone and sent Adalynn a text message.

"I need your help, please."

"What happened, sweetie? Are you okay?"

"I need to leave here and I haven't gotten word yet on my apartment."

"Enough said. You can stay here for as long as you need to."

"Thank you. I'll call a cab because I can't take the car."

"We can pick you up?"

"No, I don't want to run the risk of Ian seeing you. I'll see you soon. Thank you."

"See you soon and I'll open a bottle of wine and box of chocolates."

I took the bag down from the closet shelf and packed everything I needed. I stood in the full-length mirror and stared at the necklace Ian gave me. The most beautiful gift anyone had ever given me. I removed it from my neck and laid it out on the dresser. I jumped when I heard the front door slam. I zipped my bag and left it on the bed while I went and checked the house. I walked down the hall to Ian's bedroom and I nervously knocked on the door.

"Ian?" I called.

There was no answer. I slowly opened the door and gasped when I saw the mess. The room was in shambles. All the blankets were ripped off the bed, the chair and end table were turned over, and there were clothes lying all over the floor. I walked back to my room and called the cab service. As I grabbed my bag from the bed, I walked downstairs and hit the keys on the piano one last time before I left. I heard a horn beep and I stepped outside. I threw my bag in the back of the cab and gave the driver Adalynn's address. As the cab started to pull away, I softly placed my hand on the window as a single tear fell from my eye.

Chapter 24

"Aw, sweetie, come here," Adalynn said as she held her arms out to me and Daniel took my bag.

"Adalynn, I—I…"

"I know, sweetie. Let's go sit down and you can tell me what happened."

She led me over to the couch and Daniel brought the bottle of wine and the box of chocolates over and set them on the table. I told Adalynn everything that Ian said.

"What a prick. I don't know what the hell the matter with him is. I've seen the way he looks at you and how his eyes light up when you walk into the room. He's done things for you that he's never done for other women before, including me. Maybe I should have a talk with him."

"No, please don't. Please. He's hurt me so much. I need to tell you something, but you have to promise me you will never ever repeat it. Promise me, Adalynn."

"Sweetie, I promise."

"Ian's mother didn't die. She left him when he was a child."

"What?! Are you serious?"

"Yes, and he's still so angry about it and I think that's the reason why he's closed himself off from loving anyone. I think he's afraid I'll leave him like his mom did."

"Wow. He told you that?"

"Yes, he told me she left. I'm just assuming the other is his problem."

Adalynn reached for a glass of wine and handed it to me. "Drink this, you'll feel better."

I heard my phone beep. I pulled it out of my purse and nearly had a heart attack when I saw it was from Ian.

"I figured you'd leave. Have a nice life, Rory."

I put my hand over my mouth as the tears kept coming.

"Don't respond to him," Adalynn said as she took the phone from my hand and set it on the table.

We drank a few glasses of wine and ate half the box of chocolates. Adalynn showed me to the guest room and I climbed into bed. I kept staring at the text message Ian sent me. I already missed him and I wanted to go back, but he was toxic for me. Andrew was right; he'd get tired of me and move on. I needed to think of my future. I did the unthinkable. I sent him a text message.

"You left me no choice."

A few moments later, he responded.

"I'm sorry you felt that way."

I set my phone down on the nightstand and cried for hours. The emptiness I felt was horrific and I didn't realize that I'd grown so dependent on him. The need I felt for him scared me and as much as I wanted to believe I was strong, I wasn't. I was back to that weak little girl from Indiana.

The next morning, I opened my eyes, but I couldn't gather enough strength to get out of bed. I didn't *want* to get out of bed. I never wanted to get out of bed again. The door slowly opened and Adalynn peeked her head through.

"Good morning. I brought you some coffee."

I sat up and took the cup from her.

"I'm not going to ask you how you are because I already know."

I looked down as I sipped my coffee. "I miss him so much, Adalynn."

"I know you do," she said as she took a hold of my hand. "I have to go on a business trip tomorrow for *Prim* and you're coming with me. I think it would be good for you to get out of Malibu and get your mind off of Ian."

"Where are you going?" I asked.

"Paris." She smiled.

"Adalynn, there's no way. I don't even have a passport."

"No worries about that. Daniel is getting you one. It'll be ready today. He has connections. We just need to get your picture. So get out of bed and doll yourself up." She smiled.

"I don't know."

"Rory. There's no better cure than Paris for a broken heart. Wait, isn't Paris the city of love?" Oh well, listen, you'll be surrounded by hot French men, French coffee, French chocolates, and best of all, French fucking pastries!"

I let out a laugh.

"I already purchased your ticket, it's non-refundable, and we're flying first class."

I got out of bed, showered, got dressed, and had my picture taken for my passport. My heart was heavy and I still found it hard to breathe. Adalynn tried to get me to eat, but I couldn't. Every bite of food I took made me feel sick. Adalynn said she had a few things to pick up before we left tomorrow and she asked if I would go with her. Daniel dropped me off at *Prim* and, as I walked into her office, I saw Ian sitting in the chair across from her desk.

"Rory, what a nice surprise," Adalynn said as her eyes widened.

Ian turned around and our eyes met. "I—I'm sorry. I didn't know you were in a meeting," I said nervously as I turned around and sprinted down the hall. I had to get out of there. My heart was racing and my breathing felt constricted. I pushed the button to the elevator a hundred times, thinking that it would magically make the door open faster. I didn't know where the stairs were, so I couldn't take them. I felt a hand lightly grab my arm and turn me around. It was him.

"I'm sorry. I don't want to hurt you. Please, Rory, I don't want to end things on a bad note."

"It's too late for that," I spat as I jerked my arm out of his grip.

"I can't give you what you want. I wish I could."

"And I can't give you what you want," I said as a tear streamed down my face. "Please, just let me heal."

He put his hand on my cheek, and for the first time since I'd known him, I saw his eyes fill with tears. "Fuck," he whispered as he shook his head and walked away.

****

We landed and I couldn't believe I was in Paris. I listened to music and slept most of the way. My eyes filled with tears a few times, but I managed to stop them. Even though I was with Adalynn, I still felt lost and alone. I felt like my world had crumbled, and I was left lying on the ground under a rubble of pain. I paid a visit to Stephen before I left and told him that I had to go on a trip. I spoke with the management at Hudson Rock and they told me that it would be okay to Skype with him on visiting days, during visiting hours.

We walked into the apartment that Adalynn's father owned. It was small, but amazing. I walked over to the French doors that led out to a balcony from my bedroom. I opened the doors and gasped at the beautiful sight that was out my window.

"It's gorgeous, isn't it?" Adalynn smiled as she stood next to me.

"It's amazing. Thank you so much for bringing me here."

"I want to apologize again for yesterday. I didn't know that Ian was going to show up and when I went to text you, my phone died."

"It's okay. Don't worry about it. We're here in Paris now and all thoughts of Ian Braxton have left my head. It's time to start anew and move on."

"High five." She smiled as she held up her hand. "I have to get over to my meeting. Are you going to be okay here?"

"I'll be fine. I'll go do a little sight-seeing."

"Stay close and don't get lost. When I get back, I'm taking you to one of my favorite restaurants."

When Adalynn left, I walked around the apartment and took note of the beautiful antique furniture throughout. Adalynn said we'd be here for a week, so I unpacked my clothes and placed them in the dresser drawers. I decided to go and explore the area. It was a beautiful sunny day and I wanted to be outside. As I was walking down the street and taking in the beautiful surroundings, I stopped at an outdoor market that displayed the best-looking fruits and vegetables. As I picked up a shiny red apple, I heard someone speak.

"C'est une belle journée pour une belle femme. Puis-je vous aider?"

I looked up from the shiny red apple to a French-speaking man. "I'm sorry, but I don't speak French," I said.

"Ah, you're an American. I should've known by your exquisite beauty." He smiled.

God, his accent was beautiful. He was beautiful. He wore his brown hair longish and just the right amount of scruff sculpted his face. His hazel eyes had a brightness to them when he looked at me, and his smile was warm. He was a nice distraction.

"I'm Andre, and you are?" He smiled.

"Rory." I smiled as we lightly shook hands.

"Nice to meet you, Rory. Please take that apple."

"Oh no, I couldn't. At least let me pay for it."

"No, no, no. It's a gift from me. Is this your first time in Paris?"

"Yes, it is, and thank you very much." I smiled as I began to walk away, holding up the apple.

"It was nice to meet you, beautiful Rory. Make sure to visit again."

I turned around and gave Andre a small smile and then bit into my apple and continued walking down the street. So far, I was liking my time in Paris. The bakeries were exquisite and smelled so good. On my way back to the apartment, I stopped and picked up some beautiful flowers from a flower cart on the corner. When I arrived back at the apartment, I set the flowers on the counter and looked for a vase. As I arranged the purple and pink peonies in the vase, they made me smile and that was what I needed. I set them in the center of the small dining table and then took a picture of them with my phone. I was so jet lagged, so I went and lay down on the bed for a while. For the first time, I had a dream about Ian. I dreamt that we were on the beach and he was holding me in his arms, telling me that he loved me.

"Rory, sweetie, wake up," Adalynn said as she lightly shook me.

I opened my eyes and I could feel the wetness of the tears on my face. I looked at her, still trying to focus on what was going on.

"You were crying in your sleep."

I got up and walked into the bathroom. "I had a dream about Ian."

"Aw, sweetie. I'm sorry. I know it's hard. Do you miss him?"

"Yes, I miss him so much."

"Well, come on. We're going out tonight and we're going to show this town how two American girls have fun."

I smiled and started the shower. I needed to go out and have some fun. But I secretly wished that it was Ian I was having fun with. As I let the hot water stream down me, I couldn't stop thinking about him. I wondered what he was doing, if he was with another woman, and if he was thinking of me. I was pretty sure that Andrew and Richard were happy that I was gone. I put on my little black dress, high boots, and I curled my hair. I was ready to go out and paint the town.

The restaurant we went to had a line that was around the corner of the building. Adalynn looked at me and rolled her eyes.

"You have got to be kidding me," she huffed.

"This line is obnoxious."

"I know, but they have the best food in all of Paris."

As we stood in the obnoxious long line, I saw Andre, the guy from the fruit stand, approaching us.

"Look, it's the beautiful American girl." He smiled.

"Andre, hi. What are you doing here?"

Adalynn kept elbowing me. "Oh, Adalynn, this is Andre. Andre, this is my friend, Adalynn."

"Another beautiful American girl. How did I get so lucky today? Come with me." He smiled.

I looked at Adalynn as she twisted her face. "Go, follow him. Maybe he can get us in."

We followed Andre into the restaurant and were promptly seated. "How?" I smiled.

"I have connections." He winked.

"Well, thank God for Andre," Adalynn said.

He sat and ate dinner with us. He was a funny guy and he made me and Adalynn laugh throughout dinner. For a split second, I didn't think about Ian, but that didn't last too long. Andre paid our bill, even though Adalynn fought him tooth and nail for it. It was nice to see her lose for once. As we were saying goodbye, Andre smiled at me and asked me for my phone number. I told him I wasn't sure, but Adalynn grabbed his phone from his hand and programmed my number into it. He kissed her on the cheek and thanked her.

"It was nice to have dinner with you, my beautiful American girl. I will call you to go out," he said as he gave me a kiss on each cheek.

Adalynn and I climbed into the back of the cab. "Now, tell me how you met him?"

"I met him at the fruit stand this afternoon when I was looking at the apples. I swear, if he calls me his 'beautiful American girl' again, I'm going to scream."

Adalynn laughed as she put her hand on mine. "He's a distraction, Rory, and you need all the distractions you can get right now."

I spent the next few mornings jogging around the neighborhood. It was beautiful and every time I passed by the fruit stand, Andre would wave and yell, "Good morning, my beautiful American girl." I would just give a small smile and a light wave. He came over the apartment a couple of times and brought us fruit. He was a nice guy, but I still couldn't get my mind off of Ian. I couldn't even say how many times I'd picked up my phone and almost called him, just so I could hear his voice. Everything I did and saw reminded me of Ian. I missed him so much and I started to wonder if I'd ever get over him.

"Adalynn, can you do me a favor?"

"What is it, sweetie?" she asked as she was putting on her makeup.

I bit down on my bottom lip because I was afraid to ask her. She stopped putting on her mascara and looked at me.

"Are you okay?"

"Will you call Ian and put him on speakerphone?"

"What? You're joking, right?" She asked as she looked at me. "Oh my God, you're serious."

"I just want to hear his voice. Just for a minute. Please."

"Rory, we're leaving tomorrow. Maybe you should go see him."

"I'm not going back with you. If it's okay, I'd like to stay here for a while longer."

"I don't like the thought of you being in Paris by yourself."

"I'm not. I have Andre," I said as I looked around.

Adalynn sighed and dialed Ian's number. "I just want you to know that I'm doing this against my will."

"Hello," Ian answered.

"Ian, darling, how are you?" Adalynn asked.

"I'm okay. How's Paris?"

"Paris is fabulous as always. What have you been up to?"

Hearing his voice was music to my ears. As pissed as I was at him, I still found comfort in his voice.

"Not much. I've been busy with work."

Adalynn looked at me and shrugged. "Well, Ian, I just called to say hi and that I'll be flying home tomorrow. We should have dinner when I get back."

"Sounds good, Adalynn. Have a safe flight home."

"Thanks, darling. Bye."

"Bye."

"Thank you, Adalynn," I said as a tear fell from my eye.

She looked at me and cocked her head. "Come here, you poor thing," she said as she hugged me. "When I get back, I'm going to have a long talk with him."

"It doesn't matter. What's done is done and I could never be with someone like him. I just have to get over it and move on. That's why I want to stay here a while longer."

"Christmas is in a couple of weeks. You'll be back for Christmas, right?"

I shook my head. "No, I don't want to be anywhere near Malibu when Christmas comes."

"Well, you can stay here as long as you want. But I don't want you alone on Christmas."

"Don't worry about me and Christmas. I'm a big girl, and I can take care of myself."

There was a knock at the door and Adalynn and I looked at each other. I walked to the door, looked out the peephole, and saw Andre standing there, holding flowers in front of his face.

"Hello, my beautiful American girl." He smiled. "I wish I could take credit for these beauties, but they were just lying by the door when I walked up."

"Thanks, Andre. Come on in." I smiled.

I took the beautiful red roses from him, cut the stems, and arranged them in a vase. "There isn't a card. Are you sure these aren't from you?"

"I swear, Rory. They're not. They were propped up against the door when I walked up."

Adalynn walked out from her bedroom and looked at the flowers. "Oh, pretty. Who are they for?"

"We don't know. There wasn't a card and Andre said they were propped up against the door when he got here."

"Andre, I need to have a word with you."

"Did I do something wrong, Adalynn?" he asked.

"No, of course not. I'm leaving Paris tomorrow, but Rory has decided to stay for a while longer. I need you to keep an eye on her while she's here."

"No problem. I will keep my beautiful American girl company every day."

I rolled my eyes because he was driving me crazy. "I appreciate that, Andre, but I'll be fine."

"A beautiful girl should not be alone in Paris, Rory. It's not safe," he said.

I sighed as I walked to the kitchen and took the vegetables from the refrigerator. Since it was Adalynn's last night in Paris, she wanted to stay in and the three of us cooked an amazing dinner.

Chapter 25

Adalynn had been gone two days already and, as promised, Andre hung around. The thing I found a little strange about him was that he didn't try to hit on me. In fact, he was just being more of a friend than anything. He came over after he closed up the fruit stand and we cooked dinner together. I didn't have romantic feelings for him. I was still not over Ian and it wasn't getting easier. Everyone said that time heals all wounds, but this wound wasn't healing with time. It was just as open as it was when I'd left. I had talked about Ian to Andre. Maybe that was why he wasn't hitting on me, he didn't want to push me.

"You know, Rory, you're always sad. I've noticed that about you. You're terrible at faking happiness."

"Thanks, Andre," I said.

"Sorry, my beautiful American girl, but it's the truth." He smiled as he touched my chin.

"Have you ever been in love, Andre? I mean really, deep in your bones, you can't live without the person, love?"

"No, not to that extent. I've had many girlfriends, and I have loved some, but not to that extent. I'm still looking for her." He winked.

I hoped to God that wink wasn't directed at me. That was the last thing I needed.

"Rory, you came to Paris to forget about that man. So why do you keep focusing on him?"

I set the salad bowl on the table. "I don't know. We're connected somehow, and I can't let go of that connection."

"You can't or you don't want to?" he asked. "There's a difference. We as humans can do anything we want."

I pondered what he said as I took the chicken out of the oven. "I've been thinking about moving here."

"What?!" he exclaimed.

"Of course, I'll need to find a job first and then look for my own apartment. But I think it will be good for me, and then I can look into psychiatric hospitals and move Stephen here."

"That's a major decision, Rory."

"I know it is, and I've been thinking about it since I came here."

"If you need any help finding an apartment, let me know." He smiled. "What are your plans for Christmas? It's coming next week."

"I'm going to stay here, cook myself something, and watch Christmas movies."

"That's boring. You're more than welcome to come with me to Germany and spend the holiday with me and my family."

"That's very sweet of you, Andre, but I'm afraid I won't be good company. I'd rather just stay here."

"And wallow in self-pity, right?"

I smiled as I cut into my chicken. After dinner, we finished off the bottle of wine and Andre gathered his things to leave.

"Good night, my beautiful American girl." He smiled as he kissed my cheek.

"Good night, my amazing French boy."

Andre winked and walked out the door.

The next morning, I got up early and went for my morning run. As I ran by the fruit stand, Andre yelled out to me.

"Me and you tonight, Eiffel Tower. I'll text you."

I gave him a thumbs up as I ran by. I hadn't been to see the Eiffel Tower yet and it was only fifteen minutes away from the apartment. As I ran, my mind kept thinking about what Ian was doing for Christmas. I was sure he'd spend it with his father and Andrew. For once, I was glad I wasn't in Malibu.

I stopped at the bakery on my way back and picked up some French pastries. When I got back to the apartment, there was a tall – okay, it was about four feet tall – thing wrapped in paper. I called it a thing because I wasn't quite sure what it was. I opened the apartment door and set my box of pastries down. I propped the door open with a chair and dragged inside what seemed to be a plant. "What the hell?" I said out loud. I looked around for a card and there wasn't one on the outside. As I carefully ripped the paper from the plant, I gasped when standing before me was a four-foot tree made entirely out of fresh pink and purple roses and white carnations. It was the most beautiful thing I'd ever seen. Tears filled my eyes as I stared at the beauty of it. I searched around the flowers to find a card, but there wasn't one. I was positive this was delivered to the wrong apartment. Either that or Andre sent it. I took my phone from my pocket and sent him a text message.

"Did you send me a tree made of flowers?"

"Huh?"

I took a picture of it and sent it to him.

"That's pretty, but no, I didn't send it. There's no card again?"

"No, and I'm worried that these things are being delivered to the wrong apartment."

"Oh well, then the delivery people should be more careful. Enjoy it. By the way, meet me at the Eiffel Tower tonight at eight o'clock. You mentioned you wanted to see it, so I think tonight is a good night since I'm leaving tomorrow. I have to restock the fruit after the stand closes, so I'll just meet you there."

"Sounds good. See you then."

I couldn't stop staring at the tree as I sat at the table drinking my coffee and eating my French pastries. I felt bad because if it was meant for someone else, they were missing out, so I went around to all the apartments on my floor and asked them if they knew anything about it. Everyone said no, except for the people that lived next door; they weren't home. I looked at the clock and had some time to take a nap before I had to get ready and meet Andre. I was excited because I'd always dreamed of seeing the Eiffel Tower, and now, I was finally going to get to. I set the alarm on my phone and drifted off to sleep. I had another dream about Ian and when I woke up, my heart was racing and my eyes were wet. *Was I ever going to get over him?*

****

The cab was beeping his horn outside my window. "Okay, okay, I'm coming." I locked the apartment and flew down four flights of stairs so the impatient cab driver would stop beeping his horn. I opened the door and climbed in the back.

"I heard you the first twenty times you beeped the horn," I said.

"I'm sorry, Madame, but the horn was stuck."

"Oh," I said in embarrassment. "I need you to take me to the Eiffel Tower, please."

"Have you ever been, Madame?" he asked in a heavy French accent.

"No. This is my first time."

"You're not going to the Eiffel Tower alone, are you?"

"I'm meeting someone there."

"Very good." He smiled.

As the driver drove down the street, I could see the Eiffel Tower in the distance. The cab stopped as close as he could. After paying him what I owed, I got out of the cab and walked the rest of the way until I was standing in front of the one thing I've always dreamed of seeing.

"Isn't it beautiful?"

My heart leaped into my throat at the sound of his voice. As I slowly turned around in disbelief that it was actually him, I gasped and my eyes filled with tears as he stood there a few feet away from me with his hands in his coat pocket.

"Ian, what are you doing here?"

He never took his eyes off me as he slowly walked to where I was standing. "It's so good to see you, Rory. I've missed you so much," he said as he cupped my face in his hands.

"How—"

"Shh." He smiled. "Just let me kiss you first and then I'll explain everything," he whispered as he leaned in and brushed his lips against mine.

His lips, his kiss, his hands on my face, were pulling me back in. Suddenly, flashes of memories of the night I left flooded my mind. I pulled away.

"No! I won't let you do this to me," I exclaimed as I held up my finger.

"Rory, please listen to me. I need you to listen to me, sweetheart."

"I'm meeting someone here. In fact, he should be here any second," I said nervously as I looked around for Andre.

"That's what I'm trying to tell you. Andre isn't coming. He set this up for me; for us."

My head was in a ball of confusion and I didn't understand what was going on. My heart was racing at the speed of light and I felt like I was losing my mind.

"What? What are you talking about?"

"I can see you're really upset. Please calm down, and I promise I'll explain everything. Please, Rory. I traveled a long way to see you."

Taking in a deep breath, I stood there and stared at him. He was so handsome and he was pleading with me to hear him out. I started to calm down and nodded my head. "Go ahead and tell me why you're here."

"I missed you, and it's been really hard for me since you left. You're on my mind every second of every day. I dream about you every night, and I can't get you out of my fucking head. Everything I do, and everything I see, reminds me of you. I hate it that you're not at home with me. Since the day you left, I've slept in your bed because it smells like you, and I miss your scent. I miss you. I miss us. I miss everything we shared."

The tears that had filled my eyes started to pour down my face and I turned away from him. *Was he just saying these things to get me back, and then once I went home, would things go back to the way it used to be?* "There is no us," I whispered.

"Please, don't turn away from me, and please don't say that. I'm willing to give it all up for you. The company, the house, the money, everything. I'll walk away from it all just to be with you. You were right. The way I am does have to do with my mother. I can admit that now because I refuse to lose you. I'm just so scared that you'll leave me like she did. I was afraid to love because I saw what it did, not only to me when she left, but what it did to my dad. I know now that I can't live that way anymore. I want us to share a home, Rory. I want us to be a couple, and I want to go on dates with you and travel with you. I want to scream to the world that you're mine."

I swear my heart stopped beating. I turned around and he was standing there with tears falling down his face. I ran to him, jumped in his arms, and kissed him like I never had before.

"I missed you too. I missed you so much that it felt like parts of me were dying every day."

"I know, sweetheart. I felt the same exact way. I love you, Rory Sinclair. I'm in love with you and I have been since the night you laid your head across my lap in the limo. I just couldn't admit it, and then when you left, reality hit me. You and I are supposed to be together. The both of us were at the right place at the right time. We were destined to meet. I know that now. I'm so sorry for hurting you and saying those awful things to you, and I will spend eternity making it up to you. I love you so much, and I can't live without you."

"I love you too, Ian."

He smiled as we kissed passionately for a few moments and then he broke our embrace. "I was so scared that you were going to turn me down and tell me to go to hell."

I laughed as I hugged him. "I would never turn you down. I think you better take me back to my apartment. We have some serious making up to do." I smiled.

"You bet we do and I don't want to waste a second of it."

Ian picked me up and carried me back to his cab. Once we climbed in the back, our lips locked all the way back to the apartment.

****

When we walked into the apartment, I flipped on the lights and looked at the beautiful tree that was sitting in the corner. Ian looked at me and smiled.

"Do you like it?"

"Did you send it?"

"Yes, I did." He smiled.

"I love it. It's beautiful. I've never seen anything like it."

"Did you like the roses?"

"Did you send them?"

"Yes." Ian laughed.

"I loved them."

"Good. That's my beginning to being a perfect boyfriend." He smiled. "Because that's all I want to be to you."

"You're perfect no matter what. Now, you have five seconds to take me to bed."

"I can do it in one," he growled as he picked me up and carried me to the bedroom.

Chapter 26

I lay there wrapped in Ian's arms, the sheets tangled between us, from the best sex we ever had. I was on Cloud Nine and nothing could bring me down. The passion that I felt when we made love was like nothing I'd ever felt before. I lifted my head and looked at Ian's smiling face.

"I think you need to explain about Andre."

"I was wondering when you were going to ask me about him. I found out you were here from Adalynn's assistant. That reminds me, Adalynn and I are going to have quite a talk when we get back because she lied to me about you."

"Leave Adalynn alone." I smiled.

"Anyway, I knew where this place was because it's been in her family for years and I'd stayed here a few times when I came to Paris. I've known Andre for a long time, and I figured you'd be checking out the fruit stand since it was so close, so I sent him your picture, asked him to be on the lookout for you, and asked him to keep an eye on you until I could get here."

"So that's why he didn't hit on me."

"He didn't hit on you because I threatened him. Believe me, he would have."

"You arranged to meet me at the Eiffel Tower. That was very romantic." I smiled.

"I'm trying to be, Rory. I know I said all that shit about romance and stuff, but the truth is, I've never wanted to do any of those things until I met you. Oh, that reminds me," he said as he got up and pulled a box from his pants pocket.

"Here," he said as he handed me a small box.

He climbed back into bed and I opened the box, revealing my key necklace that he'd given me before. "Thank you, Ian. I've missed this."

"It's a new one. Your other one is still sitting on the dresser where you left it."

"What? I don't understand."

"When I gave that other one to you, I told you that it represented that you'll always have a place to stay. I wanted to give you a new one that represented something else. This necklace is the key to my heart because you've unlocked it and you filled my heart with love. I want you to know that my love for you will always protect you."

He took the box from my hand and removed the necklace from it. I lifted up my hair as he put it around my neck. "There, it's right where it's supposed to be," he said as he lightly kissed the back of my neck.

I turned around and looked into his eyes. Eyes that were happy and full of life. I placed my hand on his cheek. "I love you so much. I've never felt this way before."

"I've never felt this way either. I love you too, Rory," he said as he kissed the palm of my hand. "Christmas is in a few days and, if you don't mind, I would like to spend it here, in Paris. No family or friends. Just us. I want to spend Christmas alone with my girlfriend."

"I would love that. What about your dad? Won't he be mad?"

"I had a long talk with my dad and I told him how much I loved you and that I was coming to Paris to get you back. He told me to do what I had to do and we'll talk after the holidays. I also wanted to tell you that I went and visited Stephen before I left."

"You did? Why?" I asked as I kissed his bare chest.

"Because I wanted to tell him how much I loved you and that I promise to take care of both of you."

"Ian," I whispered.

He took my hand and interlaced our fingers. "I'm so sorry for everything, Rory. I really need you to know that."

I sat up and cupped his face in my hands. "I know you are. I'm sorry too. I shouldn't have pushed you the way I did."

"No, you doing that really opened my eyes. I thought for days about how much I loved you and how I needed to tell you, but I couldn't. I was too scared. Scared of everything that love represents."

"Are you still scared?" I asked.

"A little bit. I'm afraid I'm going to fuck up and you'll end up leaving again."

"We need to promise each other that we'll be open and honest about everything. As long as we talk about how we're feeling and what's bothering us, we'll be fine." I smiled as I kissed his lips. "I'm so happy you're here."

"Me too, sweetheart," he said as he pulled me into an embrace. "I'm never letting you out of my sight again."

"Promise?" I smiled.

"Promise. I need to make love to you again, right now." He smiled.

"What are you waiting for? I'm more than ready." I winked as I took his hand and placed it between my legs.

"Damn, I love you!" He smiled as he rolled me on my back and hovered over me.

****

The next morning, after two rounds of making love, we got dressed and walked down the street to the fruit stand. Andre looked at me and winked as he and Ian shook hands.

"You." I smiled as I pointed my finger at him.

"You deserve to be happy, Rory, and I was happy to make it happen for you. You're my beautiful American girl."

"Hey! Watch it," Ian said.

Andre laughed as he threw him an apple.

"I thought you were leaving today," I said.

"I'm leaving tonight."

I gave him a hug and a kiss on both cheeks. "Have a Merry Christmas, Andre," Ian and I said as we walked away.

"I'll be coming to Malibu to visit my beautiful American girl," he yelled.

Ian held his hand up and flipped him off from behind and I heard Andre's loud laughter throughout the streets.

Ian hailed us a cab and had the driver take us to the Eiffel Tower. "Why are we here again?" I asked.

"We're here as an official couple. I wanted us to look at it together because it's something you've always wanted to see and I want to share it with you."

"You're an amazing man, Ian Braxton."

We stood in front of the Eiffel Tower, and I held the hand of the man who was the love of my life. The man who saved my life. The one who took me in, healed me, protected me, and showed me a world that I had only ever dreamed of. I looked up at the tower and then over at him. He looked at me and smiled.

"I love you, Ian."

"I love you too, sweetheart," he whispered as he leaned over and kissed my lips.

Ian and Rory's journey of love continue in the second book of the Millionaire's Love Series:

When I Lie With You (A Millionaire's Love, #2)

Make sure to read the first chapter of *Collin* at the end of the book!

Playlist

White Flag -.Dido

Say Something - A Big World featuring Christina Aguilera

Unchained Melody - The Righteous Brothers

Raining In Paris - The Maine

Story of My Life - One Direction

Satisfied – Acoustic - Jewel

Everybody Hurts - R.E.M.

Iris - The Goo Goo Dolls

Everytime - Britney Spears

In her Eyes - Joshua Radin

Somewhere Over the Rainbow - .Jewel

Madness - Muse

Fake Plastic Trees - Radiohead

Cry - James Blunt

Best Of Me - Daniel Powter

Let Her Go - Passenger

Head Over Feet - Alanis Morissette

Jar of Hearts - Christina Perri

Sandi Lynn

About The Author

Sandi Lynn is a New York Times, USA Today and Wall Street Journal bestselling author who spends all of her days writing. She published her first novel, Forever Black, in February 2013 and this is her sixth published novel. Her addictions are shopping, romance novels, coffee, chocolate, margaritas, and giving readers an escape to another world.

Please come connect with her at:

www.facebook.com/Sandi.Lynn.Author

www.twitter.com/SandilynnWriter

www.authorsandilynn.com

www.pinterest.com/sandilynnWriter

www.instagram.com/sandilynnauthor

https://www.goodreads.com/author/show/6089757.Sandi_Lynn

Collin
Chapter 1

I looked at the time on my phone while I was stuck in the famous New York City traffic. My mom was going to kill me if I was late for dinner again. I was expected to be at home for dinner two nights a week. The two nights that Julia and Jake came over, we'd all have dinner as a family. I should've left Black Enterprises earlier, but I had an unexpected visitor and she was smoking hot. One thing led to another, we had sex, and now I was going to be late. I parked the Range Rover and took the elevator up to the penthouse. As I walked through the elevator doors, I headed straight to the kitchen, where I heard everyone talking. Thank God, they hadn't started eating yet.

"There you are," my mom said as she walked over and kissed me on the cheek.

Something was going on. Everyone was way too happy. Julia smiled as I kissed her on the cheek and I shook Jake's hand.

"What's up? I'm sensing there's a celebration or something."

Julia looked at me and grabbed my hand. "I'm pregnant. You're going to be an uncle." She smiled.

"What?! Congratulations!" I exclaimed as I pulled her into an embrace.

"Thank you, little brother."

I reached over and gave Jake a light hug. "Congratulations, bro. Wow. I thought you guys were going to wait a couple of years?"

"Yeah. So did we. But it happened, and we couldn't be happier." Jake smiled.

I turned to my dad, who was grinning from ear to ear. "Well, looks like you're going to be a grandpa." I smiled as I hooked my arm around him.

"Yeah, and I think one grandchild is enough for now. You reek like perfume and I'm assuming she was the reason you're late."

"I was working, Dad. I got the contracts ready for tomorrow's meeting."

"Really, because when I left the office three hours ago, you were almost finished." He sighed.

I walked away because I didn't need his shit. He didn't understand what I was going through and I was in no mood for a Connor Black lecture. My mom and Julia called us to the table and we all sat down and enjoyed a family dinner. I was happy for Julia and Jake; they were going to make amazing parents. She was glowing, Jake was all smiles, my parents were ecstatic, and I was happy that now there was something other than me on which Connor and Ellery could focus.

I hadn't been the model son since Hailey left. I wanted it to work, but she said that with her being in Italy, and me in New York, it wouldn't. She left to study fashion when she was accepted by one of the top schools of design and was interning with a well-known, up-and-coming designer. It was a once-in-a-lifetime opportunity for her and the thing that hurt me the most was that she wasn't even willing to try and have a long distance relationship. She left without even so much as a sorry. My twenty-second birthday was the next week and we had been seeing each other for almost six years. How do you just throw the past six years of your life away? I thought we had something, and I thought that I meant something to her. The more I thought about it, the angrier I became. Well, those days were gone now. I'd never let another woman do that to me. Since she left, I'd partied too much, drunk too much, had sex with every woman that looked my way, and I'd been labeled New York's Most Eligible Playboy. Much like my dad, women fell all over me. My mom called it the Black Curse. I'd decided that many women were better than just one. No relationships, no strings, no frills, nothing. Just good sex and a sweet goodbye. When one woman left, another stepped into her place.

"Are you okay, Collin?" my mom asked.

I looked at her as she stared at me with her blue eyes. "Yes, I'm fine. Why?"

"You seem distant. Your sister asked you a question and you didn't answer her."

The truth was that I was lost in my thoughts about Hailey that I didn't hear her. "I'm sorry, Julia. What did you say?"

She looked at me with pursed lips. "We'll talk later, after dinner."

"Okay." I smiled as I finished eating.

****

As I pulled my phone from my pocket, I went upstairs to my room and sat down on my bed. Julia knocked lightly on the door and asked if she could come in.

"Hey." I smiled as I held out my hand to her.

She took it and sat down next to me. "I'm worried about you, Collin."

"Don't be, sis. I'm all right." I smiled.

"It's been a couple of months since Hailey left. Have you talked to her?"

"No. She made it clear that it would probably be best if we didn't because it would make things harder. What the fuck ever. I'm over her, and I'm moving on."

Julia put her arm around me. "I don't think you're over her and there's no way you can be. It hasn't been long enough, and I know damn well that when you've been in a relationship as long as the two of you were, it's just not that easy to get over."

"Yeah, well, you're wrong. I've wasted the last six years of my life on a bullshit relationship. I won't ever do that again. I'm exploring, going out, and having fun. I'm doing what I should've been doing the past six years instead of being tied down to one girl."

"I know you don't mean that, Collin."

The truth was maybe I did mean it. I was still angry at her for leaving our relationship behind. I looked at my watch and saw it was time to hit the bar with Aiden. I gave Julia a kiss on the cheek and got up from the bed.

"Listen, I have to go now. I'm meeting Aiden in about thirty minutes. Congratulations again. You and Jake are going to make really great parents."

"Thanks, Collin, and stay out of trouble," she said as she pointed at me.

"That I can't promise." I winked as I walked out the door.

I walked into the bathroom and brushed my teeth before walking out of the penthouse. I dabbed on some more cologne and, as I walked downstairs, my mom stopped me.

"Collin, where are you going?" she asked.

"Out with Aiden."

"Do you think you can stay home at least one night? We hardly see you anymore." She pouted.

"Mom, come on. I'm almost twenty-two. The last thing I want to do is hang with my parents when I can go out with my friends. Plus, Dad sees me every day, all day long at the office."

"Yeah, well I don't, and I miss my son."

"I love you, Mom," I said as I kissed her on the cheek and stepped onto the elevator.

I felt bad. I loved my mom so much, and I hated when she made me feel guilty, but fun was to be had and that was exactly what I was going to do; no matter what she said.

****

I took a cab to Club S because I knew that I'd be drinking and wouldn't be able to drive. My dad was in the process of hiring a new driver. Denny had retired; my dad forced him into it because he had some health issues and it was becoming too much for him. My dad seemed to be taking his time with hiring the new driver, and I believed that it was because he couldn't see anyone else driving him or us around besides Denny.

Aiden was standing outside Club S, waiting for me, when the cab pulled up to the curb. I got out, we high-fived, and walked inside. The music was blaring and the floor was thumping. It was more crowded than usual tonight and the girls were gorgeous. I was getting hard just looking at them. I walked up to the bar and ordered my usual scotch, and Aiden ordered his whiskey. This club had become our usual hangout over the past couple of months. The girls were smoking hot and they sure knew how to have a good time. I think if my parents knew that I hung out there, they'd be pissed. We sat at the table and kicked back our drinks. This pretty girl kept eyeing me from the bar. When I gave her a wink and a smile, she strutted over to our table and sat down next to me.

"You're really cute." She smiled.

"Thanks, babe. You're pretty cute yourself."

"Can I buy you a drink?" she asked.

"No. But I can buy you one."

I raised my hand and signaled for Amber, our waitress, to bring us a couple of shots each. As soon as she set them in front of us, we brought our shot glasses together and then slammed them as fast as we could. After we slammed both shots, she grabbed my hand and led me to the dance floor. As I grabbed her waist, she moved her hot ass up and down my body, causing me to become instantly hard. Her dress was really short, which allowed my hands easy access to cup her bare ass. She welcomed it and threw her head back when I squeezed it. When the song changed, I led her back to the bar for some more shots, and when we approached the table, Aiden already had some hot girl sitting on his lap. The four of us drank more than we should've and, before I knew it, we were outside the club and I had my girl's back pressed up against the side of the building.

"Let's go back to your place." She smiled as she nipped my bottom lip.

I turned around and hailed us a cab that took the both of us back to the penthouse.

"We have to be really quiet. My parents are sleeping," I whispered as I carefully shut the front door.

She laughed as I picked her up and tried to carry her up the stairs. Needless to say, I stumbled and we both fell. We started to laugh, and I put my hand over her mouth as we got up and went to my bedroom, closing the door softly behind us.

****

"Collin, get down here, NOW!" my dad yelled up the stairs.

I rolled my eyes and went down to his office. "What?"

"You know what, Collin."

I sighed as I crossed my arms. I knew what this was about. It was about the hot brunette I brought home last night. "Dad, calm down. She's a nice girl." I smiled.

"Really? What the hell is her name?"

Shit, he put me on the spot. If I remembered correctly, I didn't catch her name, but if I told my dad that, he'd flip, so I gave her a name. "Her name is Darcy."

"Bullshit! Her name is Renee. Ask me how I know, Collin. Go ahead and ask me," he yelled.

"How do you know her name is Renee, Dad?"

"Because she introduced herself to me this morning when I was walking down the hall and she came out of your room, naked! Your mom is in the kitchen, ready to kill you. You've been out of control since Hailey left and this stops today. Do you understand me? Now get your ass in the kitchen and apologize to your mom, and maybe, just maybe, when I walk back in there, you'll be alive."

My head was already killing me from last night's alcohol binge and my dad's yelling made it worse. Now, I had to go and face my mom. The last thing I wanted to do was disappoint her, but lately, that was all I seemed to do. I walked out of the office and straight into the kitchen, where my mom was sitting at the table.

"Sit down, now!" she said with anger in her eyes.

"Mom, I'm—"

"Don't. Don't you dare say a word until I'm finished saying what I have to say."

She pointed her finger at me. Something I didn't ever remember her doing. She was pissed and she kind of scared me.

"I know you're hurting, Collin. I know how hard it's been on you since Hailey left, but you are way out of control. You go out every night. You come in during the wee hours of the morning, and you reek of alcohol. I don't appreciate naked girls coming out of your bedroom in the morning. It's rude, disrespectful, and I won't have it in my house. What the hell were you thinking?"

As I looked into her angry, but sad eyes, I hated myself for making her so mad. "Mom, I'm sorry. I wasn't thinking, and it'll never happen again."

"You're right; it won't happen again. Connor, get in here," she yelled from the kitchen.

My dad walked in and looked at me. "Still alive, I see."

I rolled my eyes and my head felt like it was going to explode. My mom got up from her chair and started getting the stuff out for the hangover cocktail she always made. God, I hated that shit.

"Connor, don't you have something to tell Collin?" she said.

My dad looked at me as he sat down in the chair. "I've decided that you're attending the meeting at the office this morning and then, after that, I have some things I need you to take care of."

"No way, Dad. Today's my day off."

There was no way I wanted to sit in that meeting with a hangover. I didn't get much sleep last night, and all I wanted to do was go back to bed.

"I've changed your day off and today isn't it," he said as he got up from the chair.

My mom walked over to me and handed me a glass with the cocktail in it. "Here, my darling son, drink up because you're going to need to feel a hundred percent before you go into the office." She smiled.

My dad sipped his coffee and, as he walked out of the kitchen, he turned around, looked at me, and then looked at his watch. "You have about fifteen minutes to get ready. I'll be waiting by the elevator. You better not be a minute late."

Sandi Lynn

Manufactured by Amazon.ca
Bolton, ON

11041929R00179